TEAGAN HUNTER

Editing by Editing by C. Marie

Proofreading by Judy's Proofreading & Julia Griffis

Cover Design: Emily Wittig Designs

For anyone who has ever had their heart broken by the wrong man…
I hope you found the right one.
P.S. Fuck that douchebag.

DEAR READER

While this book is mostly a fun and easy read, Vanessa is recently divorced, and her ex was not faithful, so the book does touch on the topic of cheating.

For a list of all potential triggers for my books, please visit my website.

Chapter 1

LOCKE

Lawson: Hi. Hello. Hey. I miss you assholes. I can't wait to see you all.

Lawson: You're all still coming to the party this afternoon, right?

Fox: They'd better be! Lilah's expecting all of you to be there.

Keller: And if we don't show, good boy?

Hutch: I'll break your legs, rendering you useless for the Serpents this season, killing our chances at the Cup. Your fucking choice.

Lawson: Damn. That was aggressive.

Hutch: Then be here in an hour. Auden got sandwiches and shit, and she's pregnant as hell. She's the last person you want to piss off. Trust me.

Hayes: Aye aye, Captain.

Hutch: Fuck. Please don't start that shit.

Locke: Aye aye, Captain.

Hutch: Really, Locke?! I trusted you!

Keller: Aye aye, Captain.

Lawson: Aye aye, Captain.

Fox: Aye aye, Captain.

Lawson: Fuck, man. You even got Foxy scared, and this party is partly for his girl.

Fox: I'm not scared. I'm just being a team player.

Lawson: Whatever you say, Foxy Baby.

Lawson: Oh, Locke?

Lawson: LOCKE???

Lawson: WHITLOCKE!!!!

Fox: Oh, snap. He used the full name.

Lawson: No, if I used his full name, I would have said Gavin Barry Douglas Whitlocke.

Locke: How the fuck do you know my full name?

Keller: Why the fuck do you have two middle names?

Hutch: Excellent question, Kells.

Locke: It's a family thing.

Keller: Weird family, especially with names like that. Makes you sound even older than you already are.

Locke: Shut up, Keller.

Keller: Great comeback, old man.

Locke: I am not fucking old!

Lawson: You are, too. Just accept it, old-timer.

Lawson: Oooh, old-timer with the great one-timer! That has a nice ring.

Lawson: Though you tend to go top shelf more often than not.

Lawson: Anyway, like I was saying…

Lawson: Do you, like, remember black-and-white TV, Lockey Poo?

Locke: First of all, never call me that again. Secondly, how old do you think I am?

Lawson: IDK. Old? You were born in the '80s, after all.

Locke: Fuck's sake. Being born in the '80s doesn't make me THAT old.

Keller: He kind of acts like it, though. Did you hear him groan when he jumped over the boards during the playoffs last season? It was fuckin' loud. I heard him from the ice.

Hayes: I heard him, too.

Fox: Come on, guys. Let's be nice to Locke.

Fox: We might not have much time left with him.

Lawson: OH SNAP!

Lawson: Even the good boy called you old!

Fox: Please. I am begging you. Stop calling me that, Lawsy.

Lawson: Only if you stop blushing every time I do.

Hayes: You're a fucking menace, you know that? Leave Foxy alone.

Lawson: That's why they call me Lawless Lawson, baby!

Hutch: Literally nobody calls you that.

Hayes: You can't give yourself your own nickname. That's not how nicknames work. We've been over this.

Keller: Yeah, Lawson. Let me give you a nickname. I have plenty already locked and loaded.

Fox: Be nice, Kells…

Keller: What? I am being nice. I didn't list a single one for the buttmunch.

Hutch: Is it stupid that just made me laugh?

Hayes: I'm right there with you, Hutchy.

Hutch: There's just something so silly about being called a buttmunch.

Lawson: Yeah, yeah. Keller is SO funny. Back to my thing.

Lawson: Locke?

Locke: My grandparents had a black-and-white TV.

Locke: But it was a family heirloom! It's not like we gathered around and watched it every night or anything. I'd just watch Saturday morning cartoons on it sometimes.

Lawson: SATURDAY MORNING CARTOONS?

Lawson: Fuck, I miss those. We should bring them back.

Lawson: Let's do a slumber party one Friday night, then eat sugary cereal and watch cartoons on Saturday morning.

Keller: Abso—and I cannot stress this enough—fucking-lutely not. Never. Ever.

Hutch: Gotta go with Keller on this one. I'm not giving up time with my fiancée for you morons.

Hayes: Yeah, no. Besides, I already do Saturday morning cartoons with Flora.

Lawson: Boooooo!

Fox: I'll watch Saturday morning cartoons with you. Can Lilah come?

Lawson: What? No! This is for the boys only! NO GIRLS ALLOWED!

Lawson: Locke?

Locke: No.

Lawson: WHY DO YOU ALL HATE ME SO MUCH?

Fox: We don't. We love you, Lawsy.

Keller: Speak for your damn self, Foxy.

Lawson: I think this is a perfect plan. Let's make it happen.

Hutch: Or not.

Hayes: Yeah, no. I'm out.

Lawson: COME ON!

Locke: I'll pass.

Keller: Do I really need to say it again?

Fox: I'll still come, Lawsy!

Lawson: Fine. Then Foxy Baby and I
will have our OWN slumber party.
None of you dicks are invited!

Hutch: Good.

Locke: Perfectly fine with that.

Hayes: Hallelujah!

Keller: Literally none of us are upset
about this.

Lawson: By the way, have I told you
lately how much I missed you? You
guys are, like, my favorite people.

Lawson: Well, aside from Rory.

Lawson: She's amazing. Last week,
she let me be her assistant for a whole
day. A WHOLE DAY! Sure, I had to
watch her manipulate doggie anal
glands, but it was magical still.

Keller: Please don't make me barf.

Hayes: Let's not get into this again.

Hutch: She's about to be my sister-in-law. I already know how amazing she is.

Lawson: Damn, Hutchy. That was almost sweet of you.

Hutch: Tell no one.

Lawson: Sorry, bud. Screenshots are forever.

Hayes: You're screenshotting our group chats?

Lawson: Of course I am. I have a whole folder dedicated to Keller telling me he loves me.

Keller: I have never said those words to you.

Lawson: Sure you have. You just say it in your own way, Kells.

Keller: The fuck I do!

I shake my head at my teammates as the group keeps going, my phone screen exploding with new messages. This time, it's mainly between Lawson and Keller, the team's neediest and grumpiest players, who are always at each other's throats. It's usually Lawson trying to get

Keller to admit he loves him, which is quite entertaining.

That's just how we show we love each other. Most days, our chats are obnoxious. On other days, they're *really* obnoxious. But some days… Well, they're still obnoxious. I wouldn't trade being teammates with them for anyone else in the league, though. We've gone through a lot over these few years together, and we're truthfully like family, even if some of us can't admit it.

My phone continues to blow up, but I bow out of the conversation, instead trying to enjoy my last few minutes of peace before heading to Hutch's place for the party. I know the second I step through Hutch's door to celebrate his fiancée and Fox's girlfriend launching their company, it will be bedlam again. Lawson and Keller will still be arguing. Hayes and his girlfriend, Quinn, will be there with Flora, and likely Pickles, because the cat goes everywhere with her. Hutch will hover over a very pregnant Auden, and Fox will fawn over Lilah. And I'll just be standing there, taking it all in and wondering how we got to this point in the first place.

When we joined the Seattle Serpents, we all agreed we would stay single until each one of us lifted the Stanley Cup over our head. Two years later, that plan has been blown to hell thanks to several guys falling madly in love.

I don't fault them for it. Who wants to be lonely? Who can even control that kind of thing? It was inevitable that something like this would happen, but now it means only two members of the Serpents Singles Club—a ridiculous name—actually remain single, and I'm one of them. The other is Keller, who we all know will never find love. I've never met anyone so vehemently against it before. It'll be a cold day in hell before he ever lets that happen.

Unlike him, though, I'm not so against it. I never really have been. It's hard to be when it's all around me. My parents are still together and happily married. Each of my siblings is married and has children. Now, almost all of my teammates are in committed relationships too. It's everywhere, so of course I believe in it. I'm just not so sure it's going to happen for me. Any time I've tried in the past, it hasn't lasted. Not to mention I haven't felt anything even remotely close to having feelings for someone since…

No.

I don't let myself go there. Back to New York. Back to *that night.* The one I've done everything to forget.

"Can I grab you anything else?"

I'm relieved when the barista breaks my thoughts apart. She's at the front counter of The Coffee Spot, a rag in her hand as she wipes down the espresso machine. It's getting close to closing time, and I assume this is her polite way of telling me to get the fuck out.

I grin. "I'm good, Kayla. Thank you. I'm heading out now. Thanks for letting me stay so late."

"You know you're always welcome here, Locke. Even if I do close in five minutes." She tosses me a teasing wink.

I rise from my chair, then set my mug in the dirty dishes bin before sending her a wave on my way out the door. I climb behind the wheel of my SUV, which I parked just down the block, and cut my way into Seattle traffic. The drive to Hutch's place isn't long in distance, but that means nothing with the one-way streets, the closures for no real reason, and the overall shitty driving. By the time I pull into his driveway, my mood is sour, and all that peace I was striving for is nowhere to be found.

It's been like that a lot lately. I search for calm, and all I find is chaos, this unruly feeling inside me like I'm being wrung out like a towel after a long day at the pool. I don't know if it's just me itching to get back out on the ice and start the season or what, but I know I need to do something to relieve all this tension or I won't be worth a damn to my teammates.

Loud music—that's certainly not coming from my speakers—rattles my SUV, and I look in the rearview mirror just in time to see Keller stop his Audi R8 inches from my bumper. When he catches me looking, he flips me off before flinging his door open. I meet him outside just as he pushes his sunglasses to the top of his head.

"You almost owed me a new AMG," I say as a greeting.

"Please, I had plenty of time to stop. I'm still young with good reflexes, old man."

There's no smile. Not even a hint of one. But if I listen closely enough, I can hear the teasing in his voice.

"Whitlocke," he says with a nod, even though I haven't seen him since the exit interviews after we lost in the conference finals. Some guys stick around and do more training, some head home for the summer and train there. Others go on extended vacations. I went up north, and he went wherever it is he runs off to.

"Keller," I return.

Then, against his will, I haul him into a hug, which he reluctantly returns with a single pat on my back.

"Good summer?"

He shrugs, looking off into the distance. "Was fine."

Leave it to him not to reveal too much. He's always been that way, always keeps his cards close to his chest and never lets anyone know what he's truly feeling. I envy him sometimes. I wish I could be that detached and not give a shit, but it's never been in my nature.

I blame my parents for that. They always forced us kids to share our feelings and talk about things. That's not a bad thing, but sometimes…I don't know. Sometimes I just want to shut it all off and let loose. Have fun. Not give a fuck.

It'd be an excellent trick for the ice, too. Maybe even improve my game, and everyone knows I could stand to get a little quicker. Could stick handle a little better. Check harder. Do all the little things just a bit better to keep myself in the league for at least a few more years.

"My summer was good, too. Thanks for asking."

His lips twitch at my sarcasm, and it's as close to a smile as Keller gets. There's a commotion behind us, and we turn in time to see Lawson sprinting out the door, his girlfriend, Rory, attempting to hold him back.

It's useless. He slips out of her grip, then charges right toward us, his arms wide open.

"My boys!"

He barrels into me, folding me into a hug that could rival that of a gorilla before quickly shoving me away. He grins right at Keller, who is already glaring.

"Don't even fucking think about it, Lawsy."

"Kells…" he says, tipping his head to the side, his

smile widening. He takes a step toward our grumpiest teammate, who takes a step back.

"I'm so serious, Lawson. I will punch."

"You won't."

"I fucking will," he promises.

Lawson is either stupid or…well, stupid, because he launches toward Keller anyway. The latter bolts, making a run for it, and it takes Lawson all of two seconds to catch on and chase after him. I stand in disbelief, watching my teammates chase each other around the front lawn like a bunch of six-year-olds playing a game of tag at recess, only this game will likely end in violence.

Even Hutch, Auden, Fox, and Lilah stumble out of the house to watch the debacle unfold. Finally, after what feels like forever, Lawson catches Keller, throwing his arms around him and hugging him close.

"I got you! I got you! Now love me, you fucker!"

"Never!" Keller yells back, fighting him off easily. He then turns around and socks Lawson right in the gut, as promised.

"Hey!" Rory yells, already marching off the porch toward the two like *she* will be the one to stop this.

Her twin sister grabs her. "Let the boys play, Rory."

"But he's beating up my boyfriend," she pouts to Auden.

"To be fair, he probably deserves it. I bet Keller even told him he'd get punched."

"He did," I confirm, going to stand by them as Lawson tries yet again to hug Keller. I give Hutch a quick hug. "Good to see you."

"You too, man. Feels like forever. We hoped you'd stick around Seattle a bit this summer, maybe have a few grill sessions."

"I told you he'd spend the whole time in Vancouver," Auden says, poking Hutch playfully in the ribs before pushing her way between us and wrapping me in a hug—or a semi-hug. It's the best she can do with such a big belly at this late stage in her pregnancy. "Good to see you, Locke."

"You, too." I look down at her stomach. "How's it going? Everything as it should be?"

She grins, running her hand over her bump. "I hate every minute of it and cannot wait to get this baby out of me, but other than that, it's wonderful. Everything is growing appropriately, and with any luck, I'll deliver in the next week or so."

"Launching a company *and* having a baby in the same week?"

"She's superhuman, huh?" says her best friend Lilah, softly nudging Auden out of the way to hug me. "Good to see you again, Locke."

"Congratulations on the business, Lilah. I'm so happy for you."

"Happy enough to be a client of ours?" She raises her brows at me as she pulls away.

"Bet his nieces and nephews would love a pool too," Fox says, elbowing his way in next. He wraps me in a hug that can only be described as warm and accepting before pulling away, patting my cheek with a proud grin. "Missed you, bud."

It feels like a family reunion, complete with that one crotchety member who never wants to be touched. I nod at Rory, whom I know better than to try to hug. It will never cease to amaze me how she and Lawson ended up together, especially since they're total opposites. I grin at her, then look back at the lawn, Lawson still running after Keller.

Hayes pulls into the driveway with a quizzical look on his face as he enters the scene. He steps out of his SUV and lets out a loud whistle that would have even the unruliest kids listening.

"Enough!" he hollers, sounding every bit like the dad he is, and they come to a halt, both leaning over to catch their breath.

We all snicker. Nobody ever expected Hayes, known for being a bit of a wild card, to settle down with his own family, but that's precisely what he has done after getting guardianship of his niece. Quinn climbs out of the other side, Flora coming to stand beside her, Pickles by her feet as I suspected she would be.

"Are they playing tag? Can I play too, Just Quinn?"

I grin at the nickname Flora hasn't let up on. Apparently, it was a sarcastic moment that turned into an inside joke, and it has continued since.

"Sure. Go on. Try to catch Uncle Keller and give him lots of huggies. He loves those."

"Roger that!" she shouts as she takes off toward the grown men.

Once they spot her, they take off as well, trying to catch her as she giggles and darts away. It's adorable, and maybe the most animated I've ever seen Keller.

It makes me miss my nieces and nephews instantly. As much chaos as they are, they're so fun to be around, and I hated having to leave them and the rest of my family behind. Even though I love hockey and can't imagine doing anything else with my life, I don't exactly love the instability it can bring, which is part of why I've never bothered to settle down. I don't want to put that burden on my partner, having to figure out shit like moving during a school year or missing all those little moments with my kid. First steps and first words. Kindergarten graduation and recitals.

If I'm going to have a family of my own, I want to be present for all of it, not just some of it. So, until I hang up my skates—something I don't plan to do for quite a while—single is what I'll remain.

Everyone laughs, pulling my attention back to what's happening on Hutch's front lawn, and I look just in time to see Flora skid to a stop, turning the tide on Lawson and Keller as she begins chasing *them*. The guys play along, letting her "catch" them, and I swear I see Keller actually smile. It's brief, but it happens, and it's kind of unsettling. Just as quick as it comes, it's gone, and they're all three trudging back to the porch, out of breath as Lawson carries Flora on his shoulders.

"I gave Uncle Keller lots of huggies like you said, Just Quinn!" the little girl announces with a big grin.

She snickers, either ignoring or not caring about the glare the hockey player throws her way. She just reaches up and high-fives the kid before we all head into the house. Everyone gathers in the expansive kitchen except Flora, who scampers off to chase Pickles around. Lilah passes out flutes of champagne as everyone chatters about their summer.

Hutch and Auden obviously got engaged and have been planning for the baby. Hayes and Quinn talk about spending time with Flora, and Lawson goes on a ten-minute diatribe about how much he learned about dogs and their anal glands…*again*. His fascination is concerning, but Rory just looks at him like he's the most amazing man in the world. Keller says nothing, which is no surprise to anyone.

"Let me guess—family time for you, Locke?" Lawson says.

"Yep. Spent my time in Vancouver, except when we went to Disneyland. Might have overspent a bit. When's hockey starting again?"

We all laugh, but I'm only slightly joking. It's what I do, though. Each offseason, I always take my nieces and nephews on a vacation of their choosing. I figure it's the least I can do since I can't be there for them during the season. I'm always exhausted afterward and spend far too much money, but it's well worth it. Those are memories they're going to cherish for a long damn time to come.

"Well?" Auden says, looking at her best friend. "Shall we?"

Lilah smiles nervously, reaching for Fox for reassurance. I'm not even sure if she realizes she's doing it, but the goalie is right there in an instant, wrapping his arm around her waist, and soothing away all her worries.

"I'm ready," she says, her concern nowhere to be found.

We move to the dining room where a laptop sits open in front of an *It's a girl* banner that's been crossed out and replaced with *It's a Maddison Sinclair Designs!* in some of the worst handwriting I've ever seen. I'm guessing that was all Fox and Hutch's doing.

We gather around, Lilah and Auden in the middle. They both take a deep breath.

"Three, two, one!" Lilah counts down, then slams her thumb down on the space bar, and just like that, they've launched their luxury design company that caters to building you the perfect home from the ground up, including the interior.

Everyone cheers, with Hayes, Quinn, and Flora blowing into noisemakers. *Where did those come from?* Even Keller claps, seeming semi-enthused. Of course, Fox and Lilah start to make out to the point that Lawson has to pull them apart.

"Okay, break it up, break it up," he says, pulling our goalie away from his girlfriend. "This is a party, not your sex den. Let's celebrate!" He picks up a red cup and holds it in the air. "To Lilah!"

"Hey!" we all say, holding our flutes up as well.

"To Auden!"

"Hey!" we cheer again.

"And to Hutch's inability to pull out, which means we're getting a second generation! Long live the Serpents Singles group chat!"

"What's pull out mean?" Flora asks, sending everyone who is not Hayes or Quinn into a fit of laughter.

Hutch smacks Lawson on the back of the head, making me laugh harder.

The doorbell chimes, and Lawson races off toward it like he lives here or something.

"Anyone else think he's getting extra exhausting lately?" Hayes asks.

"He's *always* extra exhausting. It's like you people never listen to me," Keller grouses.

"That's because you hate everyone and everything. You don't count," I say.

Keller shrugs.

"Uh, Hutchy?" Lawson calls, walking back into the room.

"Yeah?" our captain answers.

"Someone's at the door for you."

"Who the hell is it?" Hutch growls, irritated by Lawson's vagueness.

"Was hoping you'd tell us."

Our star forward steps aside, revealing a tiny blonde woman standing behind him. Everything inside me freezes, but only for a moment, because it suddenly thaws, and I'm vibrating, from my fucking head right down to my toes tucked tight into my shoes. Every damn inch of me is shaking with...well, I'm not entirely sure what.

Someone gasps, but not even that pulls my attention. I am too focused on the woman clutching her bag tightly. Too fixated on the blonde locks I know feel like fucking silk. Too damn engrossed in the way she drags her tongue across her bottom lip, the one that tasted like pink and cherries. I didn't even know it was possible to taste colors, but I swear, if that one had a flavor, it would be her lips.

I am just too fucking distracted to pay attention to anyone else right now. Anyone other than *her*.

"Uh, who is that?" Lawson asks. I'd laugh at his piss-poor attempt to whisper, but I'm still too busy staring.

Hayes answers with, "I think that's his sister."

"*Step*sister," Hutch corrects. "What are you doing here, Vanessa?"

Vanessa.

I haven't heard that name in… I guess technically I haven't heard it at all. She wasn't Vanessa to me. She was someone else. She was Nessa.

"Sorry, I…I didn't mean to intrude." She pushes her hair behind her ear. "It looks like you're having a party. I just…"

Her dark green eyes find me, and I hold my breath. I've waited months to see her look at me again, but there's nothing. Not a smile. No spark. Not even a flicker of recognition. Not a single hint of the night we spent together in a New York hotel room.

There's emptiness, and it hurts. Almost as badly as knowing the last person I felt something for…is my captain's stepsister.

And she is completely off-limits.

Chapter 2

VANESSA

Five months ago

"Happy divorce day. Congrats on being Vanessa Meyers once again," I mutter to myself, picking up my celebratory amaretto sour and slinging back half the contents in one gulp.

I set the glass down, pressing at my lips with a napkin, careful not to mess up my lipstick because I worked too damn hard to look this good. The last thing I wanted to be doing today was sitting in a bar alone in New York City. I thought this day—now that it has *finally* come—would be celebrated with friends and family, but no. It's just me.

Alone. *Again.*

I've finally accepted reality—Neal won our friends in the divorce. I guess I should wonder if they were ever really my friends at all if they can pick that cheating, lying sack of shit over me, but it still wouldn't make it hurt any less that I'm sitting here all alone on such a life-altering night.

Not even my dad and stepmom are here. They're out with my hockey-playing stepbrother. I get it—Reed rarely comes to New York these days unless his team, the Seattle Serpents, is playing, but did they really have to ditch me to hang with him? On today of all days? Sure, they invited me to go along with them, but I wasn't feeling like being the awkward fifth wheel since my brother's girlfriend is here too.

I wanted tonight to be about *me*. Selfish? Perhaps, but it wouldn't be the first time someone said I was. In fact, people have said a lot of things about me over the last year-plus. They've called me cruel. Vindictive. Bitchy. *Vengeful*.

None of it bothers me. Why should it? They'd be the same way if they found out their husband of less than six months—the man I gave five years of my life to—somehow managed to fall dick first into his secretary. *Of fucking course* I'm mad at the world. I have every damn right to be.

I just wish all that spite and revenge actually meant something. Sure, Neal lost his fancy high-paying job when I sent the video of him banging his secretary to his boss, but it didn't feel nearly as good as I hoped it would. Much like this celebratory drink doesn't feel as good as I wanted it to.

If I'm being honest, nothing about this day feels good. I've been looking forward to my divorce being finalized for sixteen long months, thanks to Neal dragging it out far longer than he needed to, but it doesn't feel as freeing as I thought it would.

It just feels…sad. *I* feel sad.

"Hey there, sweetheart."

I turn to find a guy who looks to be about my age slipping onto the stool next to me. Crisp white polo and pressed slacks. Loafers. Dark blond hair slicked back in a way that looks purposeful yet effortless all at once. He looks like a total boy-next-door kind of guy.

I remember when I fell for that once upon a time.

"How do you know?"

"Pardon?" he says into his half-empty beer as he brings it to his lips, a shiny silver watch catching the bar lights and nearly blinding me.

I lean closer, not missing how his eyes drop to my cleavage. I wore my very favorite dress tonight, the silky midnight-blue one that hugs every curve and leaves little to the imagination.

"How do you know? How do you know I'm a *sweetheart*?"

He chuckles. "Well, I suppose I don't. But you sure look sweet, and I'd love to find out if you are."

He rolls his tongue over his lips, eyes sweeping over me appreciatively, and I'd be lying if I said I didn't enjoy the attention. But unfortunately, this guy is doing nothing for me. He reminds me too much of everything I lost for that to be the case.

The familiar ache that settled into my chest the night I found out about Neal's indiscretion makes itself known again. I've never been one to feel bad for myself, at least not until The Video happened. Since then, I've been finding myself alternating between anger and sadness, and I hate it. I want my old life back. I want to go back to being the girl who always held her head up high and commanded a room. Not the girl who got cheated on and can barely hold it together half the time.

A hand lands on my arm, and I glance down.

A wedding ring.

Suddenly, I don't want to be ogled or flirted with. I want to be left alone to sulk.

There go those damn mood swings again.

"Want to go somewhere a little quieter and get to know each other?" he asks, not realizing I've caught on to his game.

"While the offer is *oh so tempting*," I say, each word dripping with sarcasm, "I'm fine where I am."

I shake his hand off me and give him my shoulder. To anyone else, it would be obvious I'm dismissing them. This guy doesn't take the hint, though. He leans in closer, his breath smelling like a horrible IPA, and I scrunch my nose in disgust. It doesn't deter him.

"Come on, sweetheart," he says, dropping his voice low. "What do you have to lose?"

"My dignity. Now go away."

"I—"

"Pretty sure she said no, buddy. Twice now, actually."

We both whip our heads toward a new voice. A man—a very handsome one at that—sits two seats away. He's not looking our way, but it's obvious he's talking to us.

"I suggest you listen to her." His words might be calm, but there's no denying the underlying threat in them: *I suggest you listen to her, or I'll make you listen.*

Chivalrous, really, but I don't need someone to fight my battles, especially not some random guy who is probably just as bad as all the rest.

"I can take care of myself," I snap at him before turning back to Married Guy. "He's right. I did say no. Now, get lost before I take a picture of you and blast it all over social media with the hashtag *cheater*. I guarantee you it'd reach your wife before the end of the night, *sweetheart*."

His eyes widen with surprise, then just as quickly fall to slits. Everything about him changes in that moment. He goes from smiling and playful to angry, as if it's *my* fault he's trying to cheat on his wife.

"You didn't need to be such a bitch, you know," he mutters, climbing off the stool and taking his foul-smelling beer with him.

"Better a bitch than a no-balls-having cheater!" I yell to his back before slamming back the rest of my drink to calm myself.

I set the glass down, unaware I was shaking until now. It's not that I thought the guy was a real threat, but it still has me on edge, and I'm sure that has everything to do with my increasing distrust of men.

A deep, hearty laugh draws my attention, and I swing my head to the right, ready to tell Sir Eavesdropper he really needs to mind his own business, but the words never come out. I'm too distracted. I was wrong before; he's not handsome—he's *hot*. Really, really hot.

So hot it immediately puts me on alert. *What's his game? What does he gain by playing the knight in shining armor to a stranger? What does he want from me? How can he break me?* Just the thought of being broken again has that same anger from before flooding my veins, and I go from being enchanted by his looks to annoyed in a second flat.

"What's so funny?" I snipe.

Another laugh, and all it does is piss me off more.

I glare at him. "What the hell is your problem, man?"

Finally, he turns to me, and if I thought his profile was hot, it's nothing compared to getting a good look at him straight-on. Dark brows sit over a pair of hazel eyes that would make anyone stop and stare. Green peppered with flakes of gold I can see even from two seats away. A hint of scruff that's entirely too enticing and dark hair peppered with a few gray streaks, making me wonder just how old this guy is.

And while he's wearing a light blue button-up and gray dress pants, he doesn't look like he's trying too hard to impress people like Married Guy was. No, he looks comfortable. At ease. And possibly even a little familiar.

I squint, trying to figure out where I might know him from, but nothing comes to mind. I don't know this man at all, which makes it even more annoying that he's inserting himself where he doesn't belong.

"Well?" I prompt when he says nothing.

He raises a single brow, then lifts his drink—some kind of whiskey from the looks of it—and takes a swig before he flicks his chin toward the empty glass sitting in front of me. "Want another drink?"

I glance down at it, then back at him. It's on the tip of my tongue to say no. To tell this guy off. Tell him to mind his own business and that I don't need someone to rescue me. That I'm doing just fine on my own.

But instead, I say, "Yes."

He grins and waves the bartender over. "Another Macallan, please. Neat. And whatever the lady wants."

The bartender looks at me.

"Amaretto sour. Extra cherries."

He nods, then takes off to grab our drinks while the handsome stranger gets up and moves two stools closer.

What the…

But once he sits down next to me, unlike with Married Guy, I don't get the overwhelming urge to move away.

"Hi," he says, his voice deeper than I realized before.

"Hi," I murmur back, tucking a loose strand of hair behind my ear.

Are those…*nerves?* Does this guy make me nervous? Yes, he does, but not in a bad way. More like butterflies-in-my-stomach kind of nervous. It's just as unsettling. I can't remember the last time someone made me feel that way. At least not since…

I give myself a mental shake, pushing all thoughts of my ex out of my head. This day isn't about Neal. It's about me and my freedom. It's about starting over. It's about *new*.

"You okay?"

I tip my head, unsure why he's asking that.

"The adulterer," he explains.

"Ah." I nod. "Yes, I'm fine. I really did have it handled."

He smirks. "Oh, I have no doubts about that, love."

Love.

It's so cheesy, yet it rolls off his lips so effortlessly. Not smarmy at all, like with Married Guy calling me *sweetheart.*

"So, what brings you here…" He trails off, looking for my name. Normally, I'd make someone work harder for it, but I find myself wanting to tell him.

"Nessa."

I don't know why I say it. I haven't been called Nessa since my mom was still alive over a decade ago. Everyone I know either calls me Van or Vanessa, never just Nessa, but it feels fitting. Tonight is about starting over, so maybe I *should* be someone else. Besides, what's the harm in it? It's not like I'm ever going to see this guy again.

"Nessa." He tests it out, and those butterflies make themselves known again. I swear I can feel his tongue shift over each letter. I like it far too much. "It's nice to meet you, Nessa. I'm Gavin."

Gavin. I like it. It suits him.

"Hi," I say again, though I don't know why. Ugh. I'm really a mess tonight, aren't I?

He laughs, then nods at the bartender as he sets our fresh drinks in front of us. Needing something to do, I pluck a cherry from the glass and bring it to my lips, sucking the booze off before popping it into my mouth, stem and all.

Gavin never takes his eyes off me. I know because I can feel it. I think back to my college days, where my favorite party trick was tying cherry stems with my tongue, and I do just that. I stick my tongue out, showing off the finished product.

He chuckles. "Very impressive."

"Thank you," I say, setting the knot on my napkin, then taking a sip from my drink. "Got any tricks of your own?"

He reaches over, grabs my tied stem, and points at the tip jar sitting quite a way down the bar.

"I'll make that shot."

"What? There's no way," I argue.

He lifts his brows with a silent *Watch me*. Then he flicks his wrist and *whoosh*—the stem lands right on the five-dollar bill sitting at the top.

"Wow. Impressive." I toss his word back at him dryly, though I truly am impressed.

"It's all in the wrist," he explains with a shrug, as if making shots like that is part of his everyday life.

The only other person I've ever seen do something like that is Reed, though he's always holding a hockey stick when he makes it happen.

"So," I say after a few moments of silence. "What brings you here?"

"Work trip."

"What kind of work?"

He leans into me, and even though he's sitting down, it's obvious how tall this man is. I have to tip my head back just to look at him. I should move away, should back up, because we are way closer than two strangers should be, but I don't. I'm too busy trying to figure out why he smells like warm cinnamon, cedar, and something else I can't seem to name. The scotch, maybe? I don't know. I'm far too focused on the fact that he's looking at me like he's not sure if he trusts me or not.

Satisfied with whatever conclusion he's come to, he goes back to his own space, and I breathe for what feels like the first time in minutes.

"What brings you here?" He deflects the question, and I allow it, because who cares? It's not like any of this matters. I could tell him whatever I want, and it wouldn't mean a damn thing.

I find myself being honest anyway.

"I'm celebrating." I lift my drink. "Cheers?"

He picks up his Macallan with a grin. "Do I get to know what I'm cheersing to first?"

"My divorce," I say before clinking my glass to his and taking a drink.

His smile slips…and so does his stare. Right down to the three-carat square-cut diamond sitting on my left hand, the one surrounded by tiny stones. The one that was slipped onto my finger two years ago this summer and that I've yet to take off.

I quickly hide the ring, my cheeks heating.

"Okay, so that looked bad," I say, not meeting his eyes. "I, uh, I—"

"You don't need to explain anything to me," Gavin says softly.

So softly I drag my gaze back to his, looking right into his pity-filled hazel stare. I hate it. I hate it more than the whispers and rumors and knowing Neal won all our friends. I don't want to be pitied. I want to be understood.

And I have a feeling Gavin will understand.

"I don't know why I'm still wearing the ring," I finally say. "I don't have any feelings toward the man except contempt. I just… I don't know. It's mine, you know? I picked it out. It belongs to me. Sure, it once represented something else, but now it's… It's just mine, okay?" I push my shoulders back, raising my chin slightly higher.

His lips twitch at the corners. "You don't need to explain yourself to me, Nessa. Or anyone else, for that matter. How you mourn your relationship is your business and nobody else's."

I don't know what I was expecting him to say, but it wasn't that. Sure, I've received understanding from some people, but not everyone gets it. They don't know what it's like to have something you wanted so badly fail so spectacularly, especially on such a hurtful level. They don't know what it's like to not be enough for the man you promised your forever to.

"You sound like you're speaking from experience."

He takes a long drink before saying, "Never been married. Never really cared either way if I was."

"Why does it sound like there's an *until* tacked on to the end of that?"

He reaches up, scratching at the scruff lining his jaw. It's such a simple gesture yet somehow very attractive. "You heard that, huh?" He sighs. "It's complicated."

I snort. That's the same thing Neal said to me when I confronted him with The Video. *It's complicated, Vanessa. You don't understand a man's needs. I didn't know it was recording.* Not "I'm sorry." He was never sorry. He was just mad he got caught.

"I know it sounds like a copout, but it's not, I

swear." Gavin laughs lightly, bringing me back to the present. "It's not like I don't believe in love or anything like that. I'm not jaded. I'm just… I'm kind of already married to my job, and it's a big damn commitment. It's also not something I'm ready to give up yet."

I repress my sigh. "My ex-husband was the same way. Or at least that's the excuse he used to work late hours so he could screw his secretary."

It's the same excuse he used on our wedding day, too. We were supposed to be getting the "first look" photos done, and instead of being present and in the moment, he was busy on his phone. We fought like cats and dogs over it, even delayed the ceremony, and I was *this close* to calling the whole thing off. In retrospect, I should have. Maybe it would have saved me the heartbreak, especially since I found out afterward it was his secretary he was talking to.

Instead of saying how sorry he is or commenting on this new revelation at all, Gavin holds his glass up again.

"Cheers?"

It's so out of left field that I can't help but laugh—*loudly*. So loudly that I feel several eyes on us, but I don't care about them. I'm too focused on the smile growing on Gavin's face by the second, how the wrinkles that bracket his eyes deepen.

"Sorry," I say after I've finally collected myself. "I don't know what came over me."

"You have a nice laugh."

His words send a blush over my cheeks, and I duck my head. What has gotten into me tonight? Are these amaretto sours more potent than I thought? Why am I flustered by a simple compliment?

I clear my throat, looking back up at Gavin. "So, is this your first time in New York City?"

"Not by a long shot. I make it out here at least once a year, sometimes more."

"Work?"

He nods. "Always work."

He *almost* sounds sad about that, but then I remember how much he enjoys what he does, so maybe he isn't sad at all. Maybe he's lonely, like me.

"And you? Is this your first time?" he asks.

"Not by a long shot," I echo with a grin. "I live here actually. Not in the city, but not too far away either."

"That's—"

A group of guys stumbles into the bar, their raucous conversation drawing nearly everyone's attention, including ours. They're wearing hockey jerseys, and with the way just about all of them are swaying on their feet, I assume they were at the game earlier.

"And then you should have seen that fucker from Seattle. He was *so* pissed. Put his glove in Reiner's face, and it was all bets off. Fucking yard sale out there," one of the guys says, throwing punches into the air, mimicking what I guess happened at the game.

I wouldn't know. Despite my family trying to get me into it over the years and Reed playing, I never developed an interest, so I skipped out on the game and stayed in my hotel room until I couldn't take the silence anymore.

"Anyway," I say, turning back to Gavin, "you were—"

"Do you want to get out of here?" he asks abruptly.

I pause, surprised by his words.

"Sorry. I know that sounded like a line or something." He runs a hand through his hair with a soft laugh. "It's just getting a little rowdy and I'm enjoying talking to you and I figured…" He trails off, slipping from his stool and holding his hand out my way. "What do you say, love?"

I stare up at his towering height. His broad shoulders, long legs, and toned arms. That short beard that's doing things to me it shouldn't be doing and those damn hazel eyes I can't stop looking at. I shouldn't. I should go back to the hotel and meet up with my parents. Say hi to my brother and his girlfriend. I should do anything other than say yes to leaving with this man I don't know.

But I can't bring myself to say the words or turn him down. So, I don't. I slip my hand into his and let him pull me into the night.

Chapter 3

LOCKE

The vibe of the party shifts instantly. Hutch stares at his stepsister—the one we've only ever heard is evil—and Auden rubs at his back while her other hand rests on her belly. Nobody else moves, though, and it's clear we aren't exactly sure what to do. It's like we're out on the ice, waiting for our captain's instructions.

Or at least everyone else is. I'm still too damn busy staring at *Vanessa*. Hutch's *stepsister*—his *evil* stepsister, apparently.

I can't believe… This can't be the same person he's talked about. My Nessa can't be his Vanessa. That night in New York proved to me otherwise. She was sweet. She was funny. Sure, she was feisty as hell, but she was so much more than that too.

"Well, this is awkward."

I guess not all of us are struck stupid after all. Hayes groans at Lawson, and Keller reaches over and smacks him upside the head.

"Shut the heck up," he barks at our team's golden retriever.

Any other time, I'd acknowledge that Keller just censored himself around the little ears listening in and make fun of him for it, but I don't. I am *still* looking at *her*. Willing her to recognize me. To say something. To show me *anything* to prove our night wasn't all in my head.

But she doesn't.

"Surprise?" she says hesitantly to her brother.

Hutch laughs humorlessly. "That's one damn way to put it."

She winces, and I hate it. I hate that Hutch isn't making her feel welcome. That he's staring at her like he'd rather she be anywhere else in the world right now.

"What are you doing here, Vanessa?"

"I, uh…" She tucks a long strand of blonde hair behind her ear, her eyes flitting around the room.

I silently beg her to let them linger on me, but they don't. She moves on like I'm nobody, catching everyone's gaze before staring back at Hutch. It stings.

"Can we talk privately?"

He sighs, nods once, and mutters, "Excuse us for a moment."

Then he strides from the room, Auden struggling to catch up to him, and Vanessa follows along, looking unsure with each step. I hold my breath, waiting for her to look back at me, but she doesn't. I don't release it until she's gone, but even then, it feels like a struggle, like she took all the air in the room with her. It's the same way I felt when I woke up to find the bed beside me was cold.

"That is the *evil* stepsister, right?" Lawson asks once they're out of earshot. Or at least I hope she is.

"That's her," Lilah confirms. "I've seen photos from when Auden went to New York for Christmas."

"She seems nice," Quinn remarks.

She is *nice*, I want to scream, but I keep my mouth shut. I remain still, even though I want to follow her so badly. I'm rooted to my spot, which is why I can clearly see Fox staring at me. I don't like it. Not one damn bit. Especially with that little smirk on his lips like he knows something nobody else does.

My fingers twitch with the urge to flip him off, but I don't. It's Fox. He's the nicest guy I know, and I can't be an asshole like Keller. I cut my gaze away, straining to hear anything I can from the living room where they went, but it's pointless. Whatever they're saying is drowned out by my teammates bickering like a bunch of children.

"Why do you say the dumbest crap ever, Lawsy?"

"Why do you have to be such a…" Lawson looks down at Flora, who isn't paying them any attention. "…a pecker, Keller?"

Hayes snickers. "Pecker."

"Why is pecker funny? I like those on my pizza," Flora says, apparently paying attention after all.

Quinn shoots him a look, then bends down to Flora's height. "You like peppers, not peckers. And it's not a funny word. Uncle Adam is just in a goofy mood, is all."

The kid nods, then goes back to playing with Pickles, who is batting at her softly, all while Lawson, Keller, and Uncle Adam himself try to hold back their laughter.

"Does anyone know why the stepsister is here?" Rory asks.

"Not a clue," Lilah says. "But I know I'm curious as hell." She tiptoes closer to the living room to catch a bit of their conversation, but Fox grabs her elbow, stopping her.

"Come on, sugar. Let them have their privacy. Besides, I'm sure Auden will give you the rundown later," her boyfriend says.

"Always the *good boy*," Keller mutters, and Fox has a physical reaction to the two words.

Nobody misses it, nor the way Lilah's cheeks redden.

Lawson laughs, then holds his hand up for a high five. "Nice one, Kells."

In a rare moment of solidarity, Keller reciprocates, leaving Rory staring open-mouthed at the teammates. I'd find the whole thing comical if I didn't have one eye on the living room, willing *Vanessa* to return so I can get a glimpse of her again. Maybe I was wrong. Maybe it wasn't her. Maybe it was just someone who looked eerily like her. Maybe it was—

Oh, who am I kidding? It was her. I'd know those green eyes anywhere, know that golden hair of hers and that smile from a million miles away. It was her, and I want to know why she acted like she didn't know me.

"Where are you going?" Fox asks.

It takes me a moment to realize he's talking to me. I didn't even know I was moving, but I am. I'm heading right for where Hutch and his sister took off to.

"Bathroom," I say, catching his gaze.

That same fucking knowing smirk from before. What does he know? Not shit.

Even so, his expression haunts me as I turn into the restroom that's tucked in the hall between the dining and living rooms. It's still there, taunting me as I close the door behind me and press my ear against the wood. If I hold my breath, I can make out a few words.

"...the fuck, Van? Why here?"

"I-I...I don't know, Reed. I just needed to get away. I needed a fresh start. I needed..."

I can't hear the rest, Lawson's loud laugh from the other room covering up whatever she's saying. He quiets, and I focus back in.

"...mad?"

Hutch sighs. "I'm not mad. I'm just...fucking confused. You don't even... We don't even... I..."

Then there's silence from everywhere in the house. I'm not even out there, and I can tell it's awkward. I wish I could be out there, to see her face during all this, to gauge how she's feeling. And to maybe protect her from Hutch, who clearly doesn't like her.

I turn on the faucet and pretend to wash my hands, making my getaway before anyone can discover I came in here to eavesdrop. I flick the light off, stepping into the hallway—and right into someone.

"Shit, sorry," I say, reaching out to steady them.

Soft skin. Wildflowers. Lavender.

Nessa.

Her green eyes collide with mine, and I'm breathless again.

"Sorry," she says softly, stepping back and out of my grasp, leaving me feeling like I'm reaching for a ghost.

It's fitting, really, but I try not to think about that. I'm too focused on how she's looking at me like she first did in New York—like a complete stranger.

Actually, no. That wouldn't be true. She never looked at me like that, not even then. But now…

"I was just…" She points to the door behind me, like she can't wait for me to be gone and out of her way.

I nod, swallowing down the realization that she really doesn't remember me.

"Right. Sure. My bad."

She gives me a polite smile, one so small it's barely noticeable. But I notice it. I notice everything about her. Her tired eyes. How her hair is just a little out of place, like she's been running her hands through it repeatedly. How scratchy her voice is, as if she hasn't slept in days. I notice it all. I did then, and I do now.

I just fucking wish she'd notice me too.

"Oh, and hey?"

She turns, looking back at me. She rolls her tongue over her lips, the same ones that tasted like cherry. "Yes?"

"Welcome to Washington…*Nessa*."

A flinch. A sharp inhale.

I know all I need to—she remembers, and fuck if that doesn't spark the tiniest flame of hope. Hope for what? I don't know. She's still Hutch's stepsister. She's still his family. She's still so fucking forbidden it's not even funny.

But that flame flickers anyway…and I don't dare make a move to extinguish it.

Chapter 4

I sag against the door as it clicks shut behind me.

I'm exhausted, and I don't just mean a little. No, it's that grogginess you get after you stay up too late until the sun is cresting the horizon. When you're so sleepy you get the chills. When you're so tired you could fall asleep mid-conversation and have no regrets. That's what I feel like right now, and my cross-country trip is only part of the reason.

Gavin is here. How in the world is Gavin *here*? In Seattle? And why is he in my brother's house?

Logically, I know why. There's no other reason *why*. I just don't want it to be true.

I pretended not to remember him. It killed me, but I couldn't risk Reed knowing. How could I convince him to let me stay here if he knew I know his teammate…*intimately*? And how the hell am I going to go back out there and pretend some more? How am I going to act like Gavin is a stranger, especially when I know his lips taste like scotch and his hands feel like heaven?

Because I remember him. *Of course* I do. Every detail, from our meeting at the bar and how he looked at me like I was the only girl in the room to him asking me to leave and me saying yes. Our time in the hotel. The way he kissed me…touched me…I remember it all. Every damn part of it.

Even the one where I walked away.

I squeeze my eyes shut and bounce my head off the door. Maybe if I hit hard enough, I can forget all my awful mistakes, like walking away from him without a way to get in touch. Or I can forget why I came to Seattle in the first place. Now that would be a treat.

I'm not sure I even meant to come here. I just wanted to get away from New York and everything awful there. I got on my phone and booked a flight to the first place I could think of. Now, here I am, with no plan, no place to go, and a brother who is pissed I'm in his house.

I move to the sink, wash my hands, and try hard not to look into the mirror. I don't need to see how lifeless my eyes are or how messy my hair looks. I already know I look haggard. I just really wish it wasn't happening in front of Gavin. The last time he saw me,

I was dressed to the nines and to impress, not looking like a shell of myself. I still can't believe he's here. How, after all this time, is he in the last place I expected him to be? How is he here, where I ran to for a fresh start? And how does he still look so damn good?

Those hazel eyes of his…his long, thick legs… His strong arms and hands made me feel alive for the first time in what felt like an eternity. He looks good. *Too* good. Especially for someone I can't have, and not just because it's far too soon after my divorce to try the whole finding-true-love thing again. Reed already hates me. I can't add to that by starting something with his teammate.

Not that I planned to. I don't want to start anything with anyone. I still need time. The wounds… they're still much too fresh to even think about something serious. Right now, I need to focus on me, and that's it—no other distractions. Just getting back to the Vanessa I was before this whole mess.

I splash cold water on my face, using the hand towel to pat it dry. I dare a quick glance at the mirror just to make sure my hair isn't *too* ragged, and I'm shocked by what I see. I look *rough*. No, worse than rough. Like I haven't slept in months and haven't eaten in just as long. My eyes are sunken in, I don't remember the last time I actually did something with my hair other than throw it into a messy bun, and I'm rapidly working on being mistaken for Casper the Friendly Ghost.

I can't believe Gavin recognized me. I *barely* recognize myself. Maybe this move will be what I need to get back to where I was before I met Neal and lost myself, before I got married. Before I got divorced.

Before I found out that—*No.*

I push the thought from my mind. I don't need to spiral right now, not while standing in Reed's guest bathroom with him and his fiancée close by. I tuck away all the bad thoughts, roll my shoulders back, and open the door.

I hear my brother before I see him.

"What the fuck is she doing here, Mom?"

I'm not sure if I should laugh or not. Reed called his mother to find out why I'm here instead of just asking me. Does he hate me that much?

There's a long pause, and I'm sure it's Angie trying to diffuse the situation as best as she can. She's always tried to be the peacekeeper between us since she and my father got married. Sometimes I wonder if that's why Reed hates me so much. I was the baggage that came with my father, and I wonder if he felt like we were trying to replace the family he lost.

It's clear now that I was a fool to come running here. I should have stayed in New York, where everyone whispers about me behind my back.

"But why does she need to 'find herself' *here*? In Seattle? At my *house*?"

Because I have nowhere else to go, and I was hoping my brother would have my back, I want to say, but I keep my mouth shut.

"Yes, I know she's my—I wasn't going to say evil! I was just going to say *step*sister."

Ah, yes. Always adding the *step* in there, just to rub it in my face that we aren't *really* family in his eyes. I get it—he was grown and already in the NHL when our parents met. But he wasn't around to see their love blossom, to watch two broken people find each other and heal. He missed all that.

I didn't. I saw it all. I was there. We're family, and Angie feels like my family just as much as he does.

"Fine." He sighs. "But, Mom, Auden's due any day now. We have a baby coming. I can't...I can't babysit her, all right? I can't be her caretaker. If she's really here to figure her life out, *she* needs to figure it out. I can't do it for her."

He isn't wrong, but it doesn't mean his words hurt any less. It's nothing I haven't been telling myself, though. It's why I'm here: to figure my life out on my own for the first time. I just need a little help to get me started.

I know I should have thought this through more, but thinking was sort of the last thing on my mind in the moment. I just needed gone, and I needed gone fast, so Seattle it was. I knew someone here. I had a place to go. I wouldn't be alone.

But now, as I step closer to the kitchen and look at Reed's face as he ends the call with his mother, I'm beginning to believe I was mistaken on that. Springing this on him wasn't the best idea, but I didn't tell anyone about this trip aside from my dad and Angie, and that's only because my dad needed to hire a new assistant with me leaving.

My brother pinches the bridge of his nose as his fiancée comes around the island to rub his tense shoulders. It's real moments like this that almost make me forget she's a billionaire who was once a powerhouse in the hotel industry. She's so down to earth. So…normal.

"You okay?" Auden asks.

He shakes his head. "No, I'm pissed as fuck. What does she think she's doing, just showing up here? We're about to have a *baby*, Auden."

"She's looking for help, Reed."

"From *me*?"

Me comes out incredulously, and I can't entirely blame him. We haven't exactly had the best relationship through the years. We've fought more than we've gotten along and have ignored each other even more. I know he calls me his *evil stepsister* and all, but I didn't think that meant he wouldn't help me if I ever came to him for it.

I guess I was wrong.

"Yes, *you*. You're her brother. And don't you dare put *step* in front of that word," she says as he opens his mouth, likely to do just that. "You're supposed to be there for her, no matter what."

"Since when did you become Team Vanessa? I thought you didn't like her."

"Hey, I like her."

"You called her mean and vindictive the first time you met her."

"To be fair, I didn't know she had been cheated on by her husband. None of us did. All she talked about was wanting revenge, not the why. We had no idea what she was going through. Now, though…" She shrugs. "I get it. I would have been the same way, and that jerk deserved to lose everything after what he did to her."

I grin. She's right that Neal deserved it, but he didn't lose everything.

"That's fair," Reed says, dragging me back to the present. "I guess I just don't understand why me. We don't even like each other."

"Maybe that's exactly why you. Maybe what she needs right now is to get away from everything in New York, from all the people who judge her and expect certain things from her. Maybe she needs someone who won't coddle her. Maybe she needs her evil stepbrother."

How she knows better than anyone else what it is I'm looking for, I have no idea, but Auden is right. That's precisely why I came to Seattle—though I'm not sure I even knew it until now.

I clear my throat, stepping out of the shadows and fully into the expansive yet still somehow cozy kitchen. Reed whips his head my way, but Auden looks unsurprised to see me. I wonder if she knew I was there all along.

I blow out a shaky breath and give my older brother a soft smile. "I know we haven't always gotten along in the past. I was a young, bratty teen, and well, okay, a pretty shitty early twenty-something too. But I'm…" I take another steadying breath, already hating admitting this next part. "I'm not exactly doing okay right now. I'm struggling, and I need somewhere to stay while I get back on my feet and figure out the rest of my life. Not long-term, I promise. I don't want to interrupt the amazing life you've built here. I just…" I sigh. "I'm feeling lost, you know? What happened in New York… It was a lot, and I'd like to find a place to heal. A place to learn who I am now. A place I can feel safe. This was the first one that came to mind, but if you don't have the room or mental bandwidth given everything going on, I understand. Just tell me to go and I'll go. I'll—"

"Stay," Auden says, stepping forward. She takes my hands in hers, squeezing them tightly, her eyes brimming with tears. "You'll stay. That's what you'll do. Right, Reed?"

She peeks back at her future husband, but he isn't looking at her. He's staring right at me, lips slightly parted, head tilted to the side. It feels like he's looking at me for the first time, and I'm unsure how I feel about that for so many reasons, number one being *I* don't even know who I am right now.

Slowly, he rights his head, then finally nods. "You'll stay."

"Are you sure?"

He folds his arms over his chest. "I'm sure."

Relief floods me instantly. A bit of the weight on my shoulders relents, and I don't feel as tired as I did just a few minutes ago.

"But…" he says, and I hold my breath. "The baby is coming very soon. We…" He runs his hand over his jaw, reminding me so much of Gavin that I have to force myself not to look away. "We have a family we're building here, Van. I know you're going through a lot. Just because you're divorced, it doesn't mean you're automatically healed. Trust me, I know a bit about healing from heartbreak."

Auden gives me a sad smile, once more squeezing my hands, which she still hasn't let go of.

"And I'm not going to put a time limit on things, but…"

"But you want me out of your house sooner rather than later?" I finish for him.

He shrugs like he's sorry, but I know he's not. I understand where he's coming from. I truly do, and I don't plan to take advantage of his kindness in the slightest. I just need something—*anything*—to get me through until I can figure things out.

I nod. "I hear you loud and clear, big brother."

He narrows his eyes. "*Step*brother."

Auden huffs at him before pulling me into her arms and hugging me as best as she can with her enormous belly between us. The gesture catches me off guard, and I'm unsure if it's because it's so surprising or something else. Either way, I hug her back just as fiercely as she holds on to me, and something rattles loose inside me. Not by much, but still. I think I needed the hug more than I realized.

"Welcome to Washington, Vanessa," she says into my ear, and it reminds me of the way Gavin looked at me when he uttered those words. "We'll get you back together in no time."

Back together, she says. I doubt anyone can fix me at this point. I feel broken beyond repair, like I'll never be whole again no matter how much glue I use. But I want to be. I want to be my old self again. No, *better*. I want to feel like I did that night with Gavin. I want to be that person again.

I don't want to be Vanessa, the girl who got married and separated within six months. I don't want to be Vanessa, the girl whose heart was broken by the same man…*twice*. I don't want to be Vanessa, the girl who couldn't handle it and ran away.

I don't want to be Vanessa at all.

I want to be Nessa, want to feel the way I did with Gavin in New York, where I was someone else. Someone better. Someone new.

That's what I need right now, and I think Seattle is just the place to find it.

Chapter 5

LOCKE

"I should have worked out more this summer."

"Are you shitting me? You're fucking jacked, bro. If anything, I think you should have laid off the weights a bit. Should have hired you as my personal trainer instead of that guy I paid way too much money for."

"You just have to start small. One workout a day, then work your way up to two. It's nothing after that. Plus, it's a good way to get away from the kids."

"Preach, man."

I listen as my teammates Frederic and Poldzkin go back and forth on their workout routines. Some of it's good, but a lot of it is over the top and completely unnecessary. I would know—I've spent a lot more years than they have training for hockey.

Either way, it's enough to distract me from the nonstop madness that's been raging in my head since the party at Hutch's last week. I've replayed that day on a loop, like watching a game tape and trying to find my mistake that lets the other team score.

Nessa walking in. Nessa looking at everyone. Nessa looking at *me* like she looked at everyone else. Nessa in the hallway, how gorgeous her green eyes were, even though she looked like she was about two seconds away from falling asleep standing up. Nessa when Hutch kicked us all to the curb and how she was *still* looking at me like everyone else—like a stranger.

It was hard then, and it's still hard now. I want to see her again. Want to talk to her, even if just for a minute. Just to figure out why she's pretending not to know me. Then I'll be fine. I'll be *good*. I won't be wondering about this any longer and can focus solely on hockey like I should be already.

"What about you, Whitlocke?"

"Hmm?" I glance up to find Frederic and Poldzkin staring at me expectantly. I run a towel over my face as I pump my legs on the stationary bike. "Sorry, I kind of zoned out. What's up?"

"We were wondering what your routine looks like. How the hell do you stay in such good shape at your age?"

At your age. I know I'm the oldest player on the team, but do they really have to remind me of it all the time? The media does it enough already. I think the last person to not care about my age was…

I shake away the thought. It was *her*, and I can't start thinking about her again. It's too damn dangerous, especially since her brother just walked in the door.

"Legs. Lots of legs. Light, repetitious weight. I don't go for heavy. And I only lift three times a week. Maybe four if I'm feeling up for it, but nothing more. I don't see the point. On the other days, I take walks or ride the bike. Nothing too wild or time-consuming. Keep it simple and save the rest of your energy for on-ice work."

"He's right," Hutch says, picking up two twenty-pound weights and taking an open spot. "Told me that years ago, and I've been doing it ever since. Never felt better on and off the ice."

"No shit?" Frederic says. "Fuck, might have to give that a whirl. Might miss my me-time in the gym though." He walks to Hutch, clapping him on the back. "You'll get it soon, Captain. Once that kid of yours comes, you'll know those extra hours in the gym do wonders for your mood. Let the wife take care of the baby while you take care of the career, you know."

Hutch catches my eye in a look that says, *Is this guy fucking for real?*

I lift a single brow back. *Afraid so.*

My captain looks like he's about to set his teammates straight when trouble struts through the door.

"You fucking blocked me out there, dude."

"Why the hell would I block you? No way am I putting my body on the line this early in the year. Have you ever considered you just suck? Not as well as your mom does, but you still suck."

"You've never even met my mother!" Lawson fires back at Keller.

"As far as you know." Keller delivers it so deadpan you could almost believe him if you didn't know better.

"I can settle this for you two real quick, you know," Fox says, always trying to mediate.

"And I'll back him up," Hayes offers. "I was right there and saw the whole thing."

"Which means you saw Keller block my shot."

Fox and Hayes trade glances, and though I wasn't on the ice for whatever the fuck it is they're arguing about, it's clear Lawson is wrong.

"Uh, look, Lawsy," Hayes says softly, using the same tone I've heard him use on Flora when he's breaking some bad news to her.

"No, no, no." Lawson sticks his fingers into his ears, just like the child Hayes is treating him as. "I'm not listening."

"Anyone know how the fuck Rory puts up with him?" Keller grumbles.

"I heard that!"

"I thought you weren't listening?" the captain says in the middle of his bicep curls.

"Well, I'm listening now! But I'm still not talking to you."

Hutch rolls his eyes. "For fuck's sake, I didn't kick you out of my house. I had an unexpected guest I had to deal with."

"How's that going, by the way?" Fox asks. "Is your sister"—he holds his hands up when Hutch glares at him—"*step*sister settling in okay?"

My ears perk up at the mention of Nessa, but I try hard as hell to look as uninterested as possible, still pumping my legs on the bike. I've wanted to ask after her every single day since the party, but that would be incredibly suspicious. I shouldn't care about his sister, yet I do.

"Van is… Well, she's Van. She got a job, so I guess that's something. At least she's not sulking around the house as much."

"She just got divorced like, what, six months ago? Think she's allowed to sulk a bit, eh?"

Hutch is taken aback by my words, and I don't blame him. I shouldn't have said anything. It shouldn't matter to me what Nessa does or doesn't do. I guess I still can't help myself when it comes to sticking up for her.

He surprises me by nodding. "That's fair. Shit." He drops his weights on the rack, his hands going to his hips. "I need to stop being such a dick. Auden keeps telling me so, but it's just… Fuck, I don't know. Vanessa and I have never really seen eye to eye, you know? I know a lot of that might have been because she was just a teenager when our parents got together, so she was bratty as hell, but still. We're just two different people. Having her around… It's hard. And I'm nesting. Fuck, I'm nesting. I want everything to be perfect for this kid. It *has* to be perfect. I can't be expected to be away for half the season and not have my shit together. I'm not leaving that burden to Auden. She already has enough on her plate. So much. Carrying a damn baby. She's a fucking warrior. You have no idea. She's up peeing at all hours of the night, uncomfortable as hell because she can't breathe or because the baby is moving too much, and then she just smiles through the day like it's nothing. She's still putting makeup on every day. Makeup! Like I give a shit if she wears it or not. She's so damn beautiful anyway, it doesn't matter. I'm just…" He finally gulps in a big breath. "I'm scared. Shitless. I am fucking scared shitless. What the hell am I doing?"

He looks around the room, eyes wide with fear, and

I wonder if it's the first time he's expressed all this out loud because it sure as hell looks like it is. The rest of us exchange glances. That speech took a turn none of us were prepared for, not even Hutch.

"Are, uh, are you okay, Hutchinson?" Lawson asks softly, and it's probably the calmest I've seen him in a long damn time. It shows how serious this is.

"I…I don't know."

Hutch's voice is scratchy and full of panic, and it's all it takes for us to pounce on him. We gather around for an awkward group hug, minus Keller, who stands on the sidelines, arms crossed, lips pulled into his perpetual frown.

"Fuck," he mutters once we let him go, scrubbing his hands over his face. He sniffles, blinking away the tears we're all pretending aren't there. "Shit. I'm sorry. I didn't mean to unload on you guys. I'm supposed to be the captain, the leader of this team, and here I am unable to keep my shit together."

"You have nothing to apologize for," Fox says, giving him another pat. "We're here for you. Whatever you need. You know that."

"Yeah, what kind of club would we be if we weren't? Serpents Singles forever," Lawson tells him with a grin.

"We aren't a club," Keller complains. "And if we were, we wouldn't be a singles club. All you assholes are in relationships. It's just me and Locke now. We're the only two who took this shit seriously, apparently." He juts his chin out toward me.

"The fact that we're a club is still clearly up for debate, but what's not is the fact that we're still boys."

Everyone groans at that.

"What?" Lawson says. "What'd I say?"

"We aren't *boys*. That just sounds so…juvenile." Hayes shakes his head. "Let's just say we're friends, yeah? And when friends are having a hard time, we do something about it. So, I propose we take our asses down to Top Shelf and have a drink to celebrate the start of the season and the beautiful baby your fiancée is about to birth, and we just let everything else fall to the wayside for now. What do you say, Hutchy?"

Our captain exhales heavily, then nods. "I could use a beer."

Lawson lets out a loud whoop, and even Keller looks excited by this idea.

"Then let's go. I'll give Lilah a call and tell her I'm going to be late."

"Good boy," Keller mutters to our number one goalie.

Fox flips him off.

"You already know I'm in," Lawson says. "Besides, I could use some time away from the old ball and chain."

"Ball and chain?" Hayes rolls his eyes. "Please, you worship the ground Rory walks on. We all fucking know it. *Oh, Rory, you're so amazing. You look so cute in your scrubs,*" he says in a high-pitched voice.

"*Oh, Rory, you're so incredible. I might be the dumbest boy alive, but I'm still smart enough to know how lucky I am to be in your presence,*" Keller adds.

"*Oh, Rory, you're so…so…*" Fox sighs. "Shit, I can't think of anything. Rory's just really cool, you know?"

We all laugh. *Of course* that's what Fox comes up with. He's always the nice guy, even when he tries not to be.

We clean up our equipment, and I ignore how jelly-like my legs are as I hop off the bike. If they're already hurting after a simple preseason workout, I can't imagine how I'm going to feel once I'm actually on the ice, where everyone is younger and faster than me.

It's just more proof that I need to focus on this season more than anything else. No distractions, especially not in the form of a beautiful blonde bombshell with the most captivating green eyes I've ever seen. Hockey. Just hockey.

We hit the showers for a quick rinse and head out to the bar, each of us taking our own cars. I'm almost certain half the guys will make up an excuse to leave within an hour of being there. That's how it's gone since they started pairing off. One minute we'll be there shooting the shit, feeling like it did back when we first started the club. The next it'll just be me and Keller, drinking to forget how lonely we both are. He'll never admit it, of course, but I can.

I *am* lonely, and I wish like hell I weren't. But there's not much I can do about that now with everything on the line—my future as a top defenseman in the NHL, as a Seattle Serpent, and my hockey career. There's no time to think about being lonely. That's a problem for post-hockey me, and since I'm not ready to hang up my skates, I'll have plenty of time to worry about that later.

I find street parking near Top Shelf and click the button on my key fob to lock my AMG just as Hutch jogs up to me.

"Hey," he says, his shoulder bumping against mine as he shoves his hands into his pockets. "Sorry about getting a little riled up back there. Just a lot going through my mind right now, you know?"

"I know. But like Hayesy said, we're here for you. We are friends. Your *family*. We're here through it all, even if you just need to do a little venting."

He nods a few times. "Thanks, man. I, uh, I appreciate it." His voice is thick with emotion, and I can't say I blame him. He's juggling a lot right now.

Hutch clears his throat and opens the door to Top Shelf. "Now, let's have a drink, yeah?"

We step inside, and Hutch comes to a dead stop. I barely catch myself from running into the back of him.

"What the fuck?" he says.

I look around him and blink. Once, then twice. A third time for good measure. The good news is that thanks to Hutch's reaction, I'm not seeing things.

The bad news? We might have brought him to the wrong place to try to relax. Standing behind the bar is the very same blonde woman I've been trying hard to put out of my mind.

Nessa.

She's nodding at whatever the bartender says as she pours shots into a glass. Her bottom lip is caught between her teeth, her eyebrows cinched together in concentration. Even from here, I can tell she's tensed, afraid she'll drop something and mess up.

"What are you doing here?"

I hadn't even realized Hutch had moved, but suddenly he's across the room, standing at the bar right in front of her. I was too busy staring at her.

She looks up, startled. "Reed."

"What are you doing here, Van?" Hutch repeats, more bite behind each word.

I take that as my cue to join him, to hopefully keep him calm. The whole point of coming here was so he could blow off steam, not be triggered by his problems even more. I keep my eyes on his sister as I settle in beside him. She doesn't look my way even once, and I'm not sure if that pisses me off or if I'm grateful for it. I'm not entirely sure how much longer I can pretend I don't know her.

"Van? I thought you liked to go by Nessa," the bartender says.

"Nessa?" Hutch laughs. "Since when do you go by Nessa?"

"Since I want to," she answers, a bit of venom seeping into her words. She glares up at her brother. "What are you doing here?"

"What do you mean? This is my bar."

"Your bar? I didn't know you owned a bar."

He levels her with an annoyed look. "I don't mean *my* actual bar. This is where I come. My teammates and I." Hutch slaps me on the back. "Right, Locke?"

For the first time, Nessa turns her gaze to me, and I find myself holding my breath again. I don't know why I keep doing it. I'm not even entirely sure what I'm waiting for when I do it, but it happens anyway.

Hutch is looking at me, waiting for me to say something, so I exhale. "We come here after games a lot."

Slowly, she pulls her eyes from mine, looking back

at her brother. "Well, if you don't own the place, I guess I'm free to do as I please."

"Which is what?"

"Running a marathon." She lifts the glass, shaking it at him. "What the hell does it look like I'm doing? I work here now."

Hutch grinds his teeth, his jaw working back and forth as he processes that.

Finally, after several moments, he blows out a long breath and nods. "Okay."

Nessa looks surprised by his relenting. "Okay?"

"Yeah. Just don't…" He leans in closer. She follows. *Wildflowers. Lavender.*

"Just don't tell people we're related, yeah?" Her eyes widen, and I am about two seconds from punching my captain when he adds, "I don't mean that to be a dick. I mean it for your safety. For Auden's. For mine. I love my fans, and the regulars here have always left us alone for the most part, but people are fucking weird sometimes. You never know what kind of long game they're playing, and I don't want to jeopardize anyone. I just want us to be safe. *All* of us to be safe."

It might be the nicest thing I've ever heard Hutch say to or about his sister. Based on the look on Nessa's face, I'm not the only one who thinks that.

She gives him a hesitant smile. "I'll keep it to myself."

"Good." He taps the bar twice. "I'll take a whiskey, two cubes, and whatever he wants. I'm hitting the head."

His feet stomp across the floor as he walks away, leaving me alone with Nessa for the first time since the hallway. The other bartender has gone about his business but keeps one eye on me and his newest employee, just in case. I watch as she grabs a bottle of whiskey off the top shelf, plunks two ice cubes into a glass, and pours three fingers' worth of booze on top.

Silence sits heavy between us, an awkwardness that was never there in New York. I hate it. I hate that we're in this situation. I hate that we didn't exchange full names. I hate that we didn't trade numbers. I hate that she left me alone in my bed.

I clear my throat. "So, you work here now?"

"Yep." She sets Hutch's drink on the bar in front of me. "I work here now. What can I get you?"

Her words are cold. Robotic even. Like she couldn't care less that it's me sitting across from her.

It's my last straw. My breaking point.

I sigh. "Are we really going to keep pretending?"

"Pretending what?"

She says it so blasé. So unbothered.

But I know she's not. She's bothered, all right. It's evident in the way she can't seem to keep her eyes on mine, having to look away like she can't bear to keep staring at me. It's in the way she startles ever so slightly each time I speak, as if she's lost in her thoughts, and I just walked in and interrupted them. It's in how every time she dares a glance my way, her emerald eyes drop right to my lips.

"Stop pretending I don't know you wear cherry lip gloss, don't know what you sound like when you come." I lean closer, dropping my voice. "Don't know what your pretty pink cunt tastes like, *Nessa*."

The flush on her face is unmistakable. It reminds me of what she looked like that night, sweaty and satisfied on my hotel sheets.

I reach down and adjust my cock that's pressing against my zipper, then settle back on my stool. "So, are we really going to keep pretending?"

Her eyes are dilated, her pupils so big you can barely register the green. Cheeks flushed. Breaths coming in sharply. Her nostrils flare, and I have a feeling she's about to give me the tongue lashing of my life.

That's fine. I welcome it—anything to get her to acknowledge what happened between us.

"Oh, fuck off! I won! You know I did!"

We all turn our attention to the guys who just walked through the door rather loudly.

"Bullshit," Keller fires back at Lawson. "I got here first fair and square."

"No. No way. I was first. How the hell do you open the door without being first?"

"I said the first to *enter* the bar. Not my fault you stopped to be a gentleman."

"To be fair, he did say first to enter," Hayes sides with Keller.

Fox grimaces. "He did say that."

"Horseshit!" Lawson explodes, pointing at Keller. "I want a rematch."

"Rematch for a race to the place we're already at? Get a grip and buy me my drink, loser."

Lawson groans in frustration, then marches toward the bar, stopping short when he realizes who is behind it. "Holy shit. You're the evil stepsister. I—hey, ow!"

"Shut the fuck up," Hayes hisses at him after smacking him on the head.

He might be due a visit with Doc for concussion protocol before the season even starts if he keeps this up.

"Sorry." Lawson rubs at the spot, then grins at Nessa. "I didn't mean *evil*. I just meant stepsister." He holds his hand out to her. "I'm Lucas, but my friends call me—"

"No, we don't."

"Don't listen to him."

"Please, for the love of everything, shut the fuck up."

Fox, Hayes, and Keller all speak at once, interrupting Lawson, who was undoubtedly about to tell Nessa all about his self-appointed nickname.

Lawson rolls his eyes. "Sorry about them. I was going to say, my friends call me Lawson." Then he leans forward and—very poorly—whispers, "Lawless Lawson."

Nessa grins, and I hate and love it at the same time. I missed it. It's haunted my dreams since I saw her last. But I hate that it's not *me* she's smiling at.

I want it to be me.

"Nice to meet you, Lawless Lawson."

He beams, probably glad someone is finally listening to him and calling him Lawless like he's been trying to get us to do for years. He points to our goalie. "That's Arthur Fox."

"Ma'am," says the man in question, living up to his southern roots and tipping an imaginary hat at her.

She smiles, and something shifts in my chest.

Lawson points to Hayes next. "That's Adam Hayes. He banged his nanny."

"What the…" Hayes closes his eyes momentarily, likely to keep from killing his teammate, then smiles at Nessa. "Nice to meet you. Please ignore him. He loves to gossip."

"Is it really considered gossip if it's true?" Lawson shrugs. "And that's—"

"Keller. Just Keller," he interrupts.

"I was going to say Cheating Jackass Who Should Be Buying *Me* Drinks, but yeah, Keller works too." He tilts his head my way. "You met Gavin Whitlocke already, yeah?"

Our gazes collide, and if I look closely enough, I can see that pink creeping back into her cheeks.

"Something like that," she mutters before turning back to the guys. "So, what can I get you all to drink?"

They rattle off their orders, then amble over to the booth we tend to take control of whenever we're here. I don't make a move to join them, still waiting for Hutch to come out of the bathroom, where I'm sure he's calling Auden to check in with her.

Or at least that's the excuse I'm using to sit close to Nessa. She sets their drinks on a tray, adding Hutch's to the mix. Then she turns and rises up on her tiptoes, grabbing a bottle of Macallan from the top of the shelf.

She remembered.

I don't know why that delights me so much but, fuck, it really does.

She pours me three fingers' worth, then sets the glass on the tray without another glance in my direction. I watch her pick up the tray and unsteadily walk it over to the booth the other guys are occupying. I guess it's her not-so-subtle way of telling me to get lost. Funny, because she's the only thing I want to get lost in.

No.

I push that thought from my mind. She can't be the thing I get lost in. The season is just too important to let even a girl like her distract me. I pull myself off the stool just as Hutch walks back into the main room. He tucks his phone into his back pocket, confirming my suspicion that he was likely chatting with Auden.

"I miss anything?" he asks.

I shake my head. "Nah, nothing."

Still, I can't take my eyes off his sister. We settle into the booth, and I am unsurprised to find Lawson and Keller still going at it. Hutch joins the conversation right away, and I know then that this was the perfect distraction, even if Nessa is here. The guys talk around me, and I occasionally laugh or throw in a nod, but I'm not paying them any attention. Not really.

No, my focus is solely on the woman behind the bar. I watch her move around, making drinks and cracking open beer bottles. She laughs with customers. She stands too close to the other bartender, who teaches her to mix drinks. At one point, she twists her long blonde locks into a braid, letting it hang over her shoulder in a way that tempts me far too much.

But she never looks over here, no matter how much I will her to. I know she can feel my eyes on her. How could she not? I'm staring at her like some sort of stalker creep. I can't help it, though. Every time I look at her, all I can think of is that night. *Our* night. The one in New York. The last one to make me feel something.

As excited as I am for the new season to start, right now, the only place I want to be is back in that hotel, back on sheets that were a little too scratchy, a mattress that was a little too firm, and pillows that could have used replacing. None of it mattered when I had her there, and even though I shouldn't, I want her there again.

Chapter 6

VANESSA

Five months ago

"Where are we going?" I ask after we've already walked a few blocks in comfortable silence.

It's late, but New York City is still alive. It's always alive. It's one of my favorite parts about coming here. I love how the day never seems to end, even when it turns to night. It feels like you're invincible and have all the time in the world.

I haven't felt like that since the last time I was here. It was a few weeks before the wedding. Neal and I decided to get away for the weekend, a break from all the chaos of planning our perfect day, just us. It was magical—everything I could have wanted. Maybe even the last time I was truly happy.

But I don't want to think about my ex-husband right now. I want to enjoy this moment, revel in this beautiful April night, the cool breeze on my skin, and the sounds of people laughing bouncing off the buildings. I want to enjoy this time with Gavin while I still have it. Even though this is The City That Never Sleeps, tomorrow still comes, and tomorrow is when I go back to being my old self again. No more fake names to hide behind. No more half-truths. No more pretending my life isn't falling apart.

"Wherever you want." His voice is smooth like a glass of whiskey after dessert. The kind that sits on the shelf and lasts for years and years because you save it for special occasions. His touch on my lower back is just as delicious. Soft. Hot.

I wish I could say it's the alcohol making me feel this way, but I know it's not. It is the cologne that smells so familiar yet so distinct. It's how the top of my head only comes to his shoulder. And it's how he drags me closer each time somebody walks by us, like he's trying to keep me close and keep me safe.

Safe. I can't remember the last time someone made me feel that way.

I never felt *un*safe with Neal, but I guess I never really felt relaxed either. I was always *on.* Smiling at his company parties. Planning lunches and dinners with friends. Making sure everything was Instagram-worthy perfect, just like I always wanted my life to be.

So much for that.

"Are you okay?" Gavin asks, snapping me out of my awful thoughts.

"Hmm? Oh, yeah. I'm fine."

"Are you sure? I felt you tense up a bit. Everything okay?"

I nod, but it slowly transforms into a headshake. Suddenly, my eyes feel heavy, and there's a burning sensation in my nose. My throat tightens as if I've been chugging sand. I'm going to cry. I *hate* crying, and I really hate crying in front of other people.

That doesn't stop the tears from coming anyway, and once they start, it feels impossible to stop. Gavin notices, and then we're not walking anymore. No, I'm pressed against something hard and warm that smells like a bakery you walk by on a quiet street, especially in the fall when everything feels cozy and the air has that perpetual scent of cinnamon. Strong arms encircle and hold me tightly as I bury my face against Gavin's chest. This *stranger's* chest.

Oh god, what is wrong with me? Why am I a total mess? How am I unable to take a simple walk with possibly the hottest man I've ever seen? Why do I feel so damn broken?

Gavin's chin rests atop my head as his hands draw small circles on my back. It's a good hug. A comforting hug. I think the last time I had a hug like this was… Actually, I'm not sure if I've ever had one.

I like it far too much, but that's a bag to unpack another night.

Tonight, I just want to enjoy it.

The tears keep coming as so many thoughts run through my mind. Memories of meeting Neal in the city my freshman year of college. Us falling in what I thought was true love. The picnics he would spontaneously take me on and the extravagant trips that allowed me to see the world. Our home upstate where I thought we'd build a family. The home I thought we'd build a future in.

The home that's no longer a home at all.

I press my nose more firmly against Gavin's chest, letting myself get lost in him. Lost in something unfamiliar. Something that doesn't hurt. When I think I've finally cried all the tears I could possibly cry, I pull away, grimacing at the wet spot I've left on his nice dress shirt. There's even a bit of black from my mascara. I knew I should've worn the waterproof one tonight, but I promised myself no crying.

Guess I broke that rule.

"I'm sorry," I tell him as I wipe the wetness from under my eyes. "I swear I'm not usually such an emotional mess. It's just this divorce is hard, you know? Well, no, I guess *you* don't know. But it is. It's so hard, and I'm so tired of being heartbroken. I'm tired of being looked at with pity because my marriage didn't work out. I'm sick of being sad, but when I try to be happy, nothing feels right, not even my old hobbies. I used to love to paint. It was my outlet. It made me so damn happy that I was planning on transferring to art school when I realized I hated what I was studying. I wanted to open my own studio one day, but Neal told me not to, told me to keep to the path I was on because it was more stable. So that's what I did, and now I'm not even sure if I *can* paint anymore. Do I even remember how? I picked up a paintbrush a month ago, thinking I could give it a try, and nothing happened. I just stared at a blank canvas. And stared some more. Then some more and…it's still blank. That's how I feel. Blank. Like nothing. Like just…just…a failure. I feel like a failure."

The words tumble out of me, and I don't even realize what I'm saying or how true it is until I'm done. That's the worst part of this all, how big of a disappointment I feel like. Who gets married and divorced so quickly? Not people like me, that's for sure. It just all feels so…sad. And I hate it.

I gulp in breath after breath, trying to calm my hammering heart, but it feels pointless. Ugh. I can't believe I just dumped all that on him and cried on his shirt. I'm more of a mess than I realized.

There's a soft touch under my chin, and Gavin pulls my gaze to his. I expect to see a whole lot of embarrassment and pity in his eyes, but there is none —only understanding. It makes me want to start crying all over again.

"You are not a failure," he says gently and slowly, like he's trying to make sure I hear and understand every word.

"How do you know?"

"You're right. I guess I don't actually know, but I can tell just like I can tell you're going to be okay. This won't be the defining factor in your life forever. One day, you'll look back at all of it and laugh. You'll wake up and wonder why you spent so much time crying over someone who doesn't deserve your tears. You'll dust yourself off, get back out there, and find that love again. It probably doesn't feel like it now, but you will." He lifts my chin higher. "And what did I say about explaining yourself? You don't need to. Don't need to apologize. Besides, I have three sisters, so I think I can handle a few girl tears."

His words are sweet. Touching, even though I'm not quite sure he's right. It certainly doesn't feel like he is. I don't think I'll ever get over this.

"Three sisters?" I say, trying to change the subject. "Are you the only boy?"

He laughs lightly, dropping my chin. "Not by a long shot. I have three brothers as well. My parents didn't really know when to quit until they did, you know? My siblings took after them, giving me a horde of nieces and nephews to spoil over the years."

"I can't imagine having six siblings. I only have the one and, well, I'm pretty sure most days he hates me."

"If he hates you, it's his problem, not yours. And in my humble opinion, it would be a huge mistake on his part not to want to know you." He bends ever so slightly and I can see the swirls of green and brown in his eyes under the hazy yellow streetlights. "Because I think knowing you could be a great adventure, love."

Each word sends a shiver down my spine, and if his twitching lips are any indication, Gavin doesn't miss it. I'm about to tell him I want to know him too, when suddenly, I'm struck from behind. My heel gets stuck on a crack in the sidewalk, and I plummet to the ground. Gavin reaches for me—because of course he does—but he's not quick enough, and I feel my knee scrape against the concrete. I know before even having to look that I'm bleeding.

"Hey, what the fuck?!" Gavin yells at whoever just went zooming by.

I glance up just in time to see somebody on a skateboard fly around the corner, nearly knocking somebody else over in the process, their middle finger extended high above their head.

"Fucking prick," my savior says, pulling me to my feet. He brushes my hair back, cupping my cheeks in his big hands. His eyes bounce all over my face like he's checking me for damage. "Are you okay? Are you hurt?"

"Just my ego." I wince as I try to take a step. "And maybe my knee."

Against my better judgment, I glance down…and nearly go tumbling to the sidewalk again.

"Fuck," Gavin mutters as he catches me once more, this time before I hit the ground. "Nessa?"

Nessa. I grin at the name I gave him, that woozy feeling I always get whenever I see blood falling over me like a blanket. He gathers me into his arms, holding me tightly as I work to regain basic control of my body.

"Nessa? Nessa?" He holds my chin between his thumb and forefinger, looking down into my eyes.

It does nothing to help the dizziness. Something inside me snaps all at once, and I gulp in a full breath of air for what feels like the first time in minutes. Gavin looks panicked for a moment before he finally realizes what's going on.

"Shit," he mutters, resting his forehead against mine. "Shit. You scared me, love."

"S-Sorry," I say through my chattering teeth. I always get a rush of cold after an episode like this. I guess that doesn't change even if I'm pressed against a warm body. "I'm okay."

"Blood?" he asks, his own breaths a bit shaky.

"Blood," I repeat.

He sighs heavily, releasing his strong hold on me but not fully letting me go. He grasps my hand like he's afraid I'm going to fall or nearly faint again if he doesn't. He rolls his tongue against his lips, looking down the sidewalk toward even brighter lights.

"Look, I have a hotel room nearby. I can clean you up there, get you some water…you look like you could use some."

He's inviting me back to his hotel room. I know he said it's to get me cleaned up, but do I really know that? How can I be sure he's not going to expect something else? Something tells me he isn't. Something tells me he's just a good guy and truly wants to help me.

Still, I hesitate. Not because I don't trust him, but because this isn't me. I'm not the kind of girl to walk a city alone with a guy I just met, and I'm definitely not the kind of girl to go back to a stranger's hotel room, even if it is just to clean a wound. Then again, I've not been myself all night. Why start now?

"I'm sorry that was really awkward. I didn't mean anything by it. No innuendo. I just—"

"Yes."

He lifts his brows at the singular word. "Yes?"

I nod. "Yes. But just to clean my leg. Because I

really cannot stand the sight of blood, and I worry if I try to clean it myself, I'm going to end up passed out in some random bathroom in the middle of New York City, and I'd rather not do that."

My parents would lose their minds if that happened.

He grins, and it's not one of those sleazy, grimy grins you would get from just about any other guy. No, it's genuine, and it makes me feel too warm inside. With my hand still in his, Gavin leads the way. The whole walk to his hotel, he steals peeks at me, checking to make sure I'm okay and my leg hasn't fallen off somewhere along the way. Or at least I assume that's what he's looking for. Whatever the case, I like it.

He guides us into The Sinclair New York, and for a moment, I panic. *I'm* staying at this hotel too. Does he know that? Has this all been some weird elaborate game? But as he pulls me into the elevator and presses the button for a floor I'm not on, I realize it's just a coincidence.

At least the walk back to my room will be quick.

I settle back against his touch, needing it. Needing anything really. Something to reassure me I'm doing the right thing by going back to his room with him. *It's just to clean up the blood. That's all. Nothing else. It's innocent.* I repeat this to myself as the elevator climbs to the fifty-second floor. The chime says we've reached our destination, and I notice Gavin doesn't make a move to leave immediately. It's almost as if he's waiting for me, giving me a chance to change my mind.

I don't want to change my mind.

When the doors slide open, I step out of the elevator. He's right behind me, his hand still pressed against my lower back, directly above my ass. If I were to put just a little more jaunt in my step, his touch would slip lower, and I'd feel him there. A part of me wants to, too.

But I don't.

He stops in front of his room, pressing his phone against the big black circle on the door.

"Just so you know, this isn't me. My, uh, company paid for the swanky room."

"Fancy," I mutter, not mentioning that I'm staying here and not on company dime, but because the woman who created this luxury hotel chain is pregnant with my stepbrother's baby.

Gavin never did elaborate on what he does for work, but I guess that's fair. I haven't exactly told him a lot about me either. Though what am I going to say? I'm an assistant in my father's law firm and I hate every moment of it? Not because of my dad—he's amazing. It's just not exactly what I envisioned I'd be doing with my life. I wanted to travel and see the world. Experience different cultures, meet new and interesting people. I wanted to create gorgeous paintings of whatever country I found myself in.

But I never got to do any of that. I met Neal, and he became everything. He urged me to get my business degree so I could "do something practical." Then he encouraged me to forgo using it, instead staying home to support him as he rose through the ranks of his investment firm. He's the one who told me to stop with my silly drawings and focus on building our future. I'm the idiot who listened to him.

"You okay?" Gavin asks, and I wonder if he can read my mind since he seems to know when I'm stuck in it for too long.

"Yep."

He nods, then pushes the door open farther, allowing me to enter the room first. I keep waiting for my senses to tell me this is wrong and that I should bolt right out the door, but it never happens, not even as I walk deeper inside. It's a near copy of my own room five floors higher, decorated much like the rest of the hotel: a bit of modern mixed with vintage plus a bit of New York. Sleek yet cozy. Dark but not in a scary way.

The door clicks softly shut behind me, and I peer over my shoulder. Gavin takes up nearly the entire entryway. So big and so tall. Though I'm a few inches above the average height for a woman, I still feel so small beside him, and I like it a little too much.

He ducks into the bathroom, and I let my eyes wander over his things—a pair of socks near the chair, a tie wadded up on the desk, a book, and a pair of glasses near the bed. He's made himself comfortable here.

"I don't have much, but I think this will do," Gavin says as he walks into the main room.

He's holding a small first-aid kit in one hand and a wet washcloth in the other.

"What?" he asks as he gestures for me to take a seat on the bed. "Why are you smiling?"

I shake my head as I settle onto the mattress, which is, of course, perfect too. "Nothing. Just thought it was cute you travel with a first-aid kit."

"You don't?" He squats in front of me, and I notice how his pants stretch over his thighs. *Big* thighs. Thick. Muscular.

"Can't say I've ever even thought about it."

He shakes his head with a weary sigh. "Such a rookie mistake. You never know when you're going to need it."

"Apparently not. I didn't exactly have 'almost get run over by a skateboarder' on my agenda for this trip."

"No, I guess you didn't." He peeks up at me. "This might hurt a bit, so bear with me. You ready?"

I nod, holding my breath as he cleans the wound

with the washcloth. He's right. It does hurt, but it's nothing compared to how it feels having his hand wrapped around my ankle. His touch is gentle yet firm. Soft but calloused. And I don't hate it one bit. I try not to be disappointed when he lets me go, reaching into the small kit and digging out some petroleum jelly and a bandage.

"So, vacation, huh?" he asks, ripping open the ointment package.

I smile. He's trying to distract me. I love that he's trying to distract me.

"Sort of. Family thing. They're out with my brother, and I wasn't up for tagging along."

"The sounds fun. What all are you doing while you're in town?"

I don't mention the hockey game my parents went to tonight. I don't usually like telling people about what my brother does for a living, not just because we barely tolerate one another, but because I never know if someone is trying to use it to their advantage. I don't think Gavin would, but still.

"Little bit of this, little bit of that," I answer noncommittally. "Nobody wanted to go to the bar with me, and now I can see why. I felt a bit old being there myself."

"Old." He makes a displeased noise as he continues getting my bandage ready. "You're not old,

Nessa, far from it. You're young. Maybe even too young."

Those last four words feel like they're for himself, and it makes me wonder how old he is. It feels wrong to ask, though. Besides, what would it matter? I'm leaving after this, and I'll never see him again.

His brows dip closer together in concentration as he wrestles with the bandage, trying to avoid letting the sticky parts touch one another while he applies jelly to it.

"Almost got it…" he murmurs. "There." He looks back up at me. "Ready for the bandage?"

I nod again, hoping like hell he doesn't hear my quiet inhale as he touches me, this time closer to my wound. His fingers curl around my calf, sliding up ever so slowly, and I have to actively work not to shake from his touch. It doesn't stop the goose bumps, though. No, those break out over my skin anyway.

Gavin smiles at that.

"Sorry. Cold in here," I murmur as an excuse, though it's not cold at all. If anything, I'm sweating, and it has nothing to do with the temperature of the room.

It's all the man kneeling before me, the one with the gray-streaked hair and the hazel eyes that are too damn pretty to be real. His fingers massage the tense muscle as he gently places the bandage over my scrape.

I laugh when I realize what's on it. "Baby Shark?"

He doesn't look the least bit bashful when he says, "Loads of nieces and nephews, remember?"

"Ah. Makes sense."

"How are you feeling? Okay?"

"Yes," I say, but that's not exactly true. Not when his hand is still wrapped around me and he's still looking up at me, stealing my breath moment by moment.

And that's what he does—he holds on to me and he stares. It's so quiet in here I swear I can hear a clock faintly ticking away.

Tick. Tick. Tick.

But I'm not weirded out by it, and it doesn't feel awkward. It feels…I don't even know what. I just know I don't want to move, and I don't want Gavin to move. Except maybe closer. I wouldn't be mad about that.

He must feel the same way because he does. Just an inch, maybe two, but it's enough to make a big difference. Enough for me to be swimming in that cinnamon scent all over again. His fingers dance higher, skimming along the edge of my dress, and I'm suddenly very aware of how easy it would be to pull it higher and beg for his touch.

Beg for his touch? Oh, god. What's gotten into me tonight? Were those amaretto sours more potent than I thought? Or am I just that desperate to be touched?

Likely the latter. It's been…I don't even know how long at this point. Since a month after the wedding? That should have been another sign that something was wrong. What kind of newlywed isn't eager to jump in the sack and stay there? Neal, apparently.

But I don't want to think about him. Right now, I only want to think about Gavin's hand on my leg, how his fingertips have just brushed under my dress again, how badly I want them to go higher. I watch him as he plays with my dress. There are deep lines on his forehead as he pulls his lips into a frown. He's having a silent conversation with himself. I can tell. Like he's wrestling with what to do next.

I know what I *want* him to do next—kiss me. Touch me. Remind me what it's like to feel wanted and beautiful.

But he doesn't. No, he snatches his hand away like he's been caught doing something he shouldn't, then swallows thickly.

"Sorry," he says quietly, rising to his feet, and I stand along with him.

Except I misjudge just how close we really are and bump right into him. I feel myself falling backward in slow motion, and I couldn't stop it even if I tried. I don't know how it happens, and I'm not sure I want to know, but suddenly I'm lying on the bed and Gavin's on top of me. His big thighs are pressed tight against me, one leg tucked between mine. An arm is wrapped around me, his fingers digging into the small of my back, and the other is stretched out by the side of my head. In my periphery, I can see the muscles in his forearm jump.

But that's not my focus. No, it's solely on *him*. His eyes. His lips. The fact that he's so damn close that all I'd have to do is lean up and I could see if he tastes like cinnamon too. I don't have to, though, because suddenly Gavin is leaning *down*. I hold my breath, waiting for… Actually, I'm not quite sure. A kiss? Yeah, a kiss would be nice.

He doesn't do that, though. He veers right, his nose brushing along my cheek in the sweetest, softest touch. I hate it. I love it. I want him to kiss me. And in a way, he does. His lips graze gently over my cheek, moving up until he's right under my ear. A pause. A lingering kiss. Then he's dragging his mouth down, right to the corner of my lips.

Kiss me, I beg.

He doesn't. No, he repeats the action again. Then again. I groan, frustrated at being frustrated because I shouldn't want this strange man to kiss me, but I do. Gavin laughs, then pushes away just enough to peer down at me.

"Something wrong, love?"

Love.

I nod.

"What is it? Tell me. Use your words and tell me what you want."

"I want…" I poke my tongue out, running it along my bottom lip, which suddenly feels dry.

My whole mouth does, and I think it has everything to do with how I'm being looked at. Like I'm a lamb awaiting the slaughter. Like I'm…*prey*. I've never wanted to feel like that before, but something about it just feels so…right.

This feels right.

"I want you to kiss me."

Gavin's eyes darken, his brows furrowing like he's struggling to hold himself back.

"You're sure? Because once I kiss you, Nessa, I'm not sure I'll be able to stop. I'm not sure I'll want to. In fact, I know I won't. If I kiss you…" He doesn't finish his thought, but I know exactly what he's trying to say.

If he kisses me, he's going to keep kissing me.

If he kisses me, he's going to want more.

If he kisses me, he's going to *fuck* me.

And right now, I want to be fucked.

"Kiss me, Gavin," I plead.

I watch in real time as his resolve crumbles. As his brows tighten even more. As the green in his eyes slips even closer to black and his nostrils flare at my request.

And as he mutters a quiet, "What are you doing to me?"

Then he kisses me.

Gavin kisses me.

This stranger. This man I've known for less than two hours. The one who held me as I cried over my ex and bandaged my wound. The man who listened to me ramble about my failed marriage, showed compassion and said I owed no apologies, and made me feel something for the first time in over a year.

And he kisses me *good.*

His lips are soft yet hard, his scruff scratching against me in the most delicious way. His fingers tighten on my lower back, pulling me closer to him, as if that were possible. His thigh sinks deeper between my own, and I love the weight of it—of *him*—as he coaxes my mouth open.

His tongue touches mine, and I was right. He does taste like cinnamon. Scotch too, peaty, and damn is it a good combination. One I could get far too used to. I get so lost in his kiss that I don't even register my hips moving until he grunts against me painfully. He wrenches his mouth away, peering down at me with hazy eyes.

"We're playing a dangerous game," he warns.

I shrug. "I'm fine with that."

"Christ," he mutters, dropping his head into the

crook of my neck, his lips brushing against me there. He alternates between soft and hard kisses, sucking at my skin just enough to leave a mark before moving on.

It's torture. Pure torture. I want more. No, I *need* more. I roll my hips against him again, and he groans again.

"Fuck," he says against my neck as he drags his kisses back to that spot under my ear. "You're undoing me, you know that?"

I nod, sliding against him once more.

"What do you want, Nessa?" he asks softly, his tongue darting out to taste me. "Tell me what you want, and I'll give it to you."

I want to be kissed again. I want to be touched. I want to be looked at like I'm the only girl in the world. I want to be ravaged. I want to be fucked. I want to be taken slowly and softly. I want to erase the pain of the last year and a half. I want to get lost in this moment and forget everything else exists.

I want to feel like I matter.

I slip my hand over the back of his head, tugging at his hair until he hovers over me once more with his cloudy eyes and kiss-swollen lips.

"You, Gavin. I want you."

Chapter 7

LOCKE

"Earth to Whitlocke."

Fingers snap in front of my face, and I pull my attention from the woman behind the bar for the first time since we sat down.

"Sorry," I say to Lawson. "What was that?"

"I asked if your grandparents still have that black-and-white TV."

"Uh, I have no idea. Why?"

"Wanted to use it for our slumber party." He juts his chin out toward Fox, who looks like he regrets agreeing to this but is far too polite to say so.

"You were serious about that?" Keller asks.

"When have you ever known me to joke around?"

"Um, all the fucking time. You're literally one big joke."

Lawson narrows his eyes. "Screw you, Kells."

"Thanks, buddy, but you're not my type. Your mother, on the other hand…"

Lawson launches over the table at Keller, who just laughs, sipping on his drink like his teammate isn't trying to maim him.

Hutch yanks Lawson back down beside him, shaking his head at them. "Would you two knock it off? We don't need to go getting kicked out of Top Shelf."

"I'm with Hutchy on this. We like this place way too much for that," Hayes says, backing up the captain.

"Then tell Keller to leave my mother out of this." Lawson flips off the man in question, and he doesn't react in the slightest. "That woman is a damn angel and would never go for the likes of him."

Keller snorts. "Let me meet her and we'll see about that."

"Not a chance in hell."

Fox pats Lawson's back, trying to calm him down. It's rare he ever gets fired up, but anytime Keller brings up his mother, it's always like this. I swear Keller feeds off the animosity, which is a whole other bag to unpack with that guy.

"Is, uh, everything okay over here?"

I stiffen at the voice and hope like hell nobody notices. Slowly, I turn to find Nessa standing at the end of the table. That damn braid is still sitting over her shoulder, and I still want to wrap it around my fist and tug at it. I remember how much she likes that. How much she wanted my hands in her hair, pulling softly. That little noise she made every time I did it.

I clear my throat, trying to repress those memories before I do something stupid, like pop a boner with my teammates right here. With *Hutch* right here.

Don't look at her. Keep your eyes down. Don't you dare try to sneak a peek.

I repeat it again, then again. Hell, I even squeeze my eyes shut—anything to keep thoughts of her at bay.

"We're good," Hutch tells his sister. "Sorry for the commotion. Won't happen again."

There is absolutely no mistaking the threat in his words: *Straighten up or else.*

"Oh. Okay," she says quietly, and I can't help myself—I look.

I peek right over at her, and all those thoughts from our night together come racing back like I never shut them out at all. And I guess I didn't. I've thought about her every day since I woke up with her gone. Something always reminded me of her.

I think it's worse now, knowing who she is and having her so close by. I want to talk to her again. I want to know her. I want to ask her why she left. I want to see how she is since the divorce was finalized. Want to make sure she's okay. I want to touch her. Kiss her. *Taste* her.

Fuck, do I want to taste her. It's been much, much too long.

As if she can feel my eyes on her, she glances my way for a split second. It's enough to see it—that spark. That same one she had when we met. The same one that had me offering to walk a strange woman back to her hotel when the last thing I should have been doing the night before a midday game was staying out later. The one that had me inviting her back to my hotel room, something I'd never done in all my years on the road. The one that had me pressing her to my bed and giving in to every wicked thought running through my mind.

The one that still makes me want to do that.

"I'll grab you a few waters," she offers to no one in particular before practically running away.

One.

Two.

Three.

Four.

That's how many seconds I last before I mutter a pitiful excuse and race away myself. I head down the darkened hallway, hiding away in the bathroom even though I don't have to go. I just need a break. From what? I'm not sure. Pretending, maybe? Acting like I don't want to kiss the hell out of Nessa? Because I really fucking want to. Would Hutch really be that mad? I think about how I'd react if one of my sisters were dating a teammate, and I realize…

Yes.

And it's not because I don't love those guys like my brothers. I truly do. It's everything else that comes with it.

What if something goes wrong? Who would I side with? My sister or my brother who has my back on the ice? Could I ever trust him again if he hurt her? Could I resist beating the shit out of him? Would I need to call up my agent and demand a trade to keep from going to prison? Would I be able to live with the knowledge that the guy who is supposed to have my back has my sister on hers?

Fuck, that sounds so damn crude, but it's the truth. It's exactly what I would think, and I have no doubt the same would go through Hutchinson's mind, too. He might not be as close with Nessa as I am with my sisters, but it still wouldn't be right, no matter how much I wish it could be.

And that's just it. It's not right. Being with Nessa would never work. Not just because she's related to Hutch, but because we are in two different places in our lives. She just got out of a messy divorce and is trying to figure things out. I'm not looking to get tangled up in anything that could jeopardize my season, especially not when it could be my last with the Serpents. Even without the Hutch factor, it would never work anyway.

So, I have to stop thinking about her. About her long, silky blonde hair that felt like heaven between my fingers. About that freckle just to the left of her belly button that I traced with my tongue. About how she tastes like cherries, which I fucking love. And about how her pussy was—

No.

I push that last thought from my mind. If I let myself go there, I'm not walking out of this bathroom for at least another ten minutes, and I've already been in here too long. I really don't need someone coming to look for me and finding me mid-freak-out.

I do what I've done for half a year: I carefully place every memory and thought of Nessa into a box, pack it tight, seal it shut, and put it back on the shelf where I've kept it all this time. I pump a few squirts of soap into my palm and wash my hands, all while staring into the mirror, chastising myself.

Don't think about Nessa.

Don't think about Nessa.

Do not fucking think about Nessa!

When I'm absolutely sure I've gotten her out of my mind, I wrench the door open and turn right, determined to go have a good time with my teammates. Apparently, the lighting difference between the bathroom and the hallway is significant because I definitely don't see the person before I run into them.

"Shit," I say, reaching out to steady them.

The second my fingers touch skin, I know.

Nessa.

I stare down at her, taking in her wide green eyes and the pout of the lips I just promised myself I would stop fantasizing about.

"Gavin," she says breathlessly.

Fuck. Fuck, fuck, fuck. Why'd she have to say my name? Why'd she have to look up at me like that? All those thoughts I so gingerly placed into the box tumble back out, racing to the forefront of my mind, and all I can think about is kissing her.

"We've got to stop meeting like this, love."

Her eyes sparkle at the endearment, just like they did before.

"S-Sorry," she says, and I barely hold in my groan as she rolls her tongue along her bottom lip. "I didn't see you."

Her eyes slide to where I'm holding on to her, to where I can feel her skin burning beneath my palm. I let her go and step back, putting much-needed distance between us.

"It's fine."

The words are clipped, though not because I'm mad. I'm just trying that damn hard to hold myself together. We stand there awkwardly for I'm not even sure how long, but it is long enough for my fingers to start twitching with the urge to touch her again. My body to vibrate with need. It's long enough that I know it's too long, and I'm seconds away from losing control.

Nessa must feel it too, because she tucks a strand of hair behind her ear. It's her tell. She's nervous. Anxious. Unsure. Whatever you want to call it.

She clears her throat. "I should… I need to…" She points behind me toward the bathrooms.

"Right. Sure."

I move right, and she does too. I move left. She does too. She sighs, then moves again. This time I stand still as she brushes by me.

I don't know how it happens—I'm not sure if it's an unconscious effort on my part or what—but suddenly her wrist is trapped in my grip and I'm keeping her from walking away. I drop my eyes to where I'm holding on to her, right to her naked ring finger.

I swallow at the sight. "You took it off."

Her head snaps up, and I catch her gaze.

"I never put it back on," she whispers.

I don't know what it is about those words, but they're my complete undoing. In a blur, Nessa is pressed up against the wall, and I'm there. *Right* there. My thigh is pushed between hers. Her lips are inches away, so fucking close I can *feel* the strangled breaths she's taking.

It reminds me of having her in my hotel room bed back in New York. The way I fell against her and how soft she was beneath me. The noises she made when I trailed my lips just below her ear. How she looked up at me like I was the only person in the world.

Like she is right now.

Someone ambles down the hallway, and I press closer, shielding her from them as they pass by with a quiet, "Sorry."

I'm not sorry. Not when it means I'm so fucking close that all I'd have to do is dip my head *just* a bit and I'd be kissing Nessa again. I *really* fucking want to kiss her again.

I shouldn't even be back here in this hallway. I should be out there with my teammates—with her *brother*. I shouldn't be thinking about how easy it would be to slip my hand up her shirt or how fast I could make her come. I shouldn't be thinking about that at all.

Then I feel it.

It's soft and subtle, but it's there. Nessa rocks her hips against me. Slow and short movements. So damn minuscule I wouldn't even know she was doing it if I weren't so close to her. If my thigh wasn't pressed so tightly between hers. If her eyes weren't fluttering closed with each gentle pass.

Fuck, I want to grab her hips and help her. I want to slide her over me again and again until she's making those sounds I love so much, but I can't. I don't. I keep my palms pressed against the wall, my hands decidedly to myself, even though it's killing me as she continues moving.

Intentionally or not, she breaks down my walls with each glide, and I'm doing everything in my power to keep them from completely crumbling. I'm slipping, and I'm slipping *fast*. Maybe if I could just touch her a little or taste her. Something. *Anything* to take the edge off.

I press closer and she gasps lightly, our position changing just enough to make a difference, and the sound unravels me. I drag my nose along her cheek, the scent of fresh flowers overwhelming me in the best way possible. Then the lavender kicks in, and I wonder if that's the lotion she wears or maybe even her body soap. I don't know. I just know it drives me wild and makes me do unimaginable things, like press my lips to that spot below her ear.

She whines, and I grin against her. It's the first time I've felt like smiling in a week, maybe even longer. I'm not sure, but it certainly doesn't make me want to let this feeling go. I kiss her again, this time moving toward her lips, which is where I really want to be. With each kiss, she grinds against me again.

Kiss. Grind.

Kiss. Grind.

Kiss. Grind.

I'm there, just at the corner of her lips. So fucking close I swear I can already taste the cherry lip gloss I know she loves so much. If I just move a millimeter… maybe two…I'd have my lips on hers again, and I'll know for sure if that one night was just a fluke, if all the thoughts of her I can't seem to let go of are just me holding on to a fantasy. I'll know if I have any chance of staying away from her.

Then I hear it—footsteps. A cleared throat.

I freeze, and Nessa does the same beneath me.

Fuck. Shit. Fuck.

Slowly, I turn. Relief washes over me when I realize it's not Hutch, but it's gone just as quickly as I take in my teammate standing there with a wicked grin on his face and heavily tattooed arms crossed over his chest.

"Whitlocke," he says quietly. *Pointedly*.

I swallow. "Keller."

His lips twitch when he moves his gaze to the woman pinned against the wall. "Stepsister."

If possible, she stiffens even more under me. She

doesn't like that. She doesn't like that we know things about her, that Hutch has brought her up to us before. She shoves at me lightly, and I reluctantly pull away, putting a respectable amount of distance between us.

"It's Vanessa," she tells him, running her hand down her wrinkled shirt. "I…"

But she doesn't finish her sentence. She bolts, pushing past Keller and back into the bar. I wish I could be surprised by her fleeing, but given our history, I'm not. I watch her go, not moving an inch, even though I want to run after her so damn badly. I can't for a multitude of reasons, one being the hulking man taking up the hallway. We stand there like we're in some old Western film, and I can't decide which of us is going to pull a gun and fire first.

"Well, can't say I had you pegged as a sister-fucker."

"Jesus, Keller," I mutter as I squeeze the back of my neck, trying to release the tension sitting there.

"What? Is that not what I just walked in on?"

"We weren't…" I grit my teeth. "Nothing was happening."

"Really? Because it looked like she was humping your leg and you were seconds away from kissing her." He arches a challenging brow. "You telling me I need to get my vision checked by Doc?"

I sigh, then sigh again. Because no, he doesn't need

Doc to check him out. That's exactly what he saw. How stupid could I be? Pressing Nessa against the wall like that. Nearly kissing her. Letting her ride my leg. What the hell was I thinking? I wasn't thinking. Or maybe I was. I don't know. All I know is it can't happen again. It *won't* happen again.

"Fuck," I say, running my hand through my hair.

"Yeah, that's what I thought." Keller huffs out something as close to a laugh as he gets, which, to be fair, isn't close at all. "You want to talk about it?"

"I…" I don't want to talk about it, not really. But I should. I exhale heavily. "It was an accident."

"You accidentally almost fucked her?"

The look on my face must say it all.

"Oh, shit," he says, eyes wide. "You actually *did* fuck her?"

"Stop saying it like that!" I snarl. "That's not how it was."

"Then how was it? And when the hell did it even happen? We just met her last week at the party."

I wince. "Not all of us. I, uh, I met her a while ago." Five months and nineteen days ago, to be precise, but who's counting? "In New York."

"New York? But we haven't played them since…"

"April third."

I can see it all click into place.

"That was the night you disappeared on us. We

had no idea where you went. I guess now I know. You were with the stepsister."

"*Vanessa*," I correct, more heat in my tone than necessary, and Keller's brows rise at my reaction.

But she's not just "the stepsister" or "the sister," and she especially isn't the fucking "evil stepsister." She's Vanessa. *My* Nessa.

No.

Not mine. Not really. She's just a girl I knew for one night. That's all.

"I take it you had no idea who she was," Keller says.

"Do you really think I would have slept with her if I had? Siblings are off-limits. Everyone knows that."

It's an unspoken rule for all teammates in every sport, not just hockey. Sure, there might be a few exceptions, like Cameron Lowell and Collin Wright on the Carolina Comets. They're brothers-in-law now after an accidental pregnancy. So, it can work out, and that's great for them, but I highly doubt Hutch would be okay if he found out about me and Nessa.

Fuck. I didn't even think to make sure she's okay. She ran out of here so fast, I couldn't even gauge where she was after...well, whatever that was. Is she mad? Is she embarrassed about being caught? Is she okay? I want to ask her, want to leave Keller and his judgmental face right in this hallway and go find her.

But I don't. I stare my teammate down, waiting for his next question that I know is coming.

"Are you going to tell Hutchinson?"

Am I going to tell my fucking captain I had the best night of my life with his sister? Tell him I not only know what she looks like naked but also how she sounds when she comes? Am I going to tell him that even though I had no idea who she was, it doesn't make me feel any less damn guilty?

No. No, I am not telling Hutch a damn thing.

"It was nothing. Just a night of fun. It didn't mean anything. He doesn't need to know about it."

But every word feels wrong. They taste wrong. Bitter. Stale. It wasn't nothing. It wasn't just a night of fun. And it damn sure meant something.

I just wish it hadn't. It would make this situation a hell of a lot easier.

Keller studies me, and for a minute, I think he's about to call me on my bullshit. He doesn't though. He nods, then hitches his thumb over his shoulder.

"You'd better get back out there before Lawson comes looking for you. That guy can't keep a secret to save his life."

"Can you?"

This time, Keller does smile—and it's creepy as hell.

"Oh, Locke. I've got secrets you couldn't even dream up."

I'm not sure if that makes me feel better or worse, but I take it anyway.

"Thanks," I say, brushing past him.

I'm nearly to the end of the hallway when I hear my name.

"Locke?"

I turn. "Yeah?"

"It's okay if it wasn't nothing. It's okay if it wasn't just fun. And it's okay if you want it to stay between us for now, but Hutch should know eventually. While I don't begrudge anyone keeping shit to themselves, this could be something that tears the team apart, and I don't know about you, but I've got a fucking Cup to win, you feel?"

He's right. I know he is. I've barely held it together this last week, and that was without seeing Hutch every day. How the hell can I be on the ice with him and keep this shit to myself? Have this hanging between us? I can't. It'll eat me alive. I'm not that kind of guy. I can't keep a secret like that from one of my best friends.

I nod. "I feel."

"Good." Keller gestures toward the bar. "Go before they send in the good boy, or worse, the golden retriever."

I can't even laugh at his nicknames for Fox and Lawson. I'm too busy trying to school my features and to convince myself to absolutely *not* look over at the bar, no matter how badly I want to. Keller disappears into the bathroom, and I suck in a deep breath, then exhale.

In. Out. Step.

In. Out. Step.

In. Out. Step.

I slide into the booth beside Hutch, who is in the middle of a story about his time with his former team, the rest of the guys hanging on to every word.

I only look for Nessa twice.

Chapter 8

VANESSA

"It was nothing. Just a night of fun. It didn't mean anything. He doesn't need to know about it."

He's right. My brother doesn't need to know I know Gavin. It's not like I planned on telling him anyway. But *just a night of fun? It didn't mean anything?* Maybe not to him, but it damn sure meant something to me, and that's the worst part of this all.

"Nessa!" my training manager snaps—not for the first time—as I overpour yet another shot.

"Sorry. I'm sorry, Josh." I grab a towel and clean up my mess.

I've been in a daze since Gavin walked into this bar, since he sat on the stool and told me he remembers everything about our night together. I remember it too. It's burned into my brain, into my skin. No matter how many times I've tried to bury it, it always resurfaces, and it's been on my mind even more since I showed up in Seattle last week, and there he was, standing in my brother's house.

My brother, who has been surprisingly…well, not a complete dick for a change. It's not like we're buddies suddenly, but we haven't been as hostile as we have in the past. I know I have Auden to thank for the change in Reed's demeanor. Well, her and that baby that's nearly done growing inside of her. He's too busy worrying over them to give me much of a thought or pick fights with me.

While things are going okay, it doesn't make me any less eager to get out of there. The baby is coming any day now, and the last thing I want to do is burden them with my presence. This is precisely why I need to stop thinking of Gavin and our night together and the way he had me pinned against the wall not fifteen minutes ago and start thinking of what the hell I'm going to do next.

That begins with actually focusing on my new job and not screwing it up completely. In hindsight, it probably wasn't my most brilliant move to lie about my bartending skills, but it got me in the door, right?

"I thought you had experience tending bar," Josh grumbles, simmering beside me as I try again to pour a proper shot. Whoever he's giving these test drinks out to, they're certainly getting their money's worth, all this extra booze in them.

"I do."

It's not completely a lie. Once, in college, to raise money for a charity our sorority was working with, I *did* tend bar. Sure, it was mostly popping open cans, twisting off bottle tops, and pouring rum and Cokes, but still. I *do* have experience…just maybe not as much as I thought could get me through this.

"I'm just rusty, is all," I say, shooting him a smile. Thankfully, it gets him to relax a bit, and I breathe a little easier as I work on the second drink on my to-do list: an old fashioned.

Josh grunts when I put a bit too much bitters in it, but in the end, he accepts it, takes a sip, and nods.

"Not bad. Still needs work, but it's drinkable. Better than that Manhattan you tried to make earlier."

I wince at the reminder, then get to work making another drink. It goes like that for what feels like hours, even though the clock shaped like a goalie mask that's hanging on the wall says it's barely been ten minutes. I know because my eyes keep flicking that way, and it has nothing at all to do with the fact that the clock hangs over the table Gavin and his teammates are at.

Nope. Nothing at all.

I let my gaze drift down and to him, and it takes me back to all those months ago when I sat next to him at a bar not unlike this one. I was drawn to him then, and that was before I even knew what it was like to have his undivided attention, like a warm summer day, the sun shining, not a cloud in the sky.

But that was a different time under different circumstances. Before I knew who he was and just how absolutely off-limits he is.

Besides, I'm not supposed to be focusing on that now. My job, replenishing my savings account, and finding a place to live—those are my priorities, not some one-night fling that meant nothing.

"Hey, Josh?"

"Hmm?" he asks, partly distracted by counting our tips in the jar next to the register.

"Do you know of any places to rent?"

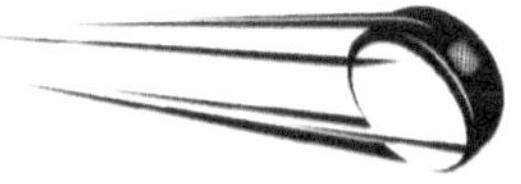

"We should talk."

I jump, letting out a too-loud squeal as I reach for the pepper spray hanging off my purse. It was sitting on my pillow a few days ago, and I have a sneaking suspicion it was Reed's doing. The sad part is if that is the case, it might be the most brotherly thing he's done for me, and it's just a can of pepper spray.

Pepper spray I don't need as I take in the sight

before me. Gavin leans against an all-black Mercedes SUV, his big arms crossed over his chest as he looks at me with serious eyes. I hate that he looks so good in something as simple as a pair of jeans and a white t-shirt that hugs him just a little too well. His dark hair that was once so soft between my fingers is hidden under a Seattle Serpents hat, and I want to reach over and pull it off. All it does is remind me of this awkward situation we seem to have gotten ourselves into.

After the guys had their fun earlier, they closed out the tab and left a far too generous tip for what little I did, then took off without another word. It was fine. It's not like I was expecting some big emotional, let's-rehash-the-past moment with Gavin after our hallway incident, especially not with his teammates around, but I didn't expect to see him standing outside my workplace tonight.

"Gavin. What, uh, what are you doing here?"

He pushes off his car, taking a few steps toward me, and it's annoying how much I enjoy the fact that I have to tilt my head back to look into his eyes. Neal isn't a small guy by any means, but he certainly isn't as big as the man before me.

"We should talk."

I cross my arms over my chest, lifting my chin higher. "You said that already. It doesn't explain why you're standing in front of my place of employment, waiting on me like some stalker."

It's hard to tell with the overgrown scruff on his face, but I swear his lips twitch.

"Not stalking you. I just didn't have any other way of getting in touch with you. Thought it might raise a few red flags if I were to ask Hutch for your number."

Not that I'd answer anyway.

"Not that I think you would have answered anyway," he says, putting a voice to my thoughts.

I try not to smile at that, keeping my face neutral.

"What do you want to talk about?"

He gives me an exasperated look, and it's almost comical. "I think you know what we need to talk about, *Nessa.*"

His patience is wearing thin. Of course I know what he wants to talk about. I just don't want to talk about it.

"We slept together once a long time ago. It was fun. Not really sure what else there is to discuss when all of it meant nothing anyway."

He flinches at my words, but I'm not sure why. He's the one who said them. I'm just repeating it. He sighs, lifting the hat and running his hand through his hair before replacing it.

"Look, can we just grab a bite to eat and handle this like adults?"

"I'd like to go home and rinse off the smell of beer. And I'm not hungry."

My stomach decides this is the precise moment it wants to convey just how hungry it really is since all I had for lunch was a limp salad, and that was hours ago while I was on my phone looking for apartments. My food was just as disappointing as what I found.

"That so?" Gavin asks, lips pulling into a smirk.

I narrow my eyes at him in warning. "That's so."

He drops the smile, then sighs again. "I just… We need to…" He frowns when the words don't come, finally settling on, "Please, Nessa?"

I hate that I'm still standing here talking to him when I should have walked away immediately. I hate that we're in this situation to begin with. And I hate more than anything that his plea is working.

"Fine," I concede. "You have one hour. I really do want to go home and shower. I smell like bar and bad cologne."

"One hour," he promises, turning back toward his car and opening the passenger door for me. He waves me on. "After you."

Neal never opened my door for me. Not once in all our years together, and it's silly how I'm just noticing that. I push the thought away as I shuffle past Gavin, sliding against the cool leather seats, inhaling that new car smell I've always loved.

He rounds the front of the vehicle, paying careful attention to traffic before pulling his door open and sliding in behind the wheel. He doesn't ask me where to go, just puts the car in drive and makes the decision for himself. Part of me wants to be a brat and make a comment, but I'm too tired to care at this point. I just want to have this conversation, put it all behind us, and move on. I *have* to move on. After all, that's what I'm in Seattle to do, right? To build a new life and put my past to rest? I can't do that if I'm still hung up on a one-night stand from months ago.

We drive in silence for roughly ten minutes—which is forever in the city—before pulling into a parking lot that's nearly full, which is surprising for this time of night. Before exiting, Gavin gives me a stern look that clearly says *Stay*. I don't know why I listen to him, but I do. He opens my door, extending a hand my way, and dammit if I don't slip mine against it.

Soft. Warm. His touch is exactly as I remember it.

I yank my hand away as soon as I'm out of the car, and I don't miss how Gavin's lips turn down at that.

"Hope you like burgers," he says as we walk across the small parking lot.

"Depends on if they're good burgers or not."

"Good is a relative term."

"So you're taking me to a *bad* burger place?"

"I wouldn't call it bad exactly. But it's cheap, and a Seattle staple."

"Don't you make millions of dollars a year?"

He grunts. "Doesn't mean I can't enjoy a bargain burger."

"Fair enough."

He opens the door, waving me ahead of him, and I step into the fast-food place. The seating options are sparse, and despite the late hour, there are plenty of people lined up at the counter as workers buzz around behind it, stuffing burgers and fries into bags and making shakes. My mouth instantly waters as we get in line. The people ahead of us rattle off their orders, the line moving so quickly I barely have time to look at the board before we're next.

"Want me to order for you?" Gavin asks, as if he can sense my panic.

I used to hate it when Neal would do that. He'd always just assume what I wanted, never bothering to ask my opinion on the matter, and I'd rarely end up with something I actually enjoyed. But I'm not as annoyed by it when Gavin offers. If anything, I'm relieved. It's been a long day, and I don't feel like making decisions right now.

"Please."

"Any requests?"

"Surprise me," I say, my stomach growling at the smell of food.

He nods, then steps up to the counter. "Can I get two Deluxe, two Special, two Cheese, two fries, four tartar, and vanilla and chocolate shakes, please?"

The worker's fingers fly over the screen as they punch it all in, and I'm amazed they could even understand everything Gavin just rattled off. I certainly didn't. I'm still too stunned by the whole deal to notice him handing them a black credit card.

"What are you doing? I can pay for my own dinner," I protest, reaching into my purse for the cash I was handed before I left the bar.

"I know."

"Then let me pay." I hand him a wad of bills, unsure what the total is but knowing this should cover it.

He looks down at the money like he's offended, then turns his hazel gaze back to mine. "I said I know you *can* pay for your own dinner, not that I'm going to let you."

He turns back to the worker, who hands him his receipt, then spins to grab our food. Everything moves so quickly, and before I know it, we're given our giant bag of burgers and fries and our two shakes. Gavin juggles it all, refusing to let me help. I'm as frustrated as I am endeared by it.

He points to two unoccupied chairs across the room. "Is over there okay?"

"Sounds good," I mumble. I don't care where we sit. I just want food. For the second time tonight, my stomach lets out a loud grumble as we settle into the chairs.

Gavin's brows inch together. "Do they not feed you at the bar?"

He seems concerned by this. Mildly annoyed even. I have a brief vision of Gavin storming into Top Shelf, demanding to speak to a manager, and giving them a stern talking-to about lunch breaks and how I need to be properly fed during my shift.

I shake the thought away. "They feed me. I just had a salad today, and that was a lot of hours ago. Guess I learned I'm going to need a little more sustenance if I'm going to be on my feet for so long."

He nods like he understands. "I had to learn that with hockey, too. I ate my poor parents out of house and home when I was a teenager. It was like no matter what I had to eat, I was still starving every night before bed. Didn't take long to realize I wasn't getting enough protein throughout the day. Now I make sure that's not a problem."

"Hence the five cheeseburgers?"

He chuckles lightly. "That and because even though it's just a basic burger that can be slapped together anywhere and absolutely nothing to write home to your family about, it's still a damn good burger."

"Hmm. I'll be the judge of that. Burger me."

He smiles as he pulls the food from the bag, setting it between us on the countertop. He holds up the two shakes next. "Vanilla or chocolate? You seem like a chocolate person to me."

"What if I said strawberry?"

Instantly, his chair is scraping across the tile, and it takes me all of two seconds to realize what's happening.

I grab his arm, stopping him. "No, stop. I wasn't being serious."

"Are you sure? Because I'll go get you strawberry if that's what you want."

The sincerity in his eyes is disarming, and I have no doubt if I said I wanted strawberry, he would go up there and get me one without a moment of hesitation. Neal would never. He would make me feel like crap for wanting the things I did.

It's weird. I never realized our relationship was like that until I had time to reflect on it. I think I was so in love and so invested in what we had that I had blinders on to all the things that should've been red flags.

"Thank you, but I'm perfectly fine with chocolate," I say as Gavin settles back into his seat.

"Perfectly fine with or that's what you want? Because those are two totally different things."

He's right. Those are two totally different things, and I love that he recognizes that.

"Chocolate is what I want. I promise."

He nods, accepting my answer, then points at the three different kinds of burgers he got, explaining the difference in each one. I settle on the cheeseburger, unwrap it, and dig in, acutely aware of Gavin watching me the whole time.

"Well?" he asks after I take my first bite.

"You're right," I say, dabbing at my lips with the napkin clutched in my other hand. "This burger is somehow the most basic thing I've ever had and also quite possibly one of the most delicious. Or maybe I'm just really hungry. I can't tell."

"It's always a little bit of both. It's witchcraft. Or science. I can't really determine which. I just know I come here way more often than the team dietitian appreciates. But that can be our little secret."

He winks at me, and dammit if that small gesture doesn't hit right between my legs. So do his words. *Our little secret.* This isn't the only secret we share, and the reality of that settles over us as we continue eating our burgers and fries in silence.

Awkward silence.

I hate it. I hate that once upon a time it was so easy

with him, and now everything is so strained. It's my fault, though. I was the one who ran, and in a way, I enforced a no-contact rule by not even giving him a chance to try to keep in touch. This awkwardness is all my doing, and I don't know how to fix it.

"So," Gavin starts after consuming three burgers and half his fries. "What brings you to Seattle?"

I inhale steadily, clutching my chocolate shake tighter as if I'm holding on to it for emotional support. In this moment, I just might be.

"My ex-husband is having a baby with the woman he cheated on me with."

His eyes widen in shock, a bit of vanilla milkshake sputtering from the corner of his lips. He drags the back of his hand across his mouth. "Sorry about that. I just didn't…"

"Expect that?" I laugh, but there's no humor behind it. "Yeah, me either. But whatever, you know? I mean, he is my *ex*-husband. I no longer have any claim over him. He can do what he wants. He can—"

"Stop, stop, stop." Gavin waves his hand. "He was your husband. At one point, he made vows to you and broke them. Now, someone else is getting the life you were promised. It's okay to be mad. It's okay to grieve what you lost, Nessa."

Tears spring to my eyes, and I will myself not to cry in front of him again. I need to be stronger than that, even if his words are something I needed to hear far more than I realized.

"Thank you." I clear my throat, blinking back the tears. I sit up straighter. "Anyway, maybe that's why I don't seem as cheerful as you'd imagine."

"Of course not. How can you be? Nobody would be happy about this."

"What about you? Are you happy?"

His mouth opens, then snaps just as quickly. "On paper, yeah. Outside of that? I'm not so sure. A lot is hanging on this season, and I'm not exactly sure I'm prepared for it. Then, of course, there's that little issue with…"

"Us," I finish for him.

He swallows roughly. "Yeah. That." He runs his hand over his jaw, scratching at the hair I know feels good between my thighs. I squeeze them together at the reminder. "Look—"

"Let's just forget about it," I rush out, cutting him off.

His dark brows turn inward, lips pinching together tightly. He almost looks mad, perhaps even a little offended. But just as quickly as the look appears, it passes.

"I mean, besides, what are we going to do about it now? It happened so long ago, and it's not like we knew about our *mutual friend*."

His lips pull into a grin. "I'd love to hear Hutch's reaction to you calling him your friend."

"He'd probably deny it, then Auden would say something wise, and he'd apologize. Rinse and repeat of the last week. Anyway, the point is… Well, what is the point? I just moved across the country for a fresh start, and you just said you need to focus on the season. It's not like we're trying to jump into something or reignite whatever spark we had that night. It happened, and now we move on like adults, right?"

He nods a few times, considering. "Right," he agrees, extending his hand between us. "Friends?"

"Friends," I repeat, slipping my palm against his.

When I do, there's something there. A flicker. A burst of lightning. Something I can't quite describe. It doesn't go away, especially when he slides his thumb back and forth gently, caressing my skin, almost like he's trying to imprint its feel into his mind.

It certainly doesn't feel like we're just friends…and I'm not too sure I want it to.

Chapter 9

Lawson: Okay, you guys can say it: That goal was fucking epic!

Hayes: It's preseason. Calm down.

Keller: Damn. Hayesy beat me to it.

Keller: But what he said. It's preseason. Chill.

Lawson: Easy for you to say. You'd never be able to pull off a goal like that in your life.

Keller: Bullshit.

Lawson: Then prove it. Make it happen against Vancouver.

Fox: No way you'd get that past their goalie.

Keller: Hundred bucks says I will.

Lawson: I will gladly take that bet.

Lawson: Speaking of bets, are we still taking them on when Auden's going to pop? How many days past her due date is she now?

Hutch: For starters, we are not taking bets on my fiancée and child.

Hutch: And secondly, can you guys shut up? I'm trying to get some rest over here.

Keller: That's a good idea because you won't be getting any for a long, long, long time. Like for the next several years.

Lawson: How would you know?
You're not a dad.

Keller: And despite what you tell yourself, you're not either.

Lawson: For the last freakin' time, my babies are MY BABIES! Just call me Darth Vader because I am their father.

Hayes: I really hate that that made me laugh.

Fox: Nice reference, Lawsy.

Keller: NERD

Lawson: Nerd who is getting laid regularly.

Fox: OH SNAP

Hayes: *whistles* Damn

Locke: Think he got you there, Kells.

Keller: The fuck you chiming in for, Locke? Unless you're getting some sort of secret action you're not telling the rest of us about, hmm?

Lawson: Locke?

Locke: Shut up, Lawson.

Keller: Answer the question, Whitlocke.

Locke: No. Fucking happy?

Keller: I'm never happy.

Fox: You really aren't. We should talk about that more.

Keller: Let's not.

Hayes: Maybe you should try to get laid, Locke. You're kind of grumpy lately.

Locke: Ever think I'm just tired of hanging out with a bunch of children?

Lawson: Hey, you don't get to play the "children" card AND get mad when we call you old. You have to pick.

Fox: That seems fair.

Locke: You're all so annoying.

Hutch: You really are fucking annoying. I'm still trying to sleep, you know. Baby coming soon and all that. Sleep is precious.

Locke: Speaking of... What's going on with your sister when the baby gets here? Is she still going to be living with you?

Hutch: Not a clue. The house is big and all, and she's pretty much always in her room anyway, so it's not like she'd be a bother, but I can't imagine someone starting their life over wants to be roommates with a newborn.

Hutch: If it weren't my kid, I'd feel that way.

Fox: Sucks she's in such an awful situation. Can we do anything to help?

Fox: Right, guys? Because we want to help.

Hayes: Oh, uh, yeah, sure.

Lawson: Definitely.

Keller: I don't.

Hutch: Unless you've magically found a place for her to rent, then no. But thanks for offering, Fox.

Hutch: Now, everyone shut the fuck up so I can nap.

Lawson: You know you can mute the chat, right?

Keller: YOU CAN MUTE THE CHAT?!

Keller: Holy fuck. This is a game changer!

Lawson: What? No, I was just kidding!

Lawson: LOL LOL LOL LOL

Lawson: I'm SO funny, aren't I, guys?

Lawson: Guys?

Lawson: GUYS?!

Lawson: Foxy Baby?

Fox: I'm still here, buddy.

Lawson: Of course you are. Always such a good boy.

Lawson: Fox?

Lawson: I WAS KIDDING! COME BACK!

Lawson: Whatever. It's fine. I don't need you guys anyway.

Lawson: I'll just go...do something.

Lawson: Help! What am I supposed to do?

Hutch: HAVE YOU TRIED SHUTTING THE FUCK UP? FOR THE HUNDREDTH TIME, I AM TRYING TO NAP!

Lawson: Damn, okay. I get the picture. Go nap.

Lawson: Sleep tight, Hutchy.

Hayes: Dude, don't…

Lawson: Sleep tight, Hayesy.

Hayes: Goddammit

Lawson: Sleep tight, Locke.

Locke: Uh, thanks?

Lawson: Sleep tight, Foxy Baby.

Fox: Thanks, buddy!

Lawson: Sleep tight, Kells. I hope you have the best dreams ever.

Keller: Please never speak to me again.

Lawson: Nice try, but you're stuck with me.

Keller: I hate this club.

Lawson: HA! You called it a club! No takebacks! Okay, love you, night night.

Keller: I TAKE IT BACK

Lawson: La la la. Can't hear you. Sleeping. Love you still.

Keller: Hate you still.

Lawson: Doubt it. *kissy face emoji*

Keller: *middle finger emoji*

Chapter 10

LOCKE

"Fuck, that felt good." Keller drops into the stall next to me, dragging his Serpents-branded towel across his face.

"It really did," I agree, already working my gear off piece by piece.

We just won our last preseason game, the regular season is five short days away, and I cannot fucking wait. I'm antsy for it in a way I haven't been in a really long damn time, and I'm not entirely sure why. Maybe it's because I feel like I have something to prove this season. Or maybe it was that electric crowd out there, telling me they're already pumped for what's to come.

Or maybe it's something else entirely. Whatever the case, all I know is it's felt damn good getting back out on the ice these last few games, and I can't wait for it to count for real.

"Holy shit. Was that an actual positive thing you said?" Hayes smarts off.

I flip him my middle finger, even though he's right. Anytime I'm off the ice, I've been in a pissy mood, and I suspect it has to do with a certain blonde I haven't seen since I dropped her back off at her car after burgers and shakes.

It's not for lack of wanting on my part, either. It's been hard as hell to stay away from Nessa, but I have. I only slipped up once in the group and have only had to stop myself from parking in front of Top Shelf four times. Sure, it probably wouldn't be too weird to stop in since I go there regularly, but with her working there, it feels different.

It also doesn't help that Keller is aware of our past. He hasn't said anything about what happened at the bar, and neither have I, but there's still this certain look he's been giving me, one that says, *I could ruin your life*, and I'm not about to put that to the test. So, I've kept my mouth shut and my ass out of the bar.

"I'd ask if we're all going to go out and celebrate the end of preseason, but I assume that's a no since the baby still isn't here," Lawson says. "What the hell is that thing's problem? Doesn't it want to meet its uncle Lawson?"

"I don't think the baby appreciates being called a *thing* or an *it*, so I can't imagine they're in a hurry to meet you," Hayes says, eyes wide with bewilderment as if he is somehow actually surprised by Lawson's general dumbassery.

"And I think if Hutch were in here, he would inform you that you are not the baby's uncle. You're just Rory's boyfriend," Keller adds.

"*Just* Rory's boyfriend? Just her *boyfriend*? That's all you think I am? We live together! We're raising children together!"

"I don't know how many times I have to say this, but pets are *not* children."

Lawson pulls out his phone, then shoves it in Hayes's face. "You're going to look at this angel and tell me this isn't my daughter? Look at her! Look at how damn adorable she is! That's my baby girl!"

Hayes smacks the phone away, and I roll my eyes at their antics. Yep, it's definitely hockey season again. The guys are bickering like brothers and annoying one another to no end.

"Where is Hutch anyway? I thought he was right behind me..." Fox says, stripping off his goalie equipment. No matter how many times I've watched him take it off and put it on throughout the years, it will never cease to amaze me just how small he actually is underneath it all, and that's saying something because Fox isn't a tiny guy by any means.

"He's in the hallway," Dash, our second goaltender, answers.

"Saw him on the phone," another teammate says.

Lawson rolls his eyes. "He's probably checking in on Auden...*again*. He's so obsessed with her."

"Want to do the honors or me?" Hayes says to Keller.

"You know what? I'll let you have this one."

"Do what honors?" Lawson asks just as Hayes reaches up and slaps him on the back of the head. "Hey! What the fuck, man?"

"You know what you did" is all Hayes says.

"All right, fine. I'll let you have that one. But I—yo, Hutchy? You okay?"

We all look toward our captain, who just walked into the locker room. His eyes are wide as he stares down at his phone, his skin at least two shades paler than just five minutes ago. I follow his gaze and see his hands trembling.

"Uh, Hutch?" Fox asks. "You good?"

"That was..." He swallows. "That was Vanessa. I... Auden..."

Oh shit. I launch to my feet. "Come on. Let's go."

"Go?" Lawson asks. "Where are we going?"

"*We* aren't going anywhere," I say, quickly grabbing my sweats and yanking them on. "Hutch and I are." I slip my feet into my shoes, forgoing my socks, then snatch my phone, wallet, and keys from my cubby. "Come on. I'm taking you to the hospital."

"The hospital? Oh, fuck. It's happening?"

"It's happening," I confirm, grabbing Hutch's shoulder. He's still staring down at his phone. I give him a shake, trying to snap him out of it. "Hey, man. Come on."

Finally, he looks up at me, and there is absolutely no mistaking the fear in his gaze. I've seen it time and time again on my siblings' and in-laws' faces over the years.

"Locke, I..."

"I know. Let's go, brother. I got you."

There's a brief flash of relief as he nods. "Okay, okay. I just have to change. I—"

"Change in the car. I have clothes in there. We gotta move."

Another nod. "Right. Okay. Thanks, man."

"Any time," I say as I steer him from the room and toward the parking garage.

As we make our way down the hall, I hear Lawson yell, "I can't believe we're having a baby!"

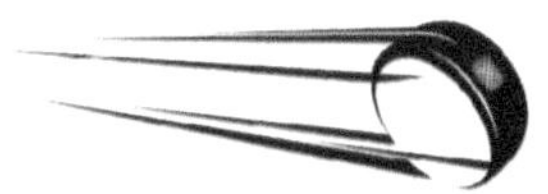

"I...I can't breathe."

"You can," I say to Hutch as I push my AMG to speeds it has never reached within city limits. "Just in and out."

"I think I'm having a heart attack." He grabs the dashboard in front of him. It's easily the most high-strung I've ever seen Hutch, and I've seen him in some pretty intense situations before.

"Dude, just breathe," I say for the umpteenth time.

What am I thinking? Of course he can't breathe. His entire world is about to change. That's a lot to take in, and it's even harder to take when you know the person you love the most in the world is hurting to make that happen.

"Did you talk to Auden? How is she doing?"

"No." He shakes his head as he inhales and exhales once again. "Just Vanessa. But I heard her. She sounded… Fuck, Locke, she was in such pain."

"I know, man. I know, but she's going to be okay. I promise. I've been through this with my nieces and nephews. It might feel like it's taking forever right now, but the baby's going to be here before you know it, and you're going to forget all about what you're feeling right now. Auden too."

He nods, another heavy inhale and exhale. I'm not sure if that helped at all, but at least he's not complaining about a heart attack. My tires squeal as I pull into the hospital parking lot, and I skid to a stop at the front entrance.

Hutch doesn't move.

"Hutch?"

Nothing.

"Hutchinson?"

Nothing again.

"Reed!"

His first name snaps him out of it, and he looks over at me, eyes wide. "I'm having a baby."

I laugh. "Yeah, yeah, you fucking are. Get in there and go meet your kid."

For the first time, he smiles, then leaps out of the car and bolts into the hospital. I chuckle as I watch him go, then drive around for ten full minutes looking for a parking spot. I'm not sure if he even wants me here, but I'm going to stick around for a while just in case.

I walk into the hospital far more casually than he did. Still, the receptionist at the desk stares up at me with surprise.

"Is the whole team here?" she asks.

I grin. "Fortunately for me, no. Can you point me toward the—"

"Maternity ward?" she finishes for me, then relays the directions.

"Thanks so much," I tell her.

"Anything for my favorite defenseman." She throws

me a wink before returning to her work, and I head toward where she directed me to go.

I settle into the back of the elevator as it takes me to the maternity floor, pulling my hat down low and pretending I don't notice people tossing second glances my way. When the doors open and everyone else files out, I see her.

Nessa.

She's sitting across the waiting room, her thumb in her mouth. She nibbles on her nails, clearly frazzled. Even in that state, I still want to cross the room and kiss her. I can't, though. Not just because Hutch could come around the corner any moment, but because we're just friends. That's what we said. I can't go back on that now, no matter how badly I want to.

I stand there staring at her for so long that the doors start to close again, and I barely catch them in time.

"Hey."

She jumps at the simple word, and I hold my hands up.

"Sorry," she mutters when she realizes it's just me. "Sorry. It's been a…day."

I point to the empty chair beside her, and she nods.

"Thanks," I say, settling into it. "How's Auden?"

"A fucking trooper." She winces. "I don't know how

she's doing it. She was in so much pain from the contractions. I can't imagine going through that."

"No kids for you, then?"

"No. I mean, yes. I mean, I don't know. I thought so with…" She sighs. "But now? I don't know anymore. I guess if it happens, it happens." She shrugs. "You?"

"Am I going to have a baby?"

She rolls her eyes. "Do you want kids?"

"Sure. Eventually."

"Eventually?"

"After hockey," I explain. "I'm not eager to drag them into this life. It's hard, and I've seen firsthand the strain it puts on a marriage. I've watched a lot of teammates struggle through the years, so I promised myself a long time ago that if I ever settled down, it would be when I'm done with my career."

"I can understand that. It's a hard life. Why force a kid into it?"

"Exactly."

A comfortable silence falls between us, and I let my eyes linger over her as she continues picking at her nails. Her hair is a bit wild, much less put together than it usually is. She's not wearing a stitch of makeup, and I'm pretty sure the socks she's wearing don't match. She looks exhausted. Still absolutely gorgeous, but exhausted.

She reaches up, rubbing at her temples.

"You okay?" I ask softly, because I'm not so sure she is.

She startles at my question, then nods, but there's no mistaking the weariness in her eyes.

"Yeah, sorry. Just got a bit of a headache."

"Want me to find you something for it?" I ask, already halfway out of my seat.

She grabs my arm, stopping me. "No, stay."

I drop back into the chair as her fingers burn their way into my skin, and fuck if I haven't missed her touch. She yanks her hand away when she notices she's been holding on to me longer than necessary, flitting her eyes away and looking anywhere but at me.

"Sorry," she mutters again.

I shake my head. "Nothing to be sorry for. Are you sure I can't get you anything? Not even a water?"

"No, I'm good. I'm just tired."

My brows pull together. "Not sleeping well at Hutch's?"

She wiggles her hand back and forth. "So-so. Late hours at the bar, too. And early mornings, trying to find an apartment."

"No luck?"

"Some luck, but not enough. It doesn't help that I don't really know what I'm looking for, you know? Or that I don't know my way around the city just yet.

Making a decision is hard when you're unfamiliar with the area. People will tell you whatever you want to hear to make a quick buck."

I want to offer to help her, but I have a feeling she's going to say no anyway. This is something Nessa needs to do on her own, something she needs to prove to herself. I respect that about her. I know she's been through a lot in the last year or so, and seeing her try to be so strong is admirable.

The same silence as before settles between us, and I have no idea how long we sit here. I don't bother checking the clock. I'm too busy watching her. Even when she slips down farther into the chair, closing her eyes, I still watch. Her breathing changes quickly, telling me she's already fast asleep. Guess she wasn't kidding about that lack of sleep. It worries me, seeing as we could still have a long night ahead of us until the baby comes.

"Locke." I jump at my name, finally dragging my eyes away from Nessa to see Hutch staring at me with surprise. "I didn't realize you were still here."

"Didn't know if you needed anything," I explain, rising to my feet as Nessa begins to stir beside me. "Everything okay?"

Hutch nods. "Good so far. She's dilated to a four, so it's going to take some time still. Her heart rate is a bit low right now, so they're monitoring it."

"So, no baby yet?" Nessa asks, her voice groggy, and I hate how adorable I find it.

"Not yet. The nurse said we could be here for several more hours."

"Do you want me to stay?" I ask.

"While I appreciate that so much, I'm okay." He looks at Nessa. "That goes for you, too. No need for you to stay. I appreciate you bringing her in."

"Oh my gosh, of course. But are you sure you don't want us here?"

"I'm sure. I promise. Besides, I know you haven't been getting a lot of sleep lately, so there's no reason for you to lose even more just sitting around here."

Nessa stares at her brother like she's shocked he's even noticed.

"What?" Hutch shrugs. "I notice things."

She smiles softly. "Well, if you're sure…"

"I'm sure." My captain looks at me. "Think you could give Nessa a lift home? Figured I'd keep the car for whenever it's time to get out of here."

"Oh, no. That won't be necessary. I can grab an Uber," she says, pulling her phone from her purse.

Like hell she will.

But I can't say that. That would be a huge red flag. It would raise so many questions, ones I don't exactly have answers for right now.

"Uh, no. Locke will take you."

"Reed, no, I—"

"It's not a big deal." I cut her off, not just because I don't want her in the back of some stranger's car, but because I'm not ready to say goodbye to her yet.

She stares at me, mouth agape, and I have to look away before I do something stupid like reach over and touch her.

"See?" Hutch says pointedly to his sister, then turns to me. "Thanks, man. I appreciate it more than you know. You're a good friend, Whitlocke."

A good friend.

It's three simple words, but they still sit so heavy in my gut. A good friend wouldn't have thought about making out with his friend's sister just twenty minutes ago. A good friend wouldn't want to kiss a friend's sister in a darkened hallway. And a good friend certainly wouldn't sleep with the sister and lie about it.

A good friend would be honest, even if it meant risking the friendship. I am not a good friend. Not by a long damn shot.

But I don't say that to him. I can't. Not today. Not when he's about to get everything he's ever wanted. Everything he deserves. I'll come clean to him later, after more time has passed. Or maybe when I'm not still wanting to kiss his sister so damn badly.

"Yeah, sure. Any time," I mutter, not really looking him in the eye.

I wait as they say goodbye and pretend I don't overhear Nessa hissing at Hutch about offering her up to some stranger. I cringe when Hutch laughs and says, "Locke would never lay a finger on you." If he only knew that not only did I already have my fingers all over her, but my mouth too.

Hutch gives me one last nod before he disappears back down the hall.

"I appreciate the offer, but I really can just grab an Uber," Nessa insists as we step into the elevator.

I don't even dignify that with a response.

"Hello?" she says, waving her hand in front of my face. "Did you hear me?"

"Oh, I heard you all right, love. I'm just ignoring you."

She huffs, crossing her arms over her chest. "Fine. Whatever."

I grin at her petulance as the car stops on the next floor. The doors open, and several more people file in, forcing Nessa closer to me. I'm instantly overwhelmed with that familiar scent of lavender and wildflowers, and it takes everything I have not to reach over and nuzzle my nose against her neck just like I did all those months ago.

I clench my teeth when the elevator stops for a second time and even more people cram inside. At this point, Nessa is so close against me that I feel like I'm at a middle school dance with her ass pressed against my crotch. I will my body not to react, thinking of anything and everything else that I can to distract me from this torture. I'm not the only one being tortured if the sudden hitch in her breath is any indication.

When the car stops for a third time, it's rough, sending Nessa tumbling into me. I grip her waist to steady her, and I'm transported right back to our night in New York. Right back to tangled sheets, soft sighs, and whispered words. I inhale shakily, then exhale just the same.

It's a fucking miracle I'm not hard as a rock right now. I don't know how, especially since all I want to do in this moment is pull Nessa's leggings down and bury my cock inside her, all these people be damned.

We finally reach ground level, and everyone starts to file out one by one. I've never been so damn grateful and annoyed all at once. Nessa steps away from me, and it's all I can do to force myself to let her go, my hand sliding from her waist in a slow free fall.

We walk silently to my car, and I grab the door for her before she can get it. She's careful to avoid my gaze as she hops into the SUV. When I slide behind the wheel, she already has her eyes closed, head resting against the window. Damn. She's more tired than she let on.

I let her rest, navigating out of the lot. I flick my

blinker on to go right, but at the last minute, I decide to go left. We barely make it to the first stoplight before she's snoring softly beside me. We drive like that for a while, me navigating the city while Nessa sleeps peacefully beside me. It's a miracle I don't wreck with the number of times I've looked over at her. I certainly get honked at for taking too long at green lights.

Twenty minutes later, I put the car into park, and Nessa finally stirs, her eyes blinking open softly.

She looks around, brow furrowed. "Where are we?"

"My place," I answer, hopping out of the car before she can protest.

When I open her door, she's already primed and ready to go, glaring over at me. "What the hell, Locke? Why are we here? I—"

"Because you're tired, Nessa. You fell asleep in the waiting room *and* in my car. You need to sleep and you're not sleeping well where you currently are, so why not try somewhere else, eh?"

Her glare wavers for only a second, then it's back again and she shakes her head. "No."

"Why not? Do you have to work tomorrow?"

"Well, no. But—"

"Then you'll stay here. You'll sleep as long as you like and you'll leave whenever you want."

"Gavin. No."

"*Nessa.* Yes." I hold my hand out to her. "Come on. Out you go."

She sighs but puts her hand in mine anyway. "Has anyone ever told you that you're obstinate?"

"Only my mother," I say with a grin, pulling her from the SUV.

She allows me to steer her into the building, and I wave to the security guy sitting near the elevator.

She whistles lowly. "Damn, this place must be fancy if you have security."

"Fancy, no, but I'm not the only athlete that lives here."

"Do other guys on the team live here?" she asks, panic lacing each word as we step into the elevator.

"Just one, but we don't have to worry about him."

She tilts her head to the side.

"Keller," I explain.

"Oh." She nods a few times. "I see. Has he, uh, said anything about…us?"

I shake my head, and she seems relieved by that. Truthfully, I am, too. I trust Keller though. Even though he's still giving me the knowing looks, I know he's not going to say anything to Hutch. That's just not the kind of guy he is.

We're quiet as the floors pass us by, but a new sense of awareness hangs between us. I wasn't even thinking about our past when I brought her here, or about anyone else seeing us together, for that matter. All I could think of was finding her a place to sleep because I didn't feel comfortable leaving her alone in Hutch's big-ass house that she's already struggling to be comfortable in.

I'm sure it's nothing against him or Auden, but it has to be weird to be suddenly shacking up with the stepbrother you already have a strained relationship with. It's clear Nessa didn't think that part through when she came out here looking for a place to stay.

We reach my floor, and I guide us toward the door at the end of the hall. I punch my code in, then push the door open, moving aside to let her pass.

"After you," I say.

She slips by me, making sure to slink as close to the other side of the doorway as she can so we don't touch. There's already been enough of that today.

"It's not much," I tell her as I slide my shoes off at the tray in the entryway. She sees me and does the same, and I pretend not to like the way her shoes look sitting there next to mine. I head for the kitchen, feeling her behind me, and open the fridge. "Are you hungry?"

"No, but I'd love something to drink."

"Water, beer, wine, juice," I offer. "I'm all out of amaretto sours."

I wink at her, and she fights a smile as she settles onto one of the stools. "Water is fine."

I slide her drink her way and grab a beer for myself, popping the top and taking a hearty swig.

"Ahh," I say, smacking my lips as I settle against the counter.

"Good?" she asks.

"Nothing beats a cold beer after a game."

"Oh, gosh. That's right. I completely forgot you played tonight with the whole baby thing. How was it? Did you win?"

"We did. Sent Edmonton home crying into their helmets, which is a great confidence booster to start the season because they're damn good at what they do."

She takes a small drink. "Are you ready for the regular season?"

"Yes and no. You'd think after doing this for as many years as I have been, I'd be ready or have things down to a science. But the game is always changing, you know? There's new talent. Guys get faster and stronger and come up with new ways to score goals. So while I'm ready in the physical sense, I'm not quite there mentally. Usually happens that way until we're a few games into the season, then I'm locked in and nothing can distract me from the game I love."

She smiles softly. "I used to feel that way about painting."

"Still feeling blank?"

"Maybe more than ever," she mutters. "Which is just sad. What twenty-seven-year-old feels blank?"

Twenty-seven. Fuck, I almost forgot how young she is compared to me. There's an eleven-year difference between us. That feels like a fucking lifetime…and another reason why nothing can happen.

I swallow down that dose of reality and say, "There's nothing wrong with a blank canvas. It just means you've got plenty of room to work."

She opens her mouth as if she's about to argue, then thinks better of it. Instead, she yawns.

"Sorry," she says, her voice dropping an octave.

I finish off my beer, drop the bottle into the recycling bin, and push off the counter. "Let's get you to bed, huh?"

We both pause, and a wave of awkwardness crashes through the room.

I wince. "I just meant…" But I don't finish the sentence.

Nessa chuckles. "It's fine. I knew what you meant. Just give me a pillow and blanket and point me to the couch."

I snort. "You're not sleeping on the couch."

"Oh, do you have a spare bed, then?"

"No, you're sleeping in my room."

Chapter 11

Gavin laughs, and the sound is low and rumbly and goes right between my legs. I squeeze my thighs together as subtly as I can, trying to push the feeling away, but all it does is make it worse.

"Don't worry, love, I'm not sleeping in there with you."

Disappointment rattles through me, and I try not to show it. I shouldn't be feeling that way anyway. We are just friends, after all, and since we're friends, it doesn't feel right to take his bed and make him sleep on the couch.

"It feels wrong to steal your bed."

"It's not stealing if I'm offering. End of discussion."

He says it with such finality that I snap my mouth closed, and I chalk it up to being so tired I can hardly keep my eyes open. He pads out of the kitchen, and I follow after him, taking in his penthouse as we go. Photos line the light gray walls, and I assume it's the nieces and nephews he's so fond of. There are multiple images of what I can only assume is his family, and even a few of him with teammates, too. I can't recall the last time I saw a guy actually *want* to display his love for his family and friends like this.

But that's not all he has that surprises me. Sitting opposite the large leather sofa that can't possibly be comfortable to sleep on is a tank.

"Is this saltwater?" I ask, bending down to peer in.

"Yep. This is my pride and joy." Gavin leans down next to me, then points to the little fish in the corner. "This is Pearl." He points to a second, smaller fish I hadn't noticed before. "And this is Rufus."

"They're clown fish? Like Nemo?"

He chuckles. "Yes, just like Nemo. And these little guys are firefish goby. They get along well, which is important. Don't want anyone getting too feisty."

"Wow," I say, watching them swim around in their home. It's full of beautiful coral and anemones and so many other things I can't even begin to name. "They're all so pretty. This tank is gorgeous. All the colors and rocks…it's all so vibrant. Peaceful."

"Thanks. I, uh, I got into fish when I was younger. Having so many siblings meant limited space in the house. We already had four dogs and two cats, so when

I wanted a pet of my own, my parents insisted it be something small so it wouldn't take up too much room. I settled on a goldfish, and it took off from there." I'm no longer looking at the fish. I'm looking at Gavin and how his eyes grow brighter with each word. It's so cute to see him so clearly excited about something. "I built this tank about six years ago. Definitely sucks when it comes time to trade teams, but I wouldn't change it. I could sit and watch them swim all night."

"Is that why there's no TV in here?"

He winces. "Is that weird?"

"Only if you tell me you don't have one at all. Then I might have to make an excuse to leave because there is no way you're not a secret serial killer."

He grins. "I have one in my bedroom."

"Phew. That was a close call."

He shakes his head, still smiling. "Come on. Let's get something to wear."

Wear? Oh, god. I hadn't even thought about not having something to sleep in. Normally, I sleep in just my underwear and a t-shirt. I can't do that here. That would be too much…right?

Gavin leads us into his bedroom, and I pause at the threshold. He wasn't lying about the TV. There's a big one mounted to the wall opposite the king-sized bed in the middle of the room. A sleek black wooden headboard matches the dresser and bedside tables. Off to the side is a big leather chair with a lamp sitting beside it, and I wonder how many nights he finds himself there with a book.

I laugh when I spot another tank, this one much, much smaller.

"Another fish?"

"Huh?" he says, popping his head out of the closet off to the side. "Oh, yeah. That would be Sir Fishsticks the Fourth."

A laugh bursts out of me. "What?"

Pink stains the tops of his cheeks. "I, well… That was the name of my first goldfish. When he passed—RIP to the little guy—I got another, and I felt it was appropriate to honor him. I just sort of kept up the tradition through the years." He grimaces. "It's hokey, I know. But I was young, all right?"

I smile, shaking my head. "Not hokey. Sweet. It actually kind of humanizes you a bit."

He tips his head to the side. "Humanizes me?"

I shrug. "Yeah, I mean, you're… Well, you're *you*. You're this larger-than-life guy who makes millions of dollars a year playing hockey. People beg for your autograph and photos. They bid on things you sign. Little kids idolize you. Fans literally scream your name. You're not exactly an average joe."

He looks surprised by this, like it's new information to him, and it might be, especially with the way he seems to carry himself. I've not spent that much time with him, but never once have I gotten the sense that he thinks he's better than anyone else. It's refreshing after spending so much time in a world where I thought I *had* to be better.

When the hell did I get so lost? When did I become that person? When did I lose who I truly am? And can I ever get her back? I don't know, but I'd like to try.

"Right," Gavin says, pulling me back to the present. He clears his throat. "Anyway, I think this will work."

He passes me a gray t-shirt, and I shake it out. *Seattle Serpents Hockey Club*, it reads. It's obviously been worn a lot, and I wonder if it's a frequent flyer of his. Something about that idea makes me feel warm, but I try to ignore it.

"Thanks," I say, taking it, then pointing to what I assume is the bathroom. "Do you mind if I…"

"Go ahead. There are towels in there if you need them for anything, and extra toothbrushes are in the drawer because I often forget them in hotel rooms and then overbuy them." He gestures toward the living room. "I'm going to make up the couch."

It's on the tip of my tongue to stop him and tell him this is ridiculous, I can't take his bed, and invite him to sleep next to me. But I don't say any of that. I just nod, then disappear into the bathroom, hiding from him…and maybe myself too.

I find a washcloth and scrub off the little bit of makeup I managed to put on this morning, then grab a toothbrush. I do everything else—including snooping in his other drawers—to avoid putting on the shirt he gave me. It's silly considering our history, but something about it feels so…*intimate*.

I'm not sure I'm ready for intimate.

After procrastinating as long as I can, I grab the shirt and trade my own for it. My nipples pebble instantly as the material slides over me, hitting just above my knees. I tell myself it's because of the cold, but I know it's because it's *his*, and something about that does things to me that it shouldn't. It smells like him, like warm and cedar. A crisp autumn day and a cozy blanket.

I attempt to push the sensation away as I pad out of the bathroom. Gavin is still in the living room, so I slip under the blankets as quickly as possible, though I don't know why. He's seen me in far less than just his t-shirt, but still.

I burrow under the comforter and relax into the bed. It's heavenly after such a long day and all the hours I've been putting in at the bar. Stepping into the bartender role has been easier than I thought. It's nothing that fills my cup to the brim, but it's something new, and I'm okay with that for now.

My body is getting comfortable, and my eyes are growing heavy.

"Good?"

I blink my eyes open. *When did I even close them?* Gavin stands in the doorway leaning against the frame with his arms crossed over his chest. He looks so good like this, so relaxed and confident.

"Very. Has anyone ever told you how comfortable your bed is?"

He chuckles, pushing off the door. "I've never had anyone else in my bed."

If I weren't so tired, I might analyze that more, but my eyelids feel like they weigh ten thousand pounds at this point.

"I'm just going to brush my teeth, then I'll be out of your hair," Gavin says.

I nod, or at least I think I do. My eyes are already closed again. I faintly hear the bathroom door snick shut as I sink deeper into the blankets. I have no idea how many minutes pass before Gavin emerges, and as much as I want to, I don't open my eyes to watch him go. He clicks off the light, then stops.

I'm not sure how I know it, but his eyes are on me. I can feel them trace over the lines of my body, settling on my face. I want to look at him, but something tells me not to. So I lie there, completely still, as he inches closer, his footfalls soft against the carpet.

Then I feel it. His lips. They're soft and warm against my forehead.

"Good night, love," he whispers.

It's the last thing I hear before sleep takes over, and I fall into the best night of rest in my life.

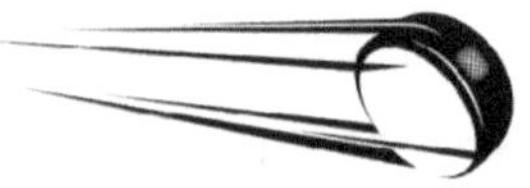

Cinnamon.

The sweet and spicy scent is the first thing I smell when I wake. Bacon is the second.

My stomach growls almost instantly, and I'm not surprised; I can't recall the last time I ate.

What I can recall—in perfect detail—is Gavin pressing his lips to my forehead. I have no idea why he did it, and I have no idea why I liked it so much, but I did.

Did he know I was still awake? Does he know I felt the kiss all the way in my toes? Does he know I can still feel his lips against me?

"You need to stop being such a little shit, Rufus. Quit stealing all the food. Pearl needs to eat too. Don't make me separate you two."

I smile. It's cute that he's talking to his fish. I'm not

quite sure what I expected Gavin's home life to be like, but it certainly wasn't this. It's so…simple. Logically, I know he's just a person with a pretty cool job, but I still expected a bit more glamour. Not waking up to him talking to his fish like they're people.

I indulge in a few more minutes in the coziness of the blankets before forcing myself to get up and start my day. I finally get a reprieve from work, but I still need to go apartment hunting, and I suppose look into getting a car at some point.

First, a pit stop in the bathroom. I do my business, then wash my hands and brush my teeth. I splash some cool water on my face, then comb my messy hair with my fingers, trying my best to look presentable. It's hard given what I have to work with, but it'll do. I reach for my pants and—

"What the fuck?" I mutter out loud.

Where the hell are my pants? I took them off last night, folded them, and set them right here on the counter. I look in the bedroom, just in case I'm remembering wrong, but they're not there either. They're gone. *Poof.* Nowhere to be found. I guess I'm walking out there with no pants on.

Gavin is standing at the stove when I reach the living room, his back to me. He's wearing a pair of gray joggers and a black t-shirt. It stretches across his back as he flips whatever is in the pan, and I'm glued to my spot, mesmerized by it. I remember watching those muscles jump when he was doing something else, when he had me pinned against the hotel wall as he drove into me again and again.

A shiver rolls down my back at the thought, and I clear my throat. He spins around at the sound, eyes wide. The surprised look on his face doesn't last for long, slowly transforming into one I am all too familiar with when it comes to him.

Desire.

His hazel gaze rakes over me slowly, from my pillow-ruffled blonde hair, over his shirt that hugs my breasts, to where the material kisses the tops of my knees. It's a carnal look. Fiery. *Hungry.* Warmth pools in my lower belly as I force myself to move closer and pretend he's not looking at me like he's thinking of having me for breakfast. He shakes his head like he's knocking himself out of his stupor and clears his throat.

"Uh, good morning," he says, his voice a touch deeper than usual. "How'd you sleep?"

"I just had the best rest of my life," I say, slipping onto a stool at the counter. "I don't know if that bed is made with heaven's clouds or what, but it's incredible."

He grins. "It is, isn't it? Makes it hard to go on the road sometimes. Not that Auden's hotels aren't up to snuff, but nothing beats your own bed."

I used to love my bed too. That was until I thought of all the times Neal could have brought his secretary there, and I began to hate it. One night in a fit of rage, I dragged it out of the house and threw it on the curb. I slept on the couch for months afterward until we finally sold the house.

I want that again, though. I want a place where I feel safe. Somewhere that feels like home. A place where I can be myself. It's why I need to get a move on finding an apartment, so I can have that back.

"What time is it?"

"Five to eleven."

"Shut the fuck up." I wince, and he laughs. "Sorry. It's just, I don't think I've ever slept this late in my life, not even in college. I must have been more exhausted than I thought. I—oh my gosh!"

I glance around the kitchen, looking for my purse.

"What's wrong?"

"Have you seen my bag?"

"I put it by the door." He points to the counter. "But your phone is here charging."

He…charged my phone for me? Did he go through my purse too? Look at my texts?

"I didn't snoop through anything, I promise. You had an alarm going off this morning, and I remember you said you didn't have to work, so I figured I'd let you sleep. I noticed your phone was at fifteen percent, so I plugged it in for you. I didn't look at anything else, I swear."

I believe him. Gavin doesn't strike me as that kind of guy. To be fair, I did nose around in his bathroom cabinets last night, so tit for tat and all that, but still.

I slide off the stool and grab my phone. I bypass the emails from apartments probably turning me down and the texts from my dad and Angie and go straight for the one from Reed.

> Reed: Born at 3:34 AM. Alana Marie Hutchinson. She's perfect.

I smile instantly, knowing Marie is a nod to Reed's mother's middle name, and my smile grows even wider when I see the photo he sent along. He's right—Alana is perfect. A little bundle of pink, her nose just like her father's, hair as dark as her mother's.

"She's cute, right?" Gavin says.

I blink away the tears stinging my eyes. "She is. She looks like Reed."

"Poor kid."

I laugh. "Poor Auden. Now she's really stuck with him."

He grins at me as he flips the food again. "You hungry?"

"Starving."

"I thought you might be. Just need to finish this, then grab the plates, and we'll be good to go."

"Oh, I can help."

I pull open the cabinet beside me, and by some miracle, it has just what I'm looking for. Unfortunately for me, Gavin is a giant, which means his plates aren't exactly reachable, even with my height. I push up on my tiptoes, trying to reach them, but it's no use. I lift my leg to climb onto the counter, and that's when I feel him.

He's behind me, and he's reaching for the plates, but it's so much more than just that. He's pressing up against me, and there is absolutely no mistaking how perfectly his cock lines up with my ass because I can *feel* it. I can feel *him*, and I want to feel more.

I want him to push my shirt—*his* shirt—up around my waist and slip my panties to the side. I want him to drop to his knees behind me and worship me with his tongue. Then I want him to slide his cock into me just like he did in the shower in New York. I just want him.

But I can't have him.

It was nothing. Just a night of fun. It didn't mean anything.

His words echo in my mind, and though they're not the ice bucket I wish they were, it's enough to clear my mind of the images assaulting me.

"Um, Gavin?" I manage to say.

"Yeah?" he asks, breath hot against my ear.

"Where are my pants?"

The question brings us both crashing back down to earth, and he pushes away from me, plates in hand. If I weren't struggling so hard to breathe, I'd think I imagined the whole thing. I settle my feet back on the floor, taking my time before turning to look at him.

"Dryer," he tells me. "I, uh, threw them in the wash this morning. I know how you hate to smell like the bar. They should be done within the hour."

He washed my clothes. I can't believe this man washed my clothes. Unprovoked. And because of something I said weeks ago. He charged my phone, he gave me a bed to sleep in because he knows I've been struggling, and he's making me breakfast. I can't remember a time I ever felt so taken care of, and I don't know what to do with that.

"Oh." I brush my hair behind my ear. "Uh, thank you. That was kind."

"No problem," he mutters before giving me his back and plating our food.

I pour us each a glass of orange juice while he does that, then settle onto the stool just as he sets the plates down. We eat in silence, and while it doesn't feel comfortable, it's not as awkward as I would expect either, and not just because I'm half-dressed.

When we're finished, I try to help clean up, but Gavin refuses, making me sit there and watch as he rinses off our plates and puts them in the dishwasher. I want to help so badly, but the last thing we need is another incident like the one that ended with me pressed against the counter.

So I don't. I sit at the counter on my phone, checking the emails I disregarded earlier. I have not one, not two, but *three* rejections from different properties I applied for. Two are because they have no units available, and the third is because, apparently, I applied to a 55-plus community complex.

"Everything okay?"

I look up to find Gavin staring at me with concern.

"It's just..." I shake my head. "It's nothing."

"Come on. We're friends, right? Friends talk."

Shit. He's got me there.

I sigh, my shoulders dropping with the weight of my issues. "I've been trying to find a place to rent that doesn't completely break my budget, and I'm not having very good luck. Everywhere I've looked is out of my price range when I get the real numbers from them or full for at least the next few months. I can't wait a few more months. Reed and Auden *just* had their baby. I'm sure they don't want to be raising their child with a freeloading, pathetic divorcee stepsister hanging around."

He gives me a sharp look. "You're not a freeloader,

for one. And two, I think I have a solution to your problem."

That has me perking back up. "You do?"

"Sure. You can live here."

And right back down my shoulders go. "Ha. Very funny."

But he doesn't smile. He doesn't say *Just kidding* or *Gotcha*. No, he stares at me stoically.

Oh my god. He means it!

"Gavin, you're… That's…" I shake my head. "Please tell me you're joking."

"I'm not."

"What."

It's not even a question because I can't wrap my head around how he'd have an answer. I can't live here. That's just ridiculous. For obvious reasons and so many others I can't quite name right now, but they exist.

He shrugs. "I'm not joking. Live here. I am days away from diving into a very intense 82-game schedule, and I'm going to be on the road for half of it. I'm not going to be here that often, so why not? You'd practically have the place to yourself. Besides, you'd be doing me a favor."

"How?"

"I need someone to take care of Pearl and Rufus."

"And Sir Fishsticks the Fourth. With parenting skills

like that, I'm starting to understand how you got to a fourth." I raise an eyebrow.

He chuckles. "And Fishsticks, too, of course. I used to have one of my neighbor's kids feed everyone, but they left over the summer for a semester abroad."

"What were you going to do, then?"

"Probably try to talk the security guard into doing it."

I can't believe his nonchalance. Not just about giving the security guard free rein to his penthouse, but about asking me to move in here.

I can't live with Gavin. It's just not possible. We have a history together. We already have secrets we're keeping from Reed—what would he think about it? I can't imagine he would approve of the idea of me living with his teammate. He doesn't seem to want me in his life all that much, and this would really be crossing a line.

Plus, I'm still clearly attracted to Gavin, and if his hard dick brushing up against my ass earlier was telling at all, the feeling is mutual. That's just a recipe for disaster.

"You're thinking about it too much." He pushes off the counter, moving closer, and I'm drowned in that scent of his I can't quite get out of my system. "It's completely innocent. Just two people helping each other out. And besides, it's not permanent. You can leave as soon as you find a place to rent, and I won't even be mad that I'm losing my pet sitter. It would just mean a good night's sleep in the meantime."

He's right. I had the best sleep of my life last night. The way his bed enveloped me as if it were specifically made for me was…ugh, it was euphoric. I want to go crawl back into it as we speak.

"I thought you said you didn't have another bedroom."

"Correction: I said I don't have another *bed*. I have two other rooms."

"Two?!"

I sound ridiculous right now. I know that, and judging by the smirk on Gavin's face, he knows that too. I'm just trying to wrap my head around how we went from having breakfast to him asking me to move in.

"I had a rookie staying with me when I first joined the team, but he's moved on to bigger and better things, so one room is practically empty, and the other holds my hockey stuff. You can take your pick on which one you want."

I nod, remembering back when Reed first started in the NHL and lived with one of his older teammates for the first year. I always thought that was such a selfless act, giving up part of your home to help someone else.

Kind of like what Gavin is attempting to do now. I know he's just trying to be a nice guy. He can say he's only offering because it benefits him, but I know better. He'd have easily found someone else to take care of his fish. He's just being kind. *Too* kind, and I can't take advantage of that…can I?

It would be wrong on so many levels, but it would also solve so many of my problems. While Reed has been nice enough over the last few weeks, he hasn't completely hidden his desire for me to move out. And I get it. I truly do. It's part of what makes this offer so tempting.

Well, that and the fact that I am having no luck finding a place on my own. The baby is here. My time is up. Should I really be looking a gift horse in the mouth?

"Look, I fully understand your reservations, Nessa," Gavin says when I don't say anything. "They're valid. But I swear it has nothing to do with New York. This is just two friends helping each other out. That's all."

It was nothing. Just a night of fun. It didn't mean anything.

There are those words again. Maybe it *was* nothing. Maybe it *was* just a night of fun. Maybe it *didn't* mean anything. Then what happened just thirty minutes ago? When he pressed against me and I felt just how *un*friendly he was feeling toward me? Was it a slip-up?

A total accident? Something that will certainly never happen again?

I don't know the answer to any of those questions, and more than that, I don't think I want to. Because he's right, this *is* just friends helping each other out, and I could really use a tick in the win column.

I exhale slowly, then nod. "All right. I'll stay here and help you with your fish—but only until I find something else. I won't take advantage of you any more than that."

"Oh, love," he says with a grin. "I wouldn't mind at all if you took advantage of me."

He's teasing. I know he is, but all it does is remind me of what a bad idea this is. Even so, I don't take back what I just said. Instead, I extend my hand over the counter. Gavin does the same, his palm sliding against mine.

Just friends, just friends, just friends, I chant to myself.

"Welcome aboard, roomie."

He smiles, and I smile back.

But on the inside? I know this man could be my downfall, and that scares me for more reasons than one.

Chapter 12

"Oh, Gavin," my mother says, her voice echoing around my SUV. She sighs, and I feel it deep in my bones. "What have you gotten yourself into?"

Sure, it's probably pathetic that I am an almost forty-year-old man and have called my parents to talk about my woes, but one thing they drilled into me from the time I was little was to talk about my feelings. So here I am, talking about them and wondering if I made a mistake by letting my one-night stand move in with me.

I don't have an answer to my mom's question because I've been asking myself the same thing since this morning, when Nessa sat across from me, looking sad about her apartment applications getting rejected, and I opened my mouth without thinking, offering her one of my spare rooms. It was such a moronic idea, and it was built on such a flimsy reason. I know that, and I'm sure she did too.

But I couldn't let her beat herself up over her situation any longer. She came all this way to start over, and if I can help in any way, I want to. She deserves it, especially after everything she's been through. Nessa is not a pathetic divorcee. She is someone who was hurt in one of the worst ways possible. So yeah, I'm going to offer her a room, even if it is the dumbest idea of the century.

I thought I was doing a nice thing by washing her clothes, but I quickly realized what a mistake it was when she walked out of my room in nothing but my old Seattle Serpents t-shirt. It took every ounce of strength I had not to march across that room and haul her into my arms and kiss her senseless.

Somehow, I resisted…until she crawled up on that counter. I couldn't help myself. I *had* to touch her. And help her, of course.

Yeah, right, you fucking perv. You just wanted to feel her against you again.

"Gavin? You there, son?"

I shake my head as my dad's voice breaks through the memory.

"Yeah, sorry," I say. "Sorry, just got distracted by… traffic."

Great. Now I'm not only lying to myself but my parents, too.

"You think I'm making a big mistake, don't you?"

"No, dear," my mother says. "You can't be making a mistake if you're trying to help someone."

I smile. Of course she would think of it that way.

"However," she continues, and the smile drops from my face instantly. "It's certainly not the brightest idea you've ever had."

My dad makes a disgruntled noise. "I'd say."

"Lars!" my mother admonishes.

"Dolly!" Dad fires back, and I grin.

My mother's name is Ruth, which is a far cry from Dolly. Neither my siblings nor I know when or why my father started calling her Dolly, but it makes us laugh either way. It's an inside joke they share, and it always makes me smile whenever I hear it.

Maybe that's why I have never settled down in the past. Maybe it's because I'm looking for something like what my parents have—that all-consuming, unconditional love that lasts for years and years. Yeah, something like that doesn't sound bad at all.

"Look, all I'm saying is the boy is supposed to be focusing on the upcoming season. He's the one who's been worried about not getting another contract. This is a bit of a distraction, no?"

"No, not a distraction," I say. "She's just a friend. What happened was in the past. We've moved on."

Even as I say the words, I don't believe them. Nessa is one hundred percent a distraction. She's *been* a distraction since April. And as sweet as my mom is for her reassurance, she's wrong. I am making a mistake, but for some reason, I can't stop myself.

I wish I had an answer for why I'm doing this, why I'm risking everything I've been working so hard for. People don't realize that when you reach a certain age in the NHL, it's easy to find yourself sitting on the bench over and over again until it becomes clear they don't need you at all. At that point, one of two things happens: you get sent back down to the AHL, or you are not offered a contract and are forced to "respectfully retire." I don't know which of those is more embarrassing, but I don't want either to happen to me. When I call it quits, I want to do so on my terms, not anyone else's. All of that is on the line by letting Nessa into my life like this.

"Well, we trust you, son," my dad says. "We know you'll do the right thing for you, whatever that looks like. If you say this girl needs your help, she needs your help, no matter the history you two have. You just keep your chin up and keep focused on your career, and whatever else happens, happens."

"Thanks," I tell him. "I appreciate it, Pop."

"We love you!" my mom calls out.

"I love you guys, too. I'm pulling into the parking lot now. Talk to you later."

We end the call, and I pull into my favorite spot. I sigh, dropping my head back against the headrest. Somehow, I have to go out there on the ice and act like I didn't just invite my captain's sister to live with me. Thank fuck Hutch isn't going to be here today, not with him and Auden just having the baby yesterday. I have some time to figure out how I'm going to tell him about Nessa.

Before she left, we made a plan for her to move in two days from now. The Serpents are starting this season with a three-game road trip, so it gives her a little time to settle in without me there to make things awkward. Plus, I have time to order another bed since I really wasn't kidding about not having another one. It's just something I never got around to. Whenever I want to see my family, I'm the one who goes to visit them. It's easier that way with all my siblings having so many kids between them. That's too many schedules to try to figure out.

When I realize I've been stewing for far too long, I finally pull myself out of the car and head into the rink. Maybe this is just what I need, a few hours out on the ice to clear my head. Something else to focus on. Something not blonde. Something that doesn't make my heart race because of the simplest things. I wave at a few of our trainers and staff as I walk through the halls to the locker room. Several of the guys are already gathered in there, getting ready for a training session, including Fox and Keller.

"Hey, man," Fox says as I tug my shirt over my head. "What a night, huh?"

I know instantly what he's talking about—Hutch and Auden. Not that I would ever bring this up to him, but Hutch texted the group chat almost immediately after Auden gave birth. We were the first people he wanted to share it with, and dammit if that doesn't intensify my guilt.

"Still can't believe Hutch is a father," Keller says.

"He's going to be good at it, too. You should've seen him on the way to the hospital. He was a wreck, but in a good way. I think anyone who is worried that much about being a good parent is going to be one."

"Man, these last few years have been weird, huh?" Fox comments.

He can say that again. So many people falling in love and starting new chapters in their lives, and here I am, clinging to a one-night stand from months ago.

"Guess it's a good thing that evil stepsister was there after all," Keller says, and I feel his eyes on me with each word.

I don't turn around and look at him, even though I

desperately want to correct him for calling her evil. She certainly wasn't evil this morning when she was in nothing but my shirt. In fact, she looked like a fucking angel.

"I'm sure Auden felt more comfortable having someone there until Hutch arrived," Fox agrees.

They continue talking about the baby, but I'm no longer listening. I'm still trying to get the image of a pants-less Nessa out of my head.

"I am an uncle!"

Several guys around the room groan as Lawson walks in. It's not an unusual reaction.

"Um, dude, you were already an uncle," Hayes says, following right behind him. "Your brother has a kid, remember?"

"Of course I remember. There's no way I could forget about Jacob and Stevie's daughter, Macie. Do you have any idea how cool that kid is? She could give Fox a run for his money in net."

"Hey, whoa," Fox says, clearly offended. "She's like twelve or some shit."

"And…?" Lawson gives him a pointed look. "Anyway, I know I was already an uncle, but I'm an uncle again."

"Not really," Keller points out. "You and Rory aren't married."

Lawson gasps dramatically. "How dare you! We

might not technically be married, but we're going to be together forever."

"Then why haven't you put a ring on her finger yet?" Hayes challenges.

Keller snorts. "As if that stops someone from leaving."

Several of us look over at him.

He glances up. "What?" he barks.

Fox's eyes connect with mine, and I shrug. I have no idea what his problem is. I usually don't.

"Because I'm waiting for the right time. I have to be careful with Rory. She spooks easily," Lawson says.

"Or maybe she just doesn't like you as much as you think she does."

Lawson flips Keller off. "She loves me. Stop being jealous."

"Of you? Never. Besides, how can I be when I have your mo—"

"Keller, I fucking swear—"

Lawson moves to go after the instigator just as our coach walks into the room.

"That's enough!" Coach Smith yells, and everyone freezes. "You two want to fight? Take it out on the ice. No throwing punches in the locker room. Now get dressed. I want you on your skates in five."

The hustle in the room picks up as we all start to get dressed just a little faster, rushing to get out there before our time is up. Coach Smith is a fantastic leader and an even better guy, but when he says he wants us out on the ice in five minutes, he means it. I really don't want to bag skate today as punishment for being late.

Five minutes later, I'm surrounded by my teammates in the rink. Just being out here already has tension easing out of my shoulders. My neck feels looser, as do my legs, and I am more than ready to feel the cold air on my face as we get practice started.

"All right, listen up. We're going to start with—"

"Sorry, sorry! I'm here!"

To everyone's surprise—but maybe especially mine—Hutch comes barreling onto the ice, looking like he barely slept a wink last night.

Fuck. I didn't expect to see him today. I thought I had more time to figure out what I'm going to say to him. My stomach churns at the idea of the conversation. What am I even supposed to say? *Hey, I slept with your stepsister who you hate, and now she's moving in with me.* No, that sounds stupid as fuck.

"What'd I miss?" he asks, coming to stand next to me.

Nobody talks for several moments, mostly just giving him stares of disbelief.

"What the hell are you doing here, Hutchinson?" Coach Smith finally says.

"Uh, practicing? Season starts in like four days, Coach."

"I'm aware. I'm also aware that your fiancée just had a baby last night. So I'm asking again—what the hell are you doing here?"

"Uh, I'm…uh…I'm the captain?"

He looks around like he's waiting for someone to step in and rescue him, but none of us speaks up because I'm pretty sure we're all wondering the exact same thing. Practice should be the last thing on his mind.

Then suddenly, everyone talks at once.

"What the fuck is wrong with you?"

"Go home!"

"Get the fuck out of here!"

"Go be with your fiancée!"

"Leave!"

I have no idea who shouts what, but it's hilarious to watch his eyes widen and him scramble to get off the ice. I breathe a sigh of relief when he's out of sight, and Keller chuckles beside me. I don't give him the satisfaction of looking at him.

"I fucking swear… You boys…" Coach Smith mutters, shaking his head and turning back to us. "Well, now that that is out of the way… Fox, you're in net first. Whitlocke, Lawson, let's run it."

So we do. We run drills and we skate. We meet

with the special teams coach and run some plays. We do all the things we need to do, and not once do I think about my captain or my new roommate or the shitty situation I seem to have gotten myself into.

Or at least that's what I tell myself.

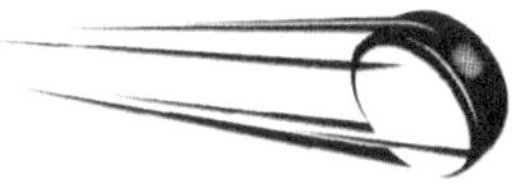

Even though he floods the Serpents Singles group chat with photos, Hutch misses the next day of practice, too, and I've never been so relieved not to see my captain.

Nessa is moving in today. In fact, I'm supposed to meet her at the penthouse after this to let her in. I had a key made for her yesterday, and it's been taunting me as it sits on my kitchen counter ever since. I can't tell if it's a reminder that I'm making a mistake, that I should talk to Hutch, or that I'm jeopardizing everything I've worked so hard for. No matter what, it's still happening.

But first, I have to survive today's practice with Hutch back on the ice.

Not that I've given him much chance to since I've practically been avoiding him, but he hasn't said anything about Nessa. This leads me to believe one of two things: he doesn't know about her new living situation, or he doesn't care.

I'm hoping it's the latter.

"That's good, that's good, that's good," Lawson says.

The pass from Poldzkin hits his stick right on the mark. He skates it toward the net, and Fox tracks his every movement. Lawson drags his arm back and releases, and the goalie drops at just the right moment to block the shot, the puck thwacking loudly off his pads.

"Fucking nice, Foxy Baby. Very nice." Lawson taps him on the pads that just stopped a beautiful shot.

The forward skates to the back of the line, and we all inch forward, watching as Thomas does the same thing, then Peirson. Fox blocks both shots, and it looks damn promising.

I get the puck from Poldzkin and rush toward Fox. He follows me, shuffling his skates as I move. And he's good, really damn good, but I've been around this league a lot more years than he has, and I know exactly what to do next. With just a quick flick of my wrist, the puck goes top shelf and hits the net before Fox even realizes what's happened.

He chuckles when he looks behind him, like he can't believe what just happened.

"Sorry," I say, tapping his pads.

"I can't even be mad about that one." He smiles at me. "That was a nice shot. Keep doing that all season long, and you're going to be our top-scoring defenseman once again."

Fuck, I wish I could be. We made it into the playoffs last year, and with each game, I felt like I was losing more and more steam. I didn't even put up a single point. That's a problem. General managers aren't just looking at what you do in the regular season. They're looking at how you perform when it gets the hardest it's going to get. If I'm not putting up numbers, there's an issue somewhere that needs to be addressed. It's a hell of a lot easier to pinpoint what it is with younger players, but with the older ones, there's usually only one thing it can be—we can't keep up.

I don't want to be the guy who can't keep up. I want to win. I want to lift that Cup over my head and have my name inscribed on it for all time.

"Fucking nice," Hutch says as I join him in the back of the line. We'll probably go through this a few more times before swapping out goalies and running it again. "Feels good to be back out on the ice again, yeah?"

"Always does. Can't wait for the season to start."

"Same. It's going to suck being away from Auden and Alana, though. I can't believe how much I already love her. It's only been a few days, but I'd lay my life on the line for her."

I grin at him. He seems happy. A bit tired, but happy, which is why this is so hard, standing here talking to him like I'm doing nothing wrong. Like I'm not hiding something huge from him. I've had this knot in my gut since Nessa first showed up, and all it does is get heavier and heavier as time passes.

"How are the girls doing, by the way?"

His smile is so big it's almost unnerving. "Amazing. I'm so damn in love with Alana already. I don't even know how it's possible, but I am. And Auden is great too. You should see her as a mother. It's the hottest thing I've ever witnessed."

I laugh. Seeing him so happy is such a one-eighty from where he was two years ago.

"Oh, by the way, I don't know if I said it—these last few days have been a bit of a blur—but thanks again for driving Vanessa home the other night."

"Oh, uh, yeah. It was no problem. How are things with your sister? I mean, with the baby home now and all?"

Yeah, that's it, Gavin. Ease into it.

"Great. She told me a few days ago she found a place and is moving out. Shit, that's today, actually."

Okay, here we go. We're doing this.

"Anyway, I offered to help her, but she laughed and

told me she has like three bags, so that would be pointless." He shrugs. "I'm happy for her. She seems to have had a weight lifted off her shoulders, and Auden gets to settle into a routine with the baby. It's a win-win as far as I'm concerned."

And that's it. That's all he says about it. He doesn't cuss me out or lay into me about moving his sister into my place, which tells me what I suspected: she didn't tell him. Hutch doesn't know Nessa is moving in with me in a matter of hours.

That knot tightens even more, and it's so damn taut I might puke. Or maybe that's all the skating I've done today, I don't know. All I know is the second Coach cuts us for the day, I get as far away from Hutch as possible. I don't sit by him like I normally would during our meeting or when we watch tapes from other preseason games. I don't even say goodbye to him before I race out to my car. I avoid him at all costs because I don't know *what* to say to him.

Twenty minutes later, when I step out of the elevator, she's there, and fuck is she a vision. Her hair is pulled up into a bun that looks intentionally messy, showing off a pair of small hoop earrings. She's wearing a simple navy t-shirt and a pair of jeans that hug her in all the right places, and she looks like a fucking knockout. Just as Hutch said, she has three bags sitting by her feet, and that's it. This time, when my stomach aches, it's for a totally different reason. She had a life at one point. A big, beautiful life. She had a house and a car and a future.

Now, all she has is this.

"Did you find it okay?" I ask as I approach, cursing myself for not thinking about giving her the code to get in.

"Kind of hard to miss the gigantic glass building, but yes."

Oh, so she's sassy today. Got it.

"Is this everything?" I nod toward the stuff by her feet.

"For now. It's all I brought with me to Seattle. I technically have a few boxes of things back in storage in New York, but it's nothing I need right now. Or at all, maybe. I haven't decided just how far I'm willing to go with this whole starting-over thing."

I get it. Sometimes you have to purge it all to really be free of whatever haunts you. I enter the code into the door, then grab all three bags and push into the penthouse, Nessa right behind me.

"I had a key made for you," I say as I set her stuff down just inside the entryway. "It's on the kitchen counter. But there's a code for the door too. It's 4646."

"So just your jersey number twice?"

That makes me smile. "You know my jersey number?"

"Don't flatter yourself," she says with a roll of her eyes. "It's literally stitched into the towels in your bathroom."

I wince. "It's a tradition from my parents. Whenever I get moved to a new team, they buy me towels with the team and my number on them. Cheesy, I know."

"Incredibly cheesy," she agrees. "But also incredibly cute."

"That's my parents for you."

"They're still together, I assume?"

"Yep. Their fiftieth anniversary is coming up next year. Us kids are planning a surprise trip to the Amalfi Coast. They're going to be so mad at first, but then they'll love us again."

She smiles softly. "Fifty years with someone sounds nice."

I've never been against relationships like a lot of the other guys in the singles group chat have been, but I've also never been in a rush to settle down. I haven't really given much thought to what fifty years could look like with somebody, but now that I'm thinking about it, she's right. It does sound nice.

Really, really damn nice.

"Anyway," she says. "Want to give me the grand tour?"

"Oh, right. You might want that, huh?"

After I offered her a room the other morning, it seemed like both of us wanted to get away from the other as fast as possible. Once her pants were dry, we settled on a move-in day, and she left. It wasn't until after she was gone that I realized I never even showed her around.

I walk her through the apartment, pointing out the secondary bathroom and the room I use to house the hockey memorabilia I've collected over the years. There's a lot of stuff in there, from commemorative photos to sticks that have too many memories attached to them to get rid of, to all the different jersey iterations I've worn.

"Wow," she says, taking it all in. "This is…wow."

I laugh. "I'm sure your brother has something similar."

"I'm sure he does, but I've never seen it. Our parents got together when Reed was already in the NHL, so he was long out of the house. As you can imagine, we haven't exactly hung out a lot over the years."

"Why is it you two don't get along again?"

"Honestly? I'm not sure." She runs her hand over the jerseys I have hanging on a rack. "I don't even remember why we disliked each other to begin with. I mean, I was a tiresome, petulant teen, and he was a young hockey star with a chip on his shoulder. Both of our families had been broken in one way or another, so maybe we thought we were trying to replace what we once had. I don't know. It's not that I don't like him, because I do. I think a lot of it is just that I don't know him. Not really."

"And is that why you didn't tell him you were moving in with me?"

She pauses. "Oh."

"Yeah, *oh*."

She shrugs. "I guess I just didn't think that was an important detail."

"You didn't think you living with your brother's teammate was an important detail to share?"

She finally looks at me, lips pinched together tightly. "Why didn't *you* tell him we were living together?"

"And how do you know I didn't?"

"Well, for starters, my phone hasn't burned a hole in my pocket, which must mean you didn't bring it up to him either."

Fuck. She has me there.

"No," I confess. "I didn't tell him."

"What? You didn't think you living with your teammate's sister was an important detail to share?"

She sounds so bratty, and it reminds me of our first meeting, when she told off that married guy for hitting on her. And I like it. Way too fucking much. So much that it makes me want to kiss her.

Gee, this is off to a great start, Gavin. She's not even been here thirty minutes and I'm already thinking about kissing her.

"Look," she says, "we're grown adults. We can do whatever we want. I don't need my brother's permission to live here, and neither do you. Besides, it's just for a few months, right? Not like it's that big of a deal."

She's right. This is only temporary. Why does Hutch need to know about it? In a few months, it'll be like this never happened.

Lies, lies, lies.

I push away the voice chanting in my head, not just because I know it's right, and nod.

"Fine. Then we don't say anything."

"Good. Now, can I see the other bedroom?"

I lead her out of the room and into the next. There's nothing in there except a few boxes left over from when I moved in.

"When you said one room was practically empty, you truly meant that."

"Yeah, what did you think I meant?"

"I don't know! That you had an air mattress or something in here and you were just trying to be nice the other night."

"Uh, no. I am far too old to sleep on an air mattress."

"I'm not. So, where am I going to sleep?"

"My bed."

Her eyes widen. "What?"

I chuckle. "We've been over this, love. You can have my bed while I take the couch. It's just for a couple of days until the one I ordered gets here."

Her gaze softens, her plump lips parting just a fraction. She's staring up at me like I just told her I rescued a kitten from a burning building, and I both love and hate it.

"You bought me a bed?"

I nod with a shrug. "It's no big deal. You loved mine so much, so I figured why not? It should come while I'm on the road."

I can tell she wants to say something else, maybe even argue with me, and I think a part of me wants that, mostly because I love the fire that ignites in her eyes when she does. But to my surprise, she doesn't.

She just nods and mutters a quiet, "Thank you."

It does something to me, and it has me wanting to kiss her again—but I *can't* kiss her again. Instead, I mumble something about needing a shower and hightail it out of the room before I do something really, really stupid like forget we're supposed to be just friends.

Chapter 13

We're surrounded by boxes of delicious takeout, from potstickers to fried rice to three different kinds of chicken and even a few dessert rolls. It's incredible food, and I can't remember the last time I was so full, but all I can think is, *He bought me a bed.*

I never once expected Gavin to go out and get me a bed. That was something I was going to do on one of my off days. In the meantime, I planned on sleeping on the couch, but of course, he wouldn't let that slide. No, he had to go and prove just how perfect he is, reminding me once again that this is a bad idea.

It took everything I had not to launch myself at him when he said he bought me the exact bed he sleeps in. Not just to thank him for the inevitably amazing nights of sleep I'm going to get, but because he took the time to remember something I liked, to do something kind for me when I didn't ask him to. I don't think Neal would've ever taken that initiative. If I were in this situation with him, he would be snuggly in his own bed while I had a fitful night of sleep on the couch. Or even the floor. He wouldn't have cared. Not like Gavin does.

I need to stop comparing the two. I know that, but the divorce is still fresh on my mind, especially with my so-called "friends" back in New York texting me about the news that's spreading like wildfire. Apparently, Neal and his secretary aren't just pregnant. They're pregnant with twins…and engaged.

Surprisingly, this new information didn't send me into a spiral when I heard it this morning. I was mad, yes, but it didn't break me like I thought it might. Actually, it made me want to draw. I don't know why, but for the first time in a really long while, I wanted to pull out my sketchbook and create something pretty and hopeful. Maybe that means I'm finally moving forward and this starting-over thing really was exactly what I needed.

"Okay, that was a hell of a feast. Remind me to let you do all the ordering from now on."

Gavin pats his stomach as he rests against the back of the couch, and I try not to think about the abs I know are hiding under his hoodie.

I chuckle, then set my half-eaten carton of chicken

chow mein on the coffee table with the rest of the food. "I just pressed a few buttons."

"Yes, but it was the combination. Those steamed green beans were perfect with the wontons."

"Guess I need to add 'excellent at ordering Chinese food' to my résumé. Maybe it'll get me somewhere other than slinging drinks at Top Shelf."

"How's that going, by the way?"

"What? The bar?" He nods. "I don't know. It's fine, I guess. It's not exactly what I wanted to do with my life, but maybe that's a good thing. The other plans I had didn't quite work out either, so why not shift goals entirely?"

"You don't want a studio anymore?"

His words surprise me. I mentioned that to him once, and that was months ago in New York. How could he possibly remember that?

"You… You remember that?"

He shrugs like it's no big deal. "Got a good memory."

But I don't think that's the case at all. The butterflies I felt in that bar with Gavin make themselves known, letting me know they're still there and aren't going anywhere. I'm not quite sure how to feel about that, so I ignore them.

"I haven't painted in a long, long time. Maybe that dream is for the old me."

"And you don't think the old you is still inside you?"

"Sometimes I hope she isn't."

"Why?"

"I…" I settle back against the couch. "I don't know. There are times when I'm not exactly proud of who I used to be. I could be mean, and I was certainly selfish. I spent a lot of my time trying to be this version of myself I thought the world wanted. I thought if I had a fancy car and a big house and the perfect partner, I was untouchable. And maybe for a while I was. Then everything came crashing down, and I wasn't just mean—I was *cruel*. To everyone. My dad and my stepmom, even when they let me stay at their place during those first few weeks after I found out about Neal. I was rude to Reed and Auden when they came for Christmas. I still can't believe they took me in when I just showed up on their doorstep. And I was certainly vicious to Neal's mistress."

"Well, I mean, all things considered…"

"She didn't deserve that, though. She was a victim like I was. He was her boss. He had power over her. He was the one breaking a promise to someone else. No matter how you look at it, he was the one to blame. I got them both fired from their jobs with the video."

Gavin sits forward. "Video? What video?"

"Oh, I didn't tell you? Not only did I find out my husband was cheating on me, I had video evidence to really hammer it home." I laugh, but it's hollow. "I guess one of the times they got frisky on his desk, he accidentally started recording, and it saved to the cloud account we shared. Imagine my surprise when I went looking for some wedding photos. I was going to have them printed and blown up to hang in our bedroom for our six-month anniversary. Instead, I found the video."

The dull ache I've had in my chest since that day makes itself known, but it's nowhere near as strong as it once was. Call it growth or letting go or whatever; I'm grateful for it. It gives me a bit of hope that I won't always be so broken.

When Gavin doesn't say anything, I dare a glance over at him. His jaw is clenched tightly, and his usually bright hazel eyes have darkened.

"Gavin?"

"Do you want me to kill him?"

I laugh, then laugh some more. Then I realize he isn't laughing too.

"Come on. You can't be serious," I say.

"I am. I'm dead serious. Do you want me to kill him? I don't know how I'd do it, but I'd do it."

I chuckle again. "While that is very sweet of you, no, I don't want you to kill him. I, uh, I kind of like having you around, and prison really isn't my scene."

His features soften almost instantly, and he relaxes against the couch once more.

"Thank you for offering, though."

"Any time." He throws me a wink. "So, about this whole you-not-painting-anymore thing…have you tried it lately?"

I shake my head. "No, but then again, I haven't had a lot of time. This move was very spur of the moment, so getting settled has been consuming all my energy."

It's the truth, but what I don't mention is the sketchbook I bought before the flight here, the one I got in hopes that something would light a spark in me and I could draw again. Nothing has though. It's still sitting blank at the bottom of one of my bags.

He waves his hand. "You're settled now."

He's right, but there's still something holding me back, and I'm not quite sure just what that is. Maybe it's my lingering anger over the divorce, or maybe it's just that I haven't felt inspired lately. Whatever it is, I'm sure I'll figure it out, and I'll get back into my favorite hobby even if it only remains a hobby.

Besides, do I really think I could open a studio? Once upon a time, I think I would've been great at it, but I haven't been *me* in so long that I don't know if I could.

But I don't tell Gavin all that. I say, "Guess we'll just have to see what happens."

He looks like he wants to say something else about that but decides not to, and I'm relieved. I'm not sure it's something I want to dive further into right now.

He yawns.

"Sorry," he says through a second one.

"Don't be. You should probably get to bed anyway. I'm sure you have a long day of travel ahead of you tomorrow."

"Not too bad of a flight to Southern California, but it'll feel long with it being the first road trip of the season."

He pushes to his feet, grabbing a few containers of food, and I follow behind him. We clean up our dinner mess, and Gavin shows me around the kitchen, pointing out where everything is. I'm sure I'll forget half of it by morning, but I love that he's trying to make me feel at home. Truthfully, I'm thankful he's leaving for a few days. It's not that I don't want him around, but it'll give me time to settle in without things feeling so awkward.

Just like the other night when I stayed here, he makes up his spot on the couch while I get ready for bed in the bathroom. I'm snuggled down in the sheets when he comes into the room.

"All done in there?" he asks.

"Yep. It's all yours."

He shuts himself inside the bathroom while I lie there, staring at the ceiling and listening to him move around. This all feels so weird, being in Gavin's penthouse, sleeping in his bed, putting him out by making him sleep on the couch. I don't like it one bit.

When he emerges, I'm still lying there, my gaze on the ceiling. I roll over to look at him as he stands awkwardly by the door.

"So, uh, good night, I guess," he says after a few moments.

"Yeah, good night," I mumble back.

He gives me a tight smile before heading toward the door, and I hold my breath as I watch him go. I don't want him to leave. I want him to stay, and not just because he has more of a right to this bed than I do. I just don't want to be lonely.

He's just about out of the room when I find myself saying, "Gavin, wait."

He pauses, then slowly turns back to me.

"Stay."

"What?" he asks, though he doesn't look taken aback by my words. It's almost as if he expected them.

"Stay," I repeat. "Please."

I hear him swallow all the way across the room. "Are you sure?"

I nod. "I'm sure."

I don't have to ask him again, and when he disappears into the living room—probably to grab his phone and pillow—I know he's coming back.

And he does. He pushes the door closed with a quiet *snick* of the latch, then settles into the bed beside me like we've done this a hundred times before. I roll over to face him.

He smiles. "Thanks."

"No need to thank me. It's your bed. Besides, I couldn't let you sleep on that couch knowing you're traveling tomorrow and won't be back in your bed for at least a week. It just didn't feel right. And also, it's not like we haven't done this before…"

Like earlier, his eyes darken again, but this time it's for a completely different reason. I wonder if he's slipping right back in time to our night together. I know I am. It's something I do often, as if that night is embedded in my memory.

But he doesn't say anything, just rolls over and flips off the bedside lamp. I do the same, and we're bathed in dark. Though this bed is huge, it suddenly feels so small. I can feel the heat radiating off him, and part of me wants to move closer to that warmth. I don't, though. I just lie there with my eyes closed, forcing myself to breathe evenly so I can fall asleep, and it can be morning, and I can be safe in the light of day.

Eventually, it works, and I'm nearly asleep when he speaks again.

"Nessa?"

"Yeah?"

"What happened that night?"

I squeeze my eyes shut even tighter. I've been waiting for him to ask this since the moment I came to town. And why wouldn't he? Of course he wants to know why I left him after an earth-shattering night.

"Why did you leave?" he continues. "Why did you run?"

"Because I was scared," I whisper.

"Of what?"

"You, Gavin. I was scared of you."

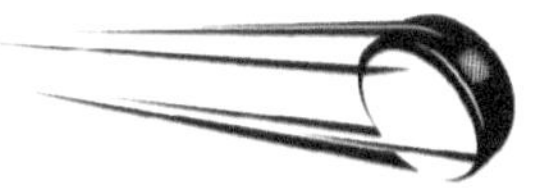

Six months ago, New York City

Gavin stares down at me with lust-filled eyes.

"Are you sure?" he asks, his voice hoarse.

I nod. "I'm sure."

It's all he needs before he's kissing me again. *Hard.*

I don't even mind. I want it like this. I want him like this, unbridled and raw. I want everything he's willing to give me, because I *need* this. Not just to put

Neal and everything he did to me behind me, but I need it for me. I need to feel alive again, whole. I can't remember what it's like, and I'm desperate for it. I think Gavin can give it to me.

Suddenly, he pulls away, and I whimper at the loss. He chuckles darkly, then kisses my throat again. Then lower, over the swell of my breasts, and I want to feel him there. I want to feel him everywhere. Bare. Nothing between us.

He continues kissing lower and lower, and it takes me a moment to realize he's pushing my dress up as he goes. His lips touch the top of my thigh, and I gasp. He laughs against me.

"Easy, love," he says. "I'm getting there."

He kisses me again, this time closer to right where I want him. Then again. And again. He does it until every inch of my thigh has been touched and I'm squirming against him with want.

Finally, I feel his lips brush against my center, and I cry out. That's how fucking desperate I am at this point. His lips graze me through my underwear, and I'm howling like a damn cat in heat. I'm pathetic.

Another rumble of laughter.

"Gavin," I say through gritted teeth, looking down at him.

"Nessa," he taunts back, and I want to wipe that smirk off his face.

"I'm…I'm dying here."

"Oh, are you?"

"Yes!"

I watch as he leans forward, pressing his lips to me again, and I want to scream. It feels so good, yet it's not even close to enough. I growl, and he laughs.

"I think I like you like this," he says. "So ready. So needy."

"Yes, I am needy. And right now, I need your mouth on me."

"Like this?" he asks before pressing his lips to my inner thigh once again.

I squirm, and he gives me yet another deep laugh. Then another kiss. And we start the process over again. On some level, I'm loving this, the teasing, the playfulness. But there's another part of me—a huge part at that—who hates every single second. I'm too damn eager to love it more. I close my eyes, lying there, hoping and praying he'll give me some relief. He must hear each request because he does.

I've been so focused on the kisses to my thighs I didn't even notice him pulling my panties to the side, but when he finally drags his tongue against me, he's dragging it against *all* of me. I buck off the bed, and Gavin grabs my hips, holding me steady as he continues to lash his tongue against me. Each touch is gentle yet firm, relentless yet flitting. It's so confusing yet so fucking good that I'm moments away from coming all over his face, even though he's barely touched me at all.

"Oh, god," I say through a moan. "Please. I need more. I need…"

Without me having to say another word, he sets my leg over his shoulder and slips a finger into me. I groan.

It's perfect. *He's* perfect.

He pumps into me, matching the rhythm of his tongue. My legs begin to shake, and though I try to hold off my orgasm to make this last as long as possible, I can't. My back arches off the bed, wave after wave hitting me. I feel it *everywhere*, my whole body coming alive in a way it never has before.

Gavin doesn't relent, though. He licks me through every second of the pleasure, flicking his tongue against me harder and faster until I can't breathe. I'm literally frozen there, all the air in my lungs trapped, my head thrown back in pure bliss.

Then suddenly my second orgasm fires through me unexpectedly, and I gasp for air, my body shaking erratically as I gulp in breath after breath.

Only then does Gavin give me a break. His touch becomes softer and slower, and my quakes become less intense. He pulls away with one last kiss, then sets my panties back in place. Honestly, I had forgotten I was even still wearing them. Hell, I'm still wearing *all* my clothes, yet I've never felt so damn naked in my life.

He rises to his feet, staring down at me with wet lips and a wicked grin, and I could *almost* come again just from the proud gleam in his eyes. He reaches for his belt, the sound of the metal clinking loud in the otherwise quiet room, and all it does is drive me forward.

I scramble off the bed until I'm standing just in front of him. I lift up on my tiptoes, placing a soft kiss against his lips before dropping to my knees before him. I push his hands out of the way to finish the job he started. I've never been too fond of giving blow jobs before, but something about Gavin has my mouth practically salivating at the idea of feeling his weight on my tongue.

Buckle undone, I unsnap the button, then pull his zipper down. Just as I'm about to reach into his dark boxer briefs, he backs away. I look up at him, puzzled, but he just backs away again. It takes another step and a flick of his wrist for me to understand what it is he wants.

He wants me to crawl.

And for some reason, I do.

I drop to my hands, following every step he takes, and fuck, it's so damn degrading, but I *like* it, and I can't believe I do. I don't even care about the scrape on my knee and how the carpet is biting into it. All I care about is getting to him so I can touch him.

Gavin is already in the chair across the room as I'm taking the last few strides toward him. He looks so good like this, like he's sitting up on a throne and I'm just a lowly peasant, begging for any scraps he'll give me. In this instance, though? I'm happy to beg. That's how badly I want him right now.

When I settle between his spread thighs, he grabs my chin in his hand, tilting my head up to look at him.

"Take my cock out, Nessa."

I don't hesitate for a moment to follow his instructions, reaching into his boxer briefs and pulling him free. Holy hell, he's beautiful. Thick and long but not overwhelmingly so. Cut and heavy with just a bit of precum leaking from the tip, like he's as ready for this as I am. Unable to stop myself, I lean forward, dragging my tongue over the drop that's taunting me.

Gavin hisses. "Don't tease. Suck."

It's all the permission I need, and I pull him into my mouth.

Warm. That's what he is. And soft. Heady. *Perfect.*

I swirl my tongue around the head, giving extra attention to the underside, before sucking him down more. I do this over and over, sucking on him before pulling back and teasing his tip again.

"Fuck, you're pretty like this, love," he says, his

fingers cascading through my hair. His touch is so gentle and sweet, and though I like it, I want more. "On your knees and taking my cock like a needy little thing. Sucking me down like you can't get enough. You can't, can you?"

I shake my head the best I can, pulling him deeper and swallowing.

"Jesus," he mutters. "You keep doing that, and I'm going to spill down your throat."

His words have me moaning, the thought of him doing so making my pussy throb. I don't understand how I can be so turned on still after coming twice already, but I am. If I were to put my hand between my legs, I would go off in seconds.

"Is that what you want?" he asks, his voice deeper now, like he's barely hanging on, too. "You want me to coat that pretty throat of yours with my cum?"

I nod, and he tightens his grip on my hair.

"I'm going to fuck your mouth now, Nessa, you understand?"

Another nod.

"If you want me to stop, pinch my leg."

It's all he says before he drives his hips forward. I gag at the intrusion, but I don't dare beg for respite. I like this. I *want* this.

He holds himself there for a moment as I struggle to breathe around him, then he backs off. His hand is still in my hair, rubbing at me softly. He does it again and again, holding me down longer each time until tears are welling in my eyes and I'm not sure if I can take much more.

"Last chance to stop, love," he warns.

I don't, and he delivers on his promise to fill my throat. He comes long and hard, so much that it's hard to keep up with it all. His seed seeps from the corners of my mouth, dribbling down my chin. It's messy and gross and yet still so fucking hot. I've never done anything like this before, and I already want to do it again.

When he finally releases me, I drop my head to his thigh, trying to catch my breath as I come down from the high I didn't know I was chasing. He gives me a few moments, then he's hauling me into his lap, his lips crashing against mine like his cum wasn't just spilling from my mouth. There's something about it that's so vulgar. So primal.

He lifts us both, kicking off his pants the rest of the way as he moves through the room, our tongues tangling the entire time. His fingers find the zipper on the back of my dress, unfastening it as far as he can in this position. When he realizes it's not enough to get me naked, he sets me on my feet to finish the job, spinning me around. Goose bumps break out all along my flesh.

Goose bumps. I don't think Neal ever gave me goose bumps.

Then I feel his lips on me. Featherlight, but they're there.

"You're gorgeous, Nessa. Do you know that?" Another kiss. "Smart too. And funny." Kiss. "*Honest.* Your ex…" He sinks his teeth into me, and I groan, dropping my head to the side to give him more access. "He was wrong," he continues. "He was so fucking wrong for not worshipping you, for not cherishing you. He didn't deserve you."

I close my eyes, taking his words to heart.

"And I don't think I do either, but I'm damn glad you're giving me this, and I promise to give you everything he couldn't, even if just for tonight."

My dress falls away, leaving me in nothing but my bra and panties. Gavin turns me back toward him, trapping me against him, my hands folding between us as he captures my mouth once again, telling me with his kisses all the things he just said over again. He breaks our kiss, resting his forehead against mine as his thumb slowly traces over the diamond on my finger.

"May I?" he asks quietly.

I know what he's asking without him fully saying it. He wants to take it off, and for the first time, I want to take it off too. I nod, and he tugs. He goes slow, watching me the whole time as he slips the piece of jewelry I thought I'd wear for all time off my finger.

And the oddest thing happens—once it's gone, I swear a weight lifts off my shoulders. I didn't even realize it was still there. I thought I was over it. I thought I was holding on to the jewelry because it's mine. Maybe I was holding on to something else too, a dream for a life that's no longer mine.

Gavin lifts my chin, pulling my eyes to his. "You belong to me now, love."

He doesn't mean it. I know he's just saying it in the heat of the moment, but a small part of me wants it to be true because I *want* to belong to someone again. More than anything, that's what I want. For now, I'll settle for this, for feeling like I'm being worshipped.

Then we're kissing again, and we land on the bed. He slips between my thighs like he was made to be there. His lips trail from my lips, down my chin and throat, not stopping until he's at my heaving chest. Unclasping my bra with one hand and tossing it aside, he closes his mouth around my pert nipple, and I sigh with relief. I could come again, just from this alone. It's that good as he plays with me, teasing me with his teeth and tongue and his hands roaming up and down my sides. It's incredible, yet I want more.

"Condom," I beg when I can't take it anymore.

He pulls away, looking down at me. His eyes are so dark right now that I can't see any green, and I like that far more than I probably should. He gives me a look, silently asking, *Are you sure?*

"Please."

The single word is all it takes for him to spring into action. He jumps off the bed in search of protection, returning just a moment later with a foil packet in hand. He drops it to the side, then hooks his fingers into my lace panties and slowly pulls them down my legs. My first instinct is to hide, which is so damn ridiculous since he's had his face buried there, but I don't. I let my legs fall open, exposing myself to him, and his nostrils flare as he reaches down and takes his cock in his hand, stroking himself.

"Fuck," he mutters, and I grin.

He reaches for the condom, ripping it open and rolling it on before settling on top of me.

"Did I mention how gorgeous you are?" he whispers.

"You did, but I'll gladly hear it again."

"You're gorgeous, Nessa." His lips ghost over mine. "Absolutely fucking stunning."

I smile against his kisses, running my hands through his hair and down his back, touching him everywhere I haven't gotten the chance to yet. Then I feel him. His cock is pressing against my entrance, and I want it. *God*, do I want it.

I pull at him, urging him on, and he listens to my

silent pleas as he slowly slides inside me. We both groan as he bottoms out, and I feel so fucking full I could burst. If I thought he was big in my mouth, it's nothing compared to how I feel stretched around him. Neither of us moves for several moments, as if we're both too afraid to. I get it. If we move, this will be over far too soon, and I don't think that's what either of us wants right now. In fact, I think I could live in this hotel room forever if I were given the chance.

Gavin calls a truce on our standoff first, moving his hips ever so slightly. He lets out a low growl.

"Holy shit," he says in my ear. "Fuck, fuck, *fuck*. You feel so good, you know that?"

"You feel good too," I tell him lamely, but I don't know what else to say. That I've never felt anything like this before? That I don't think anything could ever compare to tonight? That I'm not sure I'll ever be the same? I can't say any of that, so I don't.

Gavin picks up his pace, thrusting into me, and it's such a contrast to how rough he was earlier. So caring and unrushed. He's taking his time too, and I couldn't be happier about it. Until I'm not so happy because I *need* to come again. I don't have a choice. I might combust if I don't.

As if he knows—or maybe it's because he's right on the edge himself—he pushes up onto his knees, changing the angle, and while I miss the feel of him pressed against me, this is so, so good that I can't complain. Especially not when he hits that spot I need him to in order for me to see stars. His thumb finds my clit, and I want to cry because it feels so fucking good.

"Yes," I cry out. "More."

He gives it to me, and I gladly take it. He drives into me harder and faster, and I fall into bliss with one last tight circle around my throbbing clit. As if my orgasm sets him off, Gavin comes with a roar just behind me, so hard I feel him twitching inside me as his thrusts slow. He drops down against me, burying his face in my neck, kissing me until he has no choice but to move.

He slips out and off the bed, dropping the condom into the trash before gathering me into his arms and carrying me away. Settling me on the counter in the bathroom, he turns on the shower. Once the water is warm, he carries me inside, where he holds me under the stream and washes me from head to toe.

We fuck on the chair, then against the wall, and when he pounds into me, he whispers sweet words into my ear.

"You're beautiful, Nessa."

"This pussy was made for me, love."

"I'm not sure this will be enough."

It's magical and unlike anything I've ever experienced before.

After I don't even know how long, we find our way back to bed, my head resting against his chest, his arm holding me tight. Gavin is asleep beside me, his soft snores filling the room. But even after all that energy spent, I'm wide awake.

The last few hours are setting in, and I'm starting to panic. Not because I regret what happened, but maybe because of the opposite—I want more of it. I don't just want to *feel* cherished—I want to *be* cherished. I want to be taken care of. I want to belong to someone. I want to feel like I matter. I can easily see that someone being Gavin, and that thought is the scariest of them all.

So, very carefully, I climb out of bed. I find my ring, gather my discarded underwear and bra, and slip back into my dress. High heels in hand, I do something I've never done before—I run.

Because I think Gavin was right—this won't ever be enough, and that terrifies me more than anything else.

Chapter 14

LOCKE

"Looking good, fellas. Looking good."

Coach is right. We *are* looking good. We're up 3–1 in the final ten minutes against Los Angeles, but there's a lot of time left in the game still, and our opponents are making one hell of a push. Most of the team makes it off the ice for a change, but Frederic and Poldzkin are still stuck out there. It's been over a minute, and I know they're both tired this late in the game.

When there's finally a chance to get some fresh legs out there, Poldzkin rushes toward the bench, and I hop over. I join the play, and with a few missed passes by LA, we've got the edge once more. Hayes grabs the puck, sending it over to Frederic. They trade it back and forth a few times, Hayes unable to find an opening, too many opponents blocking any potential lanes, and all the other guys are covered.

I see a flaw, though, and tap my stick against the ice, calling for it. With just a soft, one-touch pass from Frederic, I have the puck. I drag my arm back and let it rip. Nobody sees it coming, and I let the puck fly off the end of my stick, going top shelf on the goalie just like I did to Fox in practice. The lamp lights up behind the LA net, and my teammates go wild.

"Fuck yes!" Lawson yells.

"That's my boy!" Hayes thumps me on the helmet.

I point to Frederic, letting him know it was all his play that got us the goal, especially with him having been out on the ice so damn long. I lead them down the bench, bumping fists with my other teammates as I go. Fox is standing at the end, a huge grin on his face.

"See? I told you!" He taps his helmet against mine, congratulating the other guys before skating back toward his net.

We're up 4–1 now, and our buffer is looking even better with eight and a half minutes to go. We settle down, getting back into position, and the puck is dropped at center ice. I finish out my shift, then plop down on the bench, trying to catch my breath.

"Fuck, my lungs are burning," Hayes says.

His words make me feel a little better because I feel

like I'm dying out there. It's like I'm skating through sand instead of on ice.

"Don't know how your old ass is still doing this," he remarks.

Me either.

"Hope to hell I'm half as good as you when I hit your age."

He thinks I'm playing well out there? Sure, I scored a goal, but that was only because nobody thought to cover the old guy. Still, as silly as it is, Hayes's words light a spark inside me that I didn't know I needed.

When I hit the ice for my next shift, it feels as if I'm skating a little easier. I'm still struggling and barely moving fast enough to stay out of reach of the other guys, but I'm keeping up, which is all I can ask for at this point in my career. When I get the puck, I flip it down toward LA's empty net, just barely missing. They hustle after it, and our guys are right there too, battling it out. Keller being Keller lays a big hit, and it's just enough to get the team and crowd fired up. Suddenly, sticks and gloves are flying all over the ice, and I have someone by the collar. He tries to throw a punch at me, but I dodge each attempt.

Meanwhile, Keller has someone in a headlock, practically giving him a noogie. It's hilarious and chaotic and exactly why I love this damn game to begin with. I'm not nearly as scrappy as my teammate, but that doesn't mean this isn't still fun, especially knowing one minute we could be throwing punches and the next we'd be attending each other's weddings.

There's one last meaningless puck drop before the final buzzer. The Serpents swarm Fox, patting him on the head, then congratulating each other. We just won our first game of the season, and it feels so damn good.

Maybe I've been overthinking this the whole time. Maybe I'm not too old to be out here on the ice. Maybe I can keep up and keep doing this for at least a few more years. Maybe I'm not the main course on the chopping block like I thought.

"Absolutely fucking stellar, boys!" Coach Smith beams at each one of us in the visitors' locker room. "That's how you start a fucking season off!"

He looks like such a proud dad, and I get it—I'm proud too. We played good out there.

"Hit those showers. The bus leaves in twenty."

We do as he says, the room buzzing from the win. Everyone's laughing and joking, even Keller. Well, at least as much as he laughs. Twenty-five minutes later, we're on the road to Anaheim for our next game. The bus is mostly quiet. Everyone is either on a tablet or talking quietly to their family on the phone.

"Nice goal out there," Keller says about ten minutes into the journey.

"Nice fight," I counter.

Leave it to Keller to drop the gloves during the first game of the season. He's our enforcer for a reason.

"So, how's it going?"

Something in the way he says it has me turning to him.

"What do you mean?"

He lifts his brows. "I think you know exactly what I mean."

Fuck. I do know what he means.

Nessa.

I clear my throat, sitting up higher to look over the seats to see where Hutchinson is. He's all the way up front by Coach. He has his phone out, flipping through photos of his new baby girl. I settle back into my seat, glancing over at a smug-looking Keller.

"She moved in with me."

"What?!"

Keller's outburst draws the attention of several of our teammates.

"Shh! Rory was just about to tell me what she's wearing!" Lawson says from two seats up.

I swear I hear Rory say, "I was not!"

I toss Keller a look that clearly says *What the fuck was that?*

"That's what I would like to know," he says, reading it clearly. "What the fuck do you mean she moved in with you? Into *our* building?"

I shrug. "I mean, she moved in. How hard is that to comprehend?"

He glowers, though that's nothing new for him. "Dude."

"What?"

But I know what. I do. It's so fucking stupid and reckless. I can see that now, especially after how we left things. I had every intention of sleeping on the couch, but then she looked at me with those forest eyes of hers, and I broke. Granted, it didn't take much convincing—actually, almost none on my part—but still. I really was trying to keep my distance. I was trying to be good. I was trying to stay away.

I couldn't, though. Just like I couldn't resist asking her about that night.

"You, Gavin. I was scared of you."

What did that even mean? Why was she scared of me? Did she mean scared of us? Scared of what the night meant? Because it fucking terrified me too. It still does because how the hell am I still so hung up on a one-night stand from half a year ago? How am I still so tangled up in knots over someone I spent one night with? I don't fucking know, but I am.

We didn't say anything else after that confession. I pretended to fall asleep, waiting for Nessa to do the same. Eventually, she did, and it was her soft snores that finally lulled me into slumber. I wish I had never slept at all, though. All I did was dream about that night. It felt so fucking real, like it was happening all over again.

I woke up with my cock so damn hard I had to take a cold shower. I haven't done that since I was a teenager. But there I was, a nearly forty-year-old man standing under the icy water to avoid stroking my dick to thoughts of a beautiful younger woman. I was so disgusted with myself that I left hours before I needed to just to avoid seeing her again.

"It's not that big of a deal," I mutter.

"So Hutch knows?" Keller counters.

"No, because it's none of his business. She's an adult."

He snorts. "Right. She's what, twenty-four or something?"

"Twenty-seven."

He whistles. "Quite the age gap you got there. Ten years?"

"Eleven," I say through gritted teeth. "What the fuck is your point, Keller?"

"My point is: You're too fucking old to be doing stupid shit like this, to be hiding stuff from your friends. And by the way, you wouldn't be hiding it if you didn't think you were doing something wrong."

"I *don't* think I'm doing anything wrong because

I'm not. And I'm not hiding anything. I just haven't told him yet."

"But you're going to, right?"

I can't help but laugh at the irony of this situation. Two years ago, I was having this exact conversation with Hutch when he was sneaking around with Auden, despite it being forbidden. The only thing is, I'm not sneaking around with Nessa.

But you want to, a little voice in my head says, and I try to shush it the best I can.

Keller sighs. "Look, man, all I'm saying is, be careful, yeah? You've already got one big secret regarding his sister, and now you're making it two. You're digging yourself a hole. That's not like you, Locke. You're not that kind of guy, so that tells me one of two things—you're either in over your head and just don't know how to swim out, or this girl means more to you than you're letting on. If I were a betting man, I'd say it's option two."

I open my mouth to argue, but Keller barrels on.

"But that's your thing. You deal with that however you need. I'm still firmly in the camp that this could ruin the team dynamic, and I don't want that. So whatever's going on…however you feel…figure it out and be honest about it."

He doesn't say anything else, and neither do I. How could I? It's clear Nessa means *something* to me, but I don't exactly know what that is. Is she just a damn good memory, or is she something else? I think I already know the answer to that, but it's late and I'm tired and I don't want to analyze shit anymore.

We pull up to the hotel shortly after and pile out. We get our rooms and turn in for the night, that post-win buzz from earlier having worn off by now. Besides, I'm sure most of these guys want to get to their rooms to talk to their partners some more. I know I'd be doing that if I had someone too.

I drop my bag on the chair in the corner of the room, then strip out of my dress shirt and pants, not even bothering to put anything else on. I'm just going to crawl right into bed and fall straight to sleep. I'm in the bathroom when I hear my phone rattle against the table. I ignore it.

It rings again, which sets me on edge. It's late, and the only people who would call twice in a row are my parents or one of my siblings. But it's not them.

It's *her*.

I snatch the phone up before it can go to voicemail.

"Nessa?"

"Oh, thank gosh! I am so, so sorry, Gavin! I don't know what I did!" she cries into the phone, a hiccup interrupting the last word.

"Nessa, calm down," I tell her. "What's wrong? What happened?"

"I… I…" Another hiccup. "He's just floating there! I fed him the brine shrimp exactly like you told me to but he's just floating and not moving and—"

"Who is floating there?"

"It's… I… Well, I don't know. I can't tell them apart."

I grin. The fish. She's panicking over the fish.

"Is it the big one or the small one?"

"Small. I think."

"If small, that's Rufus. The females are bigger. They're the dominant fish."

"Really?" She sniffles. "That's kind of badass."

I chuckle. "Yeah, it is. Okay, so what exactly is Rufus doing?"

She cries again. "He's…floating."

"Where at?"

"Huh?"

"Where in the tank is he floating?"

"Oh. Um, near the bottom. In the back corner. I actually couldn't find him at first, so that freaked me out, then I saw him and I just… Did I kill him?"

I try not to laugh again, especially with how upset she is. "No, Nessa, you didn't kill him. He's sleeping."

"What!" It comes out more of a screech, and this time I do laugh. "Are you sure?"

"Yes, pretty sure."

"I can't live with *pretty sure*. I'm putting you on video chat so you can see him with your own eyes."

I hear the beep come through before she even finishes her sentence, and I pull the phone from my ear to hit accept. Her face fills the screen, and my first thought is, *Fuck, she's beautiful.* I know it's been less than forty-eight hours since I saw her, and I have no right to, but I miss her.

"Look!" She flips the camera around to show me my fish. "He's just floating."

She's right. He is just floating. But I've had Rufus long enough to know that's exactly what he looks like when he sleeps. He's also in his favorite spot, which he likes to go to at night.

"Did I kill him?" she asks again, turning the phone back to her. She chews on her bottom lip, her green eyes shimmering with unshed tears.

"Nope. He's sleeping, as suspected."

Her shoulders visibly sag with relief, and she falls against the couch. There's a blanket behind her that looks suspiciously like the one from my bed, but I don't question it. I'm too busy looking at her.

"Thank god," she says. "I've been waiting for your game to end so I could call you. Definitely didn't want to give you that news during intermission."

Does that mean…

"Were you watching?"

"Hmm?"

"Were you watching?" I repeat. "My game, I mean."

"Oh." She bites into her bottom lip again. "Uh, yeah. I was."

My chest swells with excitement over that.

"That was a nice goal," she says. "I mean, I don't really know much about hockey, but it looked nice. The commentator guy said you went *top shelf, where Mama hides the peanut butter*, whatever the hell that means."

I'm so used to the different hockey slang that sometimes I forget there's a whole group of people out there who have no idea what we're saying half the time.

"It just means I scored in the upper part of the net, kind of like a mom hiding goodies from the kids in an upper cabinet. I guess it's sort of my signature move. Some hockey players have them, some don't."

"Oh. Okay, I guess that makes sense."

"What do you mean you don't know much about hockey? Your brother literally plays it professionally for a living."

She shrugs. "I don't know. Reed was already doing his thing when I came along, so it's not like it's something I grew up with. I've been to a few of his games, and I suppose I understand the basic rules, but I don't know all the phrases and sayings and the whosits and whatsits. I didn't even know who you were."

Just like that, I'm thinking of our night together again. Her hair fanned out over the bed as I slid inside her, the way she clawed at me and urged me on. How good she felt wrapped around me. Her crying in my arms in the middle of the street, confessing all her fears.

I'm thinking of all of it, and for the first time since I started playing hockey, I wish I weren't on the road right now. I want to be there with her. Even if we aren't really anything to each other, I still want that, and I'm not quite sure what to make of that.

She settles into the couch more, getting comfortable, and I do the same, climbing into my bed. She leans closer to the phone, like she's inspecting my surroundings.

"Where are you?" she asks.

"Anaheim. We'll have tomorrow off after practice, probably some press stuff, then an optional morning skate and play the next night."

"What do you do with your time off?"

"It just kind of depends on what I'm feeling that day. Sometimes I'll hit the links with a few of the boys, sometimes I'll just chill in my hotel room trying to escape Lawson."

She laughs. "I've only met him a few times, but he seems like a handful."

"Oh, you have no idea. I honestly don't know how his girlfriend puts up with him."

"He has a girlfriend?! No, wait. I knew that. It's Auden's sister, right?"

"Yep, her twin, Rory. Which means if they get married, he and Hutch will be family."

"Oh, I'm sure Reed will love that. Then he'll have a brother *and* a sister to hate."

She says it so flippantly, but I can tell her dynamic with Hutch bothers her. It makes me want to sit down and have a talk with my captain about that, but there are far more important things I need to discuss with him first, like her living in my penthouse, for starters.

"He doesn't hate you."

"No, he just thinks I'm evil." She rolls her eyes. "But whatever. I'm great, and he's just a grump. His loss."

"It really is," I agree, meaning every word.

Her cheeks redden at that, but she covers up her discomfort with a yawn.

"Oh, gosh. Sorry. The 'I think I killed a fish' adrenaline must be wearing off. Long day at the bar."

"And that's going okay still? Are they treating you right?"

She snorts. "You say that like you're going to barge

in there like some jealous boyfriend and beat them up if they aren't."

Her eyes widen as if she realizes what she said, then she shakes her head.

"Sorry. Forget I said that," she mutters.

"I would."

"What?"

"I would barge in there like some jealous boyfriend. I'd do anything to make sure you're treated right because that's what you deserve."

She stares into the camera, mouth agape, eyes shining with… Well, honestly, I'm not even sure what. Surprise? Appreciation? Who knows, but it still annoys me all the same. Wanting to protect her shouldn't be an unusual thing. It should just be standard. Makes me want to track down her ex for the hundredth time and get rid of the bastard who made her feel like she's not worthy of that. It's clear his cheating did a number on her, and I wish she could see it wasn't her fault.

"It must be late there," she says after a while. I want to point out that we're on the same coast, therefore in the same time zone, but I don't. She knows. This is just her excuse to go, and I let her use it.

"Right, and I have practice in the morning."

"Right," she echoes. "Well, good night, Gavin."

"Good night, Nessa."

We both stay on the phone for a few more seconds,

and she's the first to hang up. I miss her the second the screen goes black, and I try not to think about that too much.

Eventually, I flip off the bedside lamp and get under the covers. I lie there far longer than I should, tossing and turning, sleep evading me. When I finally do succumb, I dream of her…and what would have happened if she hadn't run.

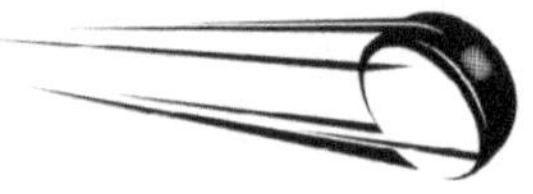

This crowd is electric, far more than Anaheim during our last game.

I'm not surprised. San Jose finished at the bottom of the league last year and picked up a damn good draft pick who everyone is excited about. I'll admit the kid has some sick hands and can skate like nobody's business, which is probably why he's made the opening roster tonight.

The rambunctious crowd just makes everything that much sweeter. We're up 4–0 in the second, keeping not only the rookie off the scoreboard, but their veteran guys too.

"What a beauty, Locke!" Hutch says as he settles onto the bench next to me.

I nod at him, the guilty feeling I've had since his

sister came to town settling into my gut. I've talked to Nessa every night of the road trip. Every night, we've found one reason or another to talk. Sometimes it's on video, and sometimes it's not. Either way, it's become like a routine, and for the first time in a long time, I don't just feel like the old guy on the team—I'm like everyone else with someone to call at the end of the night.

Sometimes our conversations last only five minutes, and I sit with a grin on my face as she tells me about her day. Other times, they last an hour or more, talking about our childhoods and telling random anecdotes. No matter what, they always fill me with something I didn't know I needed so damn badly—joy.

The only problem? Her brother. If Hutch has noticed I've been avoiding him, he hasn't said anything. I even skipped out on dinner with the main crew last night, feigning the need for extra sleep. Lawson took a few shots at me for being old, Hayes joining in on the fun, but it was the way Keller looked at me with those knowing eyes and how even Fox raised his brows that got me. They were looking at me like I was guilty, and they were right.

"Can we get a little more enthusiasm?" Hutch pushes on my shoulder. "Three goals in three games, baby! Our old man is rocking it out there!"

I shoot him a grin, and to my surprise, it's

genuine. I am feeling pretty damn good so far. We might only be three games into the season, but I'll take it. I can't remember the last time I started so hot, and that includes the season I ended up being a Norris Trophy finalist. Now, I just need to keep it going.

It does make me wonder…does it have anything to do with a certain blonde? My dad is right that she's a distraction, but maybe that's a better thing than I realized. Perhaps it's what I needed to loosen up. Who knows. What I do know is that I'm going to keep doing everything I can to continue playing this way and proving to our GM that I'm worthy of being kept around, despite my age.

Keller rams a San Jose player into the boards right in front of me, and I scoot back out of the way just in time to miss a stick to the face.

"Fuck yes, Kells! Way to play hard!" our assistant coach says to him.

He grins up at the guy, then skates off after the player he just hit, probably already looking to do it again. I shake my head at him and focus back in on the game. When I finally get my feet back on the ice again, I'm flying. Feeling so damn good, better than I have in a long time.

I could do this forever, I think to myself.

It happens so fast—one minute the puck is on the

ice and the next it's smashing into my face. I drop in an instant, cradling my cheek.

"Motherfucker! Shit, fuck!" I scream, and I have no doubt the live feeds pick it up with how silent the arena is now.

Skates stop beside me, but I'm too damn focused on the pain radiating through my face to even pay attention to them.

"Fuck, fuck!" I yell, already able to feel the blood dripping down my face.

"Easy, easy," someone says, coming into view.

Hutch.

"Just stay down," he says, trying to keep me calm.

Then he's gone, the head athletic trainer replacing him.

"Talk to me, Whitlocke," Ray says.

"Hurts. Everywhere."

"I know, I know, buddy." He presses a towel to my face to catch the mess I'm making all over the ice. "Can you get up?"

"My legs didn't get fucking hit, Ray."

He laughs. "Good to see you're still a shithead too. Come on, big guy. Let's go."

Ray and Hutch help me to my skates, then toward the bench. I hear the crowd clapping and the players tapping their sticks against the boards and ice. I send them a wave to let them know I'm okay.

"Hey, dude, I'm so sorry," someone says.

I turn to find the San Jose rookie looking awfully pale. What the fuck does he have to be upset about? I'm the one who got pelted in the face.

"Give him some space," Hutch barks, and the kid drops his head, skating away.

I can't decide if I'm grateful for my captain for sticking up for me or if I feel bad for the kid. He didn't do it on purpose. Hockey is a fast-paced game. Shit happens. Then my face throbs again, and all empathy goes out the window. So much for feeling like I'm on top of the world.

I grab Hutch before I go. "Keller."

He nods in understanding. The last thing we need is our guy to get tangled up with the rookie or another player over this. Keller got in a fight in the last game, too. No reason to start the season with back-to-back-to-*back* fights, especially when we're looking at being 3–0–0 to start the season.

I make my way down the tunnel. One stop with Doc later, and I'm out for the rest of the game. It's what I expected, honestly. I just hope it doesn't keep me out any longer.

"At least I'll get the first shower," I joke.

By the time he's done checking me out—no concussion worries, thank fuck—and patching me up, the game is nearly over. I check the TV in the hall to see we're up 5–0, and the pain in my face seems to subside just a little. I hit the shower and get out just as the guys come back in, celebrating their win.

"Locke, man, are you okay?" Hayes asks as he enters the room, coming over to pat my shoulder.

I nod. "Good as I can be."

"Holy shit! You look like hell on toast," Lawson says, reaching for my face.

"Touch me and die, Lawsy."

"Fair enough." He scuttles away, and I don't think he's ever been smarter than he is right now.

He's right, though. I look like some monster right now. There's a huge gash on my cheek where the puck split it open, and I'm already starting to swell.

"Any games?" Hutch asks, worry in his gaze, and not just for me. He's looking at the bigger picture, which I'm proud of him for.

I shake my head, wincing when I do. Doc gave me some meds, but they haven't quite kicked in fully yet. "Not officially, but it's up to me."

"So no, then." He chuckles when I nod. "Figures. Glad you're okay, man. Gave me a hell of a scare out there."

"Scared me too."

Fucking terrified me, actually. I almost lost everything in one moment. That could have been my last game in a flash. I'm glad as hell it's not.

Coach comes into the room, his eyes falling right to me. "Good?"

"Good."

He nods, then tells the team they did a good job and not to be late for the bus. An hour and some change later, we're in the air, on our way back to Seattle. I ice my face the whole time we're on the plane, and I've never been so damn thankful for a short flight in my life because the only thing I want to do is go home, crawl into my bed, and sleep. When we land back in the Evergreen State, my phone buzzes against my leg. I take it out, and the name on the screen makes my heart race.

Nessa.

I can't answer it, not here with so many eyes and ears around. So I pocket it, doing my best to ignore it when it starts to go off again. Even when I climb into my car another forty minutes later, I still don't call her back. I don't just want to talk. I want to see her.

No, I *need* to see her.

It's after two in the morning by the time I pull into the parking garage of my building.

"Come on, come on," I say as I stand in the elevator, thankful Keller and I decided not to carpool tonight. I have no idea where he is, but I'm glad it's not here. He'd know exactly why I'm so eager to get upstairs and would likely have a comment about it.

When the doors finally open on my floor, I practically sprint for my door. I punch half the code in before remembering how late it is. Is she even awake still? I know she just called an hour ago, but that was… well, an hour ago. Is she mad I didn't call her back? *Only one way to find out…*

I re-enter the code and push the door open, being quiet just in case. It's pointless. Nessa is awake all right, and based on the look on her face, she's not happy. She stands ten feet away, arms crossed as she glares at me. She's in nothing but the t-shirt I gave her the first night she stayed here, and I wonder briefly if she's been sleeping in it every night I've been gone.

But that's not important right now.

"Hey," I say after a few tense moments.

One, two, three.

That's how many seconds pass before she explodes.

"Hey? Hey?!" She throws her hands into the air. "That's what I get? You get hit in the face with a puck, ignore my calls, and I get *Hey*?!"

"Nessa, listen—"

"No!" she yells, stomping toward me. "*You* listen, Gavin. I was worried sick. I saw you crumple to the ice, and you didn't move, and my heart was in my fucking throat. I couldn't breathe, watching you lie there. I wanted to crawl through that TV and…and…"

"What?" I ask when she doesn't continue, taking a step toward her. "What did you want to do, Nessa?"

"Kiss you! I wanted to kiss you!"

Her eyes widen, her words hanging in the air between us. I take another step forward. Then another. I don't stop until we're nearly touching, mere inches separating us. Her tongue slides out against her lips, and I track the movement, my breath coming in sharper than it did when I was lying on the ice after being hit.

"You can, Nessa," I say quietly, dragging my gaze back to hers. "You can kiss me. Any damn time you want."

And she does.

Chapter 15

I'm kissing Gavin.

I have no damn idea what the hell I'm thinking, but I'm kissing him—*hard*. I can't help myself. Not after tonight. Seeing him on the ice like that… God, I feel like my heart is still in my throat.

He lay still for what felt like years, though it was only seconds, and I was terrified. I was so fucking afraid that the last time we spoke, it was about our favorite cereals. As much as I have loved our random conversations over the last few days, that's not what I wanted our last words to be.

Then he moved, and I finally breathed. But if I thought I was relieved then, it's nothing compared to now, having his hands in my hair as he holds me to him, our lips moving together. His touch is so familiar and natural, and it's like I'm floating in the clouds.

Euphoric. Transcendent. My hands go to his face on instinct, and he winces.

I pull away instantly. "Shit. I'm sorry. Are you… Are you okay?"

He nods, resting his forehead against mine. "Just a bit tender, is all."

I pull away, tipping his chin up so I can get a better look at him. He looks good because he always looks good, but he also definitely looks like he took a puck to the face. His cheek is swollen, though not as badly as I thought it would be, and his eye too. There's a nasty cut where his skin split open on impact, and I'm instantly reminded of all the blood they had to scrape off the ice. It makes my stomach turn. This time, it's not even because of my blood aversion. It's because I didn't like seeing him hurt.

Pushing up on my tiptoes, I lean forward and press my lips to his jaw, and his fingertips press into my hips where he's holding on to me. I kiss higher, then again. Each time, his grip tightens, like he's barely holding himself back. When I'm near the cut on his cheekbone, a low grumble starts in his chest, so strong I can feel it rattle against me, and when I finally press my lips to the gash, it's his undoing.

He grabs my ass and hauls me into his arms, pressing my back against the wall as he kisses me hungrily. His lips are rough against my own, his kiss nearly bruising, but I don't care. I want it. I welcome it. My hands crash through his hair, holding him closer as he continues to devour me. His tongue sweeps against mine, each stroke feeling like a promise of what's to come.

I gasp when he releases me, only for him to move his lips to my neck. He sucks and bites at me, chasing each nibble with a gentle lick. It's pure torture, my hips rocking against him, needing any sort of relief I can find. What I find isn't enough, and I claw at him, needing more.

He understands my request, pulling back just enough to slip his hand between us to unbuckle his pants. The clinking metal is such a delightful sound, especially with his lips still on me. Then his hand is on me, pulling my panties to the side and slipping through my wetness.

"Fucking hell," he practically growls. "You're soaked. Absolutely fucking drenched for me."

"All for you," I agree, biting my lips when I feel his hot, hard cock against me. "More."

"I need a condom," he says against my lips.

"No time. I need to feel you inside me now."

He pulls back slightly to look me in the eyes. "Are you sure?"

"I had an IUD put in to help with painful periods two years ago, and I haven't been with anyone since…" But I don't need to say it. I haven't been with anyone since him.

"Me either," he says, and I breathe a sigh of relief.

I didn't realize how badly I needed to hear him say it, but I did.

"Then do it. Fuck me bare, Gavin. I need this. I need *you*."

One minute I'm begging him, and the next he's buried inside me. We groan as he fills me, then again as he pulls out until just the tip is inside me and pushes in again. Over and over, hard and fast. His hips are jerky and untrained, but I don't care. I'm too damn desperate for this to give a damn.

I drag my hands through his salt-and-pepper hair, then over his back, my nails digging into his flesh as his hands do the same to my hips. He presses kisses everywhere he can as he drives into me.

"I missed this," he says, his lips now on my chin. "Missed the way this pretty little cunt feels wrapped around me." Kiss. "Missed it milking my cock like it is." Another kiss. "Fucking missed *you*, Nessa."

I missed you, too. But I don't say it out loud. It makes it all feel too damn real. Instead, I let him use me however he likes, taking everything he's willing to give and already wanting there to be a next time. I sound addicted, and maybe I already am.

That's a problem for my future self, though. Right

now, I just want to bask in this. In his touch. The way his stubble feels as he drags it over me. How good his cock feels inside me.

"I don't think I can last much longer, love," he warns.

And it's that one word that does it for me.

Love.

My orgasm slams into me, and suddenly, everything that was so blurry before snaps back into focus. It's like the last few months of heartache never happened. Gavin heals me with his touch. With his kisses. With his cock.

With a few more thrusts, he groans into my ear, and I feel his cum shoot into me. It's so damn hot that I'm nearly ready to explode again. His movements slow, and so do his kisses as we both try to collect our breath. He pulls out of me, and I groan at the loss. He laughs darkly—the sound way hotter than it should be —as he continues to press his lips to my throat.

I have no idea how long we stay like that, but it's long enough that my back begins to hurt from being pressed against the wall, and I feel his cum leaking onto my leg. As if he knows, he peels me away, carrying me through the penthouse to his bedroom. He drops me back on my feet, grabs his t-shirt, and pulls it over my head. He falls to his knees, tugging my underwear down as he goes.

"Christ," he mutters, staring at me with darkened eyes. "Do you have any fucking idea how beautiful you look with my cum leaking down your leg?"

I can't imagine it's any better than seeing him on his knees in front of me. Without warning, he leans forward, running his tongue through my slit, and I gasp. It feels so wrong. So *dirty*. But so, so fucking hot. He sucks my clit into his mouth for only a moment, flicking his tongue against it before rising again and spinning me around. He pushes me down to the bed, one hand getting lost in my hair and the other going to his cock from the sounds of it.

"Need to be inside you again," he says, and it's the only warning I have before he slams into me again.

I come instantly. It's the fastest orgasm of my life, rocking through in a split second, every fiber of my being quaking with the release. My whole body shakes as Gavin fucks me through it, and he doesn't stop there. He keeps pounding into me until my legs are jelly and my arms are numb from holding myself up. I don't care, though. It's too damn good to ask him to stop.

"Feel so fucking good, Nessa," he says, his lips at my ear as he folds himself over me. He tugs at my hair roughly, and I quiver from the pain. "Could stay in you all night."

"Please."

Though I don't know what I'm begging for, just that or something else. Either way, it spurs him on, and he slams into me even harder, his grip on my blonde locks so tight it nearly hurts. Just when I think I can't take any more, Gavin unloads inside me for the second time, and it's enough to set me off yet again.

What the hell is it about him? How does he do this to me every time? And will it ever be enough? Because right now, it doesn't feel like it.

My arms finally give way, and I drop to the bed. Gavin follows me down, falling onto the mattress beside me. He scoops me into his arms instantly, dragging me closer like he can't stop himself from touching me. I smile at that.

I love cuddling, I always have, but it was something my ex never did. Even after I told him how important it was to me—how it made me feel closer to him after baring myself to him—he still refused. He was always "too busy" or wanted to move on to something else. Even then, he had one foot out the door.

I hate that I just had incredible sex and am lying in the arms of someone who would never treat me like that, and yet, I'm thinking about Neal. It's not fair to Gavin, and it sure as hell isn't fair to me.

"What are you thinking about over there?" Gavin asks.

"My ex."

He tenses, and I don't blame him one bit.

"Sorry," I say, rolling over to face him. "It's not because I was comparing you two. I mean, I was, but not for the reasons you're thinking."

He relaxes, but only a little. "Then what are the reasons?"

I sigh. "Well, this, for starters. You're holding me."

His brows draw together. "Should I not be?"

"No, no. It's a good thing. Ne—*he* never did." I don't want to say his name out loud. Not right now. Not after everything. "He always wanted to just move on."

Gavin rolls his eyes. "Next thing you'll tell me is he never bothered with your pleasure either."

I say nothing, which says a lot.

"You're kidding."

I shrug. "Not never, but not often."

He shakes his head. "What a piece of shit."

I laugh. "Yeah, I guess he was."

I trace my finger gently over the lips that just kissed every inch of me, almost lost in a trance, caught between the present and the past.

"I asked him, you know. About why he cheated. He said it was because I was *too much*, needed too much from him. I wanted to control everything, wanted everything to be picture perfect. And I guess I did, in a way. I wanted the life they promise you when you're young, the one with the white picket fence, the two A-plus children, and the flawless family photos. I wanted *that* life. And now all I have is…" I swallow down the lump in my throat. "All I have is working at a bar and renting a room. I don't have a house or an apartment or even a car."

Gavin's quiet so long I have to talk myself into looking into his eyes, too scared of what I might see. Does he think I'm too much, too? Hell, the night we met, I cried in his arms on the freaking sidewalk. Does he think I'm too much because I called him panicking about his fish? I did have a major freak-out. Does he think I'm too much because I wanted to talk to him after he got hit? I'm not his girlfriend. I don't deserve that. Does he think I'm—

"Stop," he says softly. "You're not too much, Nessa. Stop letting him get into your head and think otherwise. There is nothing wrong with you. What Neal did falls solely on his shoulders. It's not your burden to carry. It never was, and it never will be." He leans forward, ghosting his lips over mine. "You're just enough for me."

My eyes flutter closed against his soft kiss and his words. Words that mean more to me than he can imagine. *I'm not too much. I'm just enough*, I repeat to myself.

Gavin kisses me again, and I open for him, letting

him sweep his tongue into my mouth. It's slow, languid, like he's taking his time with me, and I love every second of it. When he eventually pulls away, he smiles at me.

"Shower, then more cuddles?"

The butterflies—the ones that seem to be permanent where he is concerned—flap their wings again, and I grin right back. "That sounds perfect to me."

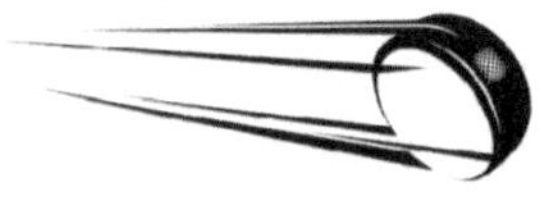

Gavin holds me all night long, and when I wake, I'm warm and satiated in a way I haven't been in a long time. I crack my eyes open, the sun filtering into the room, and stretch my legs.

"Mmm," Gavin says from beside me. "I could get used to waking up next to you."

Me too.

Maybe a little too used to it. I think I already did after my first night in the apartment. I even slept on the couch with his blanket while he was on the road because it didn't feel right being here without him. I don't tell him that, instead putting my mouth to good use by pressing kisses all over his chest. The hair there tickles my nose, and I love the way it feels against my chin.

I trail a path up, never once taking my lips off him. I trace over his throat, loving how he swallows roughly, and the dimple in his chin, up until I reach his lips. I kiss him the same way he kissed me last night—with everything I have, telling him how he makes me feel without actually saying it. After I have my way with him, I pull away and get my first look at him.

I gasp. "Oh my god!"

"What? What is it?" Gavin's eyes fly open, wide with worry as he checks me over. "What's wrong?"

I cover my mouth, pointing at him. "Your… Your face!"

"What?" He reaches up, then winces when he makes contact with the nasty wound. "Fuck, that hurts."

Somehow, with all the pleasure from last night, I forgot about him taking the puck to the face. Clearly, he did too, but now looking at him… Let's just say I won't be forgetting it for quite a while.

"How bad is it?"

I grimace as I take in his swollen cheek. It looks like he has a baseball stuffed in there or got some really, really crappy filler done. "Uh, bad."

He scrambles off the bed and into the bathroom to check it out.

"Well, safe to say I'll be wearing a fishbowl for a while," he calls out.

"Fishbowl? What's that?" I ask as I climb off the bed, grabbing my discarded shirt and tugging it over my head.

We didn't bother putting our clothes on after our shower. It seemed pointless at the time, and we were right. Gavin woke me up at six AM with his tongue between my legs, bringing me to completion before fucking me slow and sweet. I try to find my underwear but give up when they aren't anywhere to be found.

"It's a style of helmet. The NHL uses them for injuries."

"Wait—you're still playing after that?"

He chuckles, coming out of the bathroom, and I try my best not to look at his cock hanging half-hard between his legs. "Hell yes, I'm still playing. I've scored in every game this season so far. No way am I sitting out."

The look on my face must tell him exactly how I feel about it because he crosses the room, gathering me into his arms.

"Hey," he says, tipping my chin up to meet his gaze. "I'll be okay, I promise. The fishbowl will protect me, and it looks a lot worse than it feels."

I wince. "It just looks so…"

"Ugly?"

I roll my eyes. "Please, even all banged up, there is nothing ugly about you, Gavin."

"Nothing?"

"Well…"

He tickles my sides, and I squeal with laughter.

"Stop! Stop! That's so unfair!" I say, squirming in his grasp.

"Unfair how?" He continues his assault. "*I'm* the injured one here."

"Because you're stronger than me and bigger!"

He laughs. "Oh, love, I'll show you big."

I don't know how he does it, but suddenly my wrists are captured in one hand, and he holds them behind my back, pressing my tits up against his chest. He drives his hips into me, and there's no denying just how much he's enjoying me wiggling against him. Truthfully, I like it too. We're no longer laughing and messing around, the air charged with palpable sexual tension.

He runs his nose along my neck. "I could fuck you like this, you know. Holding your hands behind your back while you ride my cock."

I rub my thighs together, wanting just that.

"Or maybe I'll bend you over again, take you from behind until you're screaming my name."

I whimper as he slides his free hand between us, his

fingertips tracing along my thighs, teasing me. Always fucking teasing me.

"Play with that sweet little hole of yours I caught a glimpse of last night."

A shiver races through me, my mind chanting, *Yes, yes, yes.* He cups my bare pussy, slipping a single finger between my lips, grazing over my clit that's already pulsing.

"I could—"

Dolly Parton's "9 to 5" blares through the room, interrupting his next thought. I groan, tossing my head back, and Gavin laughs dryly.

"Work?"

I nod. "Work."

"Don't suppose I could convince you to call in?" he asks.

"Not a chance."

"Boo." He releases me, and I miss his touch instantly. "But I understand. I need to check in with Doc anyway, get this face looked at." He kisses the top of my head. "Rain check, then."

Maybe it's silly, but I'm surprised by his words. He...wants to do this again? I mean, I know he said a lot of things last night and said a few things just now, but that was just in the moment, wasn't it? Maybe not. Maybe he meant them.

I want him to have meant them.

The thought terrifies me. Not just because I have only been divorced for six months and it feels far too soon to get tangled up in something, but because of who he is—my brother's teammate. He's completely off-limits.

It's bad enough that I had a one-night stand with Gavin in New York, and even worse that I'm living with him without telling Reed. To continue sleeping with him? That's *really* bad. We shouldn't be sneaking around like this. It's wrong…isn't it?

No.

I can't tell if that's how I really feel or just wishful thinking, so I decide not to think of it at all. I'm in Seattle for a new life, a new Vanessa, and this version of me wants not to overanalyze something she doesn't have an answer for. She just wants to live. She just wants to have fun.

She just wants Gavin.

So, I kiss his cheek—the uninjured one—pat him on the chest, and tell him, "Rain check."

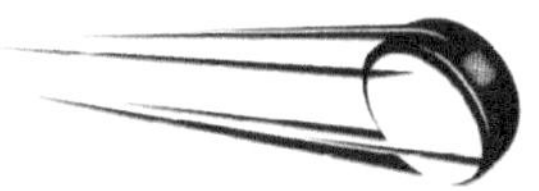

My pencil moves across the page. It's just a little doodle, but it's the first one I've made since I saw The Video.

I first got the itch last week after we finally gave in to whatever is going on between us. We haven't really talked about it, but we've certainly been enjoying it. Every night, Gavin whispers into my ear—dirty things, sweet things. It doesn't matter; I love them all. He touches me. He tastes me. He *worships* me. It's heaven. It has to be. There's no other reason for it to feel so damn good.

I'm convinced it's why I'm sitting on the rooftop of his building with my sketchbook in hand. It's where I've been planted since I washed the smell of bar off me after my shift at Top Shelf. I trade the pencil for a marker, tracing over the lines I want to be sharper and darker. While my preferred medium is painting, I figured I'd start small and get *one* sketch out, just to make sure I can still do it.

Once finished, I study the image, picking it apart. I need more color, for starters, and my lines could certainly use some finesse. But overall, it's not the worst thing I've drawn, and it feels good to flex my dormant creative muscles. That's got to be a win, right?

Feeling inspired, I flip the page to start something new. I start with the marker, trying to find what feels comfortable, and then I allow myself to get lost. I have no idea how long I keep my head bent over the pad, but it must be long because suddenly I hear footsteps. I whirl around to find Gavin striding toward me with a smile plastered on his face. He's wearing a pair of jeans that look entirely too good on his long legs and a Seattle Serpents-branded shirt that stretches across his chest just a little *too* well. There's a baseball cap spun backward on his head, and it instantly makes me want to kiss him.

"There you are." His deep timbre that I love so much spreads warmth through me, and I can't help but grin up at him.

"Hey," I say, closing my sketchbook and tucking it under one of the cushions. I don't know why. Maybe it's because I'm nervous to show him my art, or perhaps it's because I'm not ready to show *anyone* yet. I just got it back. I kind of want to keep it to myself for a while. "You're back."

"I'm back." He kisses my forehead, then settles onto the couch next to me, tugging me back against him, and I go willingly. I like that he wants to touch me so often. That's how it's been since he got back from his road trip, and it always makes those butterflies go wild. I melt into him as he asks, "How was your day?"

We left at the same time this morning. I headed to the bar in the new car Gavin helped me pick out last week for a quick afternoon shift to cover for a coworker who was at the doctor, and Gavin was attending a team event.

"Good," I answer. "While my savings account

doesn't care for it, I like the short shifts. Gets me out of the house just long enough to smell like beer, but not long enough for me to start questioning my life choices. How was your event?"

His chest rumbles with a soft laugh. "It was fun. The kids were adorable, though that's no surprise. They usually are."

"You did a skate with them, right?"

"Yeah, and there was this one kid—Jagger—he was so damn good. He's only eight, but he has a hell of a future ahead of him if he keeps it up. I thought for sure he was going to toss mitts with Keller, and not in a joking way either. He took the game *very* seriously."

His voice is full of awe, as it always is when he talks about his nieces and nephews. It's cute, and honestly, fitting for him. I bet Gavin would make a great father. Flashes of two dark-haired kids float through my mind. They're laughing as Gavin chases them through the yard, and I watch from the porch with a smile.

What the hell? Where did that even come from?

I shake the thought away. It's silly, and *so* not happening. We're just having a little bit of fun. Nothing serious. Certainly nothing that warrants thoughts like that, no matter how nice they were for a few fleeting moments. The butterflies in my belly settle, and I miss their flurries instantly.

Gavin clears his throat, then says, "So, what were you working on so intently?"

Intently? How does he know I was working intently? Was he watching me? Was he standing there much longer than I realized?

"I was drawing."

He sits forward, which sends me propelling in the same direction, and he catches me before I fall off the communal couch.

"Sorry," he says, leaning around me to catch my eyes. "I'm just… You were drawing?"

His excitement is contagious, and I find myself smiling right along with him.

"I was drawing," I repeat.

His eyes twinkle, and he presses his lips against mine lightning fast—so quick I barely have time to react—then he's back to grinning at me like *he's* the one who picked up a pencil for the first time in over a year.

"Can I see?"

I tense instantly, and Gavin doesn't miss it.

"You know what? Never mind. Forget I asked. It's your art. You don't have to share that with me, especially since you just got it back. I shouldn't have even asked."

His words echo my exact thoughts earlier, and it's almost eerie how well he understands me. I guess I shouldn't be surprised, though. It was like that our first night together, too. He never made me feel bad about anything then, even if I did give myself emotional whiplash.

I'm overwhelmed with the sudden feeling to share my drawings with him. I don't want to; I *need* to. I retrieve the sketchbook I tucked away and flip it open, handing it to him. He settles back against the cushion, his eyes tracing over the page that's full of thin and thick strokes and so many delicate curves. When he doesn't say anything for several moments, I begin to get antsy, wringing my hands in my lap.

"Well?"

He drags his eyes from the page, looking up at me. "Please don't take this the wrong way, but what is it?"

My eyes fall to slits. "What do you mean you don't know what it is?"

His eyes widen, his breath getting caught in his throat. I last all of five seconds before I break, laughing at him.

"Had you going, didn't I?"

He blows out a huff of air. "Fuck, you really did." He looks at the page again. "It's beautiful, by the way. I don't know if I said that, but it is."

"Beautiful even if you don't know what it is?"

He points to himself. "Hockey player, remember? Not an art connoisseur."

I laugh. "That's fair." I run my finger over the biggest, thickest line on the page. "Those are her hands."

"Her?"

"Yep." I trace it, showing him the outline of her jaw and chin, where her hands cradle her face. "Her lips, her nose."

His eyes widen. "Holy shit. I see it now. Her eyes," he says, taking over for me. "And her nose. She's... She's gorgeous." He leans forward, squinting at the drawing.

I see the moment it clicks for him.

His hazel eyes snap to mine. "She's you."

I grin, nodding. "She's me."

"She looks like she's sad. Like she's crying."

"That's because she is."

He smiles sadly. "Are you sad?"

"I'm—" I shake my head. "No, not anymore, I'm not."

Because of you. I don't tell him that, though.

"Is that why you used yellows and oranges and not blue?"

"Yes, this is her rebirth. Like a phoenix. Hence the feathers."

His eyes scan the drawing again, really taking it in now that he understands it. Then finally, he looks up at me, and there's nothing but pride in his eyes.

"This is stunning, Nessa. Absolutely fucking studio-worthy."

Heat flares in my cheeks at his admiration. Is it good? I guess some people would think so. But is it studio-worthy? Not a chance.

"While that's sweet, I don't think that's happening anytime soon."

"Why not?"

"Uh, because I don't even have my own place to live. Or my own bed, for that matter. Speaking of... where is that?"

"Oh, uh..." He scratches at the scruff along his jaw. "The mattress company called to reschedule for next week. Something about being short on delivery drivers. Anyway, back to this studio thing—why not?"

I huff. "Because I'm not ready for something like that. Like you said, I'm just getting back into"—I gesture toward the book—"well, whatever that is. A studio is a dream for years down the road, when I've refined my skills far, far more."

He frowns, and I can tell he wants to keep arguing about this more, but I don't bother giving him an inch, knowing he wants a mile. I grab the sketchbook, closing the cover and setting it and the phoenix-rising version of me aside, then crawl over him on the couch. I kiss his chin—right in that little dimple he has there—then up to his lips. I don't just kiss him because I want him to forget all about my art struggles, but because I missed him today. If I'm being honest, I'm missing him more and more every time he goes.

"I know you're trying to distract me," he says against me, his hands sliding over my waist and down to my ass, where he squeezes my cheeks firmly.

"So what if I am? It's clearly working." I wiggle my hand between us, palming his already hard cock.

Gavin groans, kissing me harder. I let him because it means I don't have to think about my future. I don't have to think about what I want from my art. I don't have to think about what I'm going to do when he no longer needs me around to feed his fish. I don't have to think about how much I don't want that to be all this is between us.

And I don't have to think about how maybe…just maybe…I want that future to include him.

Chapter 16

LOCKE

I'm not usually one to pat myself on the back—not when I know how fragile this game can be—but holy hell, I am on fire.

It's still early November, but this is eclipsing my Norris finalist season by miles. I'm up to six goals and almost at a point per game. According to my teammates who spend far more time on social media than I do, my name is splashed all over the place. I'm the talk of the hockey world. My agent even called me up the other day to tell me to keep my foot on the gas because this could mean a hell of a lot more than a one-year contract from the Serpents. It's everything I wanted, and while I'm happy as fuck out on the ice, it's not even close to what's causing the permanent smile on my face.

It's Nessa. We've spent the last three weeks falling

into bed together every chance we get, and while it's been incredible, it's the *other* moments, like today, that really make my heart thud.

"This place is amazing," she says, and not for the first time.

We've been walking around the Seattle Art Museum for two hours, moving leisurely from one installation to another. Sometimes she'll have an interpretation of what we're looking at, and sometimes she'll just stand there quietly, slowly falling in love with what she sees.

Me? I'm looking at her. I've *been* looking at her. Gun to my head, I couldn't describe a single piece of art we've seen together. I'm sure whatever is on the walls and in the cases is nice, but she's the most beautifully crafted thing here.

I knew two weeks ago, when I saw her sitting on the rooftop with her sketchbook, that I wanted to bring her here. She was so concentrated on her art that she didn't hear me come out there. I think it took her ten minutes before she registered my presence, and the whole time, I watched her. Her tongue kept rolling over her lips, her brows tight as she stroked her pencil against the page. She was lost in whatever she was creating, and the only other time I've seen her so alive was when I was inside her.

Then, when she showed me what she was working

on… Call me biased or whatever, but I've never seen something so beautiful before. Talking about how she's not studio-worthy—that's bullshit. She deserves to be up on these walls as much as any of the other artists do.

We mosey to the next room, and she stops in front of a giant painting of a tiger that looks like it's ready to pounce on its prey. There's a cub in the background drinking from a waterhole, its eyes focused on its parent. The whole thing is done in watercolor.

"I think this might be my favorite one."

Nessa stares up at the painting on the wall, her eyes wide in approbation, her plump lips—the ones that still taste like cherry lip gloss—parted as she takes the piece in.

"You said that about the last three pieces we saw," I point out, itching to reach over and touch her.

Not that I think any of my teammates are spending their day off cruising around here, but we've tried to maintain a healthy distance between us just in case. You can never be too careful.

"Yeah, but I think I mean it this time."

She doesn't. I know that, and she does too, but I allow it anyway.

"Something about it is so…raw," she continues, still staring up at the giant canvas. "I think it's a metaphor for life. How we can fight for our innocence, but the real world will always rear its ugly head and strip it away from us, no matter who tries to protect us from it."

It's not what I would have guessed by looking at it, but after hearing her thoughts, it makes perfect sense, and I see the image in a whole new light. We stand there for several more moments, and even though I'm done looking at this particular piece, I don't rush her. I let her take her time with it. After all, this date is for her. I'm not really into art, but it makes her happy, and that's all that matters.

"Sorry," she says after a while, finally walking away.

I shake my head. "Nothing to be sorry about. I'd stand here for hours if that were what you wanted."

She peeks up at me. "Don't say stuff like that."

"Why not? It's true."

"Because it makes me want to kiss you, that's why."

Ten words, and my resolve shatters like a plate crashing to the ground. I grab her hand, tugging her through the quiet museum, looking left and right as I go. I need somewhere I can kiss her without prying eyes.

"Gavin!" she whisper-yells, but there's no anger behind the words. She wants this as badly as I do.

I haul her into a small alcove, pressing her back

against the wall and fitting my body against hers like I've done so many times in the last few weeks.

"What are you—"

I swallow her question with my kiss, and she softens into me like she can't help but give in, not that I think she even had much fight to begin with. I slip one hand into her hair, loving the way her soft waves feel against my fingers, moving her until she's just where I want her. Her palms spread against my back, her nails digging into me and urging me on.

I shouldn't do it, but I can't help myself when I bunch that hot-as-fuck skirt she's wearing into my hand and inch it higher. I need to touch her. I need to feel her fall apart beneath me. When my fingers skim the tops of her thighs, dancing along the soft skin I've spent a lot of time kissing, she gasps, and I use the opportunity to push my tongue into her mouth. I brush my knuckle right between her legs, and she bucks her hips wildly, searching for more of the touch. More of *me*.

I bet if I were to look down where I'm rubbing against her, there would be a wet spot on her panties, and fuck if that doesn't turn me on even more. When I press against her harder, she moans into my mouth, and there's nothing quiet about it.

"Shh," I say, pulling away, kissing along her jaw. "You have to be quiet, love, understand?"

She nods, then spreads her thighs wider, giving me more access. I take advantage of it, slipping my finger into her underwear. She sinks her teeth into her bottom lip as I plunge two fingers into her warm cunt, and I chuckle at how hard she's trying not to make a noise. We're hidden right now, but all it's going to take is one wrong noise and we'll be caught.

"Shut up," she sasses, but again, there's no malice in her voice—only pleasure.

As if on cue, her eyes roll back, her lids fluttering closed.

"Keep them open," I tell her. "Keep your eyes on me, love."

She snaps her attention to me, her bottom lip so tight between her teeth I worry she might actually break skin as she rides my fingers. My cock strains against the zipper of my jeans. I don't think I've ever been this hard before, and I'm not sure if it's because of how close we are to getting caught right now or if it's simply her. My guess is the latter.

She rocks her hips, searching for more, and I know she's close. I also know just what she needs to get there. I settle my palm against her clit, the touch just enough to free her lip, her mouth now dropped open in a silent gasp.

"That's it, Nessa," I whisper. "Let me feel your

pussy squeeze me. Come all over my fingers. Make a mess—I promise to lick it off."

My words set her off, her tight cunt pulsing around me, and it's nearly enough to make me come right in my own pants. I don't, though. I just finger-fuck her through her own release, watching how her pupils grow to twice their size. Her eyes glaze over with lust, and she's lost in a haze as she comes and comes. I don't think she's ever orgasmed this long before, and I wonder if she's enjoying our public spot as much as I am.

Her body relaxes as her shakes subside and she falls back to the flats of her feet, finally pulling her nails out of my back. I miss them instantly. Slowly, I pull my fingers from her and bring them to my mouth just as I promised. The taste of her—sweet and a bit spicy—explodes over my tongue, and I feel the precum leak from my tip.

She watches intently as I lick every trace of her off my fingers, then she shocks me by grabbing my face and pressing her lips to mine. She slides her tongue into my mouth like she wants to taste both of us together, and I wish we weren't at this damn museum. I wish we were back at my place so I could bury my cock inside of her and never leave.

When we break apart, we're both starved for air, our chests brushing with how hard we're gasping for it.

Still, she smiles against me, and I can't help but return the expression.

"Want to get out of here?" I ask.

She nods. "Please."

I take her hand and lead her away, and it's the first time I've truly realized just how screwed I am when it comes to her.

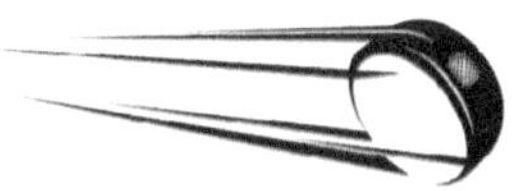

"Wait, never?"

She shakes her head. "Nope, never."

"How is that even possible?"

"Uh, did you forget I'm not from Seattle?"

"No, I know that. I'm not either, but it was still one of the first things I ate when I moved here."

"Well, sorry to burst your bubble, but nobody handed me a Seattle dog when I stepped off the plane."

"They should. I'm pretty sure that's what they do in New York with pizza."

I don't miss how her cheeks redden at the mention of New York. I'm sure it takes her right back to that night, just like it does me.

"Come on," I tell her, nodding across the street. "We're fixing this travesty."

We approach the vendor, and I order us two Seattle-style hot dogs. We find a decent spot to eat them, and I watch as Nessa takes her first bite of the cream cheese-coated bun and onion-and-jalapeno-topped meat. She looks skeptical at first—and who wouldn't be?—then when the deliciousness of it all hits her, she groans happily.

"Oh god, that's good." She covers her mouth when she says it. "Holy crap."

"See? I told you." I take a big bite of my own meal, chew, and swallow. "I was right."

She rolls her eyes, going in for another mouthful. We finish off our dinner, then toss our trash into a can. It's late. We've been out and about all day, soaking up as much November as we can before the rain inevitably settles in and drenches us all. After the art museum, we walked around Pike Place Market, then hopped across the street to the aquarium. Introducing her to Seattle dogs was my last stop, and I can tell they'll be hers too. Now that she's got some food in her, she's ready for bed. Her eyes are getting heavy, and her strides are getting shorter.

"Come on." I flick my chin in the general direction of where we parked my car hours ago. The fee is going to be astronomical, but it's worth it for her. "Let's go home."

"Home." She smiles softly. "I like the sound of that."

I don't ask if she likes it because it implies that it's *our* home, or if she's just desperate for sleep at this point. We walk through the streets, our hands brushing every few steps. A simple graze of our hands, that's all it is, but it's enough to make my body start to tingle with want.

"Speaking of home…" she asks once we hit the garage. "Anything new on my bed?"

I try to school my features not to show my panic. The truth is that her bed technically *has* already arrived. It may or may not be me who keeps delaying things with the delivery, and it's solely because I like sharing a bed with her. I'm getting some of the best nights of sleep with her lying next to me, and I'm in no hurry to change that anytime soon. It's completely selfish, but I've found that I am when it comes to her.

"What? Are you eager to stop sharing a bed with me?" I ask, trying to distract her so she doesn't start asking too many questions.

"What?" She looks horrified. "No! I was just wondering when it'll get here so I can know when I need to pay you back for it."

I stop, and Nessa knocks right into me.

"What the hell, Gavin? Walk much?"

"You can't be serious."

"About your inability to walk? Oh, I am very serious." She glares up at me, her arms now crossed over her chest, pushing her tits up and distracting me for just a moment.

I shake it away. "No, about you paying me back. Because you're not."

"Uh, yes, I am. You're not *really* buying me a bed."

"Yes, I am." I grab her hand and pull her toward the car.

She drags her feet against the ground in an attempt to pull me to a stop, but it's futile. I'm far too big for her to be able to affect my movement. "Gavin, stop. I'm being serious."

"I am too," I say over my shoulder, still charging forward.

"You cannot buy me a bed! I mean, the idea of it is really cute and all, but the execution? There are implications."

"What?" I scoff. "If those implications are that I like taking care of you, then whatever."

"Yeah, but I'm not *yours* to take care of."

This time, I do stop, and once again, she crashes into me.

"Stop doing that," she grouses, righting herself. She pushes her hair out of her face and scowls up at me petulantly, that bratty side of hers I enjoy a bit too much coming out. "What? Why are you looking at me like that?"

"Like what? Like I'm pissed?"

"Well, yeah. I didn't say anything that wasn't true." She tips her chin up, and I wonder if it's me she's trying to convince or herself.

I take a step forward, then another. We're toe to toe, so close Nessa has to lean her head back to look up at me.

"If I recall correctly, *Nessa*"—her eyes spark at the way I say her name—"I said you belong to me back in New York. And I meant it. Now, get in the goddamn car before I throw you over my shoulder and put you in there myself."

Her mouth opens, but she doesn't move. So, I do as I promised—I lift her into my arms and drop her over my shoulder.

"Gavin   whatever-the-hell-your-middle-name-is Whitlocke! Put me down—*now*!"

"It's Barry."

"Barry?!" she says incredulously.

"And Douglas."

"Oh my god, you're kidding me."

"Nope." I smack her ass, and she inhales sharply. "Now, hush."

To my surprise, she does, and I can't help but wonder if it's because she liked that slap a little too much. Knowing her, probably. When we finally reach the car, I set her on her feet and open the door for her.

"After you," I say, bending at the waist.

She huffs but climbs inside. I chuckle as I shut the door. I race around the front, slide in next to her, and pull out of the garage.

"You're kind of annoying, you know that?" she says once we hit the road.

"I can be, but I'm not annoying because of this. I just…I want to take care of you, Nessa. You deserve it. Let yourself enjoy it, okay?"

Her features soften at my words, and I hope she knows it's not some line I'm trying to feed her. I mean it. She *does* deserve it, and not just because of what happened with her douchebag ex-husband. She deserves it because she's an incredible woman. She's smart, funny when she wants to be, kind even when she doesn't think she is, and worthy of someone treating her right.

"Okay," she agrees quietly.

"Good," I say with a grin, but there's really nothing to smile about.

No, there's just tension, and a lot of it. It's nearly suffocating as I navigate my AMG through the Seattle streets. It's not a bad kind, though. If anything, it's the opposite, and it grows the closer we get to the penthouse. By the time I pull into my parking spot, it's so damn thick I can barely breathe. Or maybe that's just how badly I want her. My head is all foggy, and I can't tell the difference.

I nod to security as we slip into the elevator. Nessa settles beside me, my hand at the small of her back. I feel her lean into the touch as the doors begin to close. They're just about touching when a very familiar tattooed arm appears between them.

Keller gives me his version of a grin—which isn't one at all—as he looks at Nessa, then me. In that instant, I know he knows we're sleeping together. Maybe it's our body language that gives us away, or maybe he can feel the tension too, but he knows.

"Well, well. What do we have here?" he says as he steps into the car.

I can count on one hand the number of times I've actually run into Keller in the years we've lived in the same building. Why the hell does tonight have to be one of those times? With Nessa right here? I tug her a step closer, and he lets out a half-laugh, not missing it.

"How's it going, roomies?"

I pinch the bridge of my nose. "Don't be a dick, man."

"Me? A dick? Never. That's not my style."

We both know it is.

"Keller…"

"What? A guy can't just say hello to his

neighbors?" he says innocently, though he's anything but. "Beautiful night out, huh?"

I don't answer him, and neither does Nessa. He's being such a shithead, and if the twitch of his lips is telling at all, he knows it. When we reach his floor—a few below mine—he gives us one last look before shaking his head.

"You two have a nice night now."

I swear I hear him laugh before the doors close. Nessa relaxes, and I hate that she was even on edge to begin with.

"He won't say anything," I promise, and she nods.

The elevator doors open on my floor, and we hurry out. When we make it into the penthouse, I'm not sure who grabs for whom first, but suddenly we're nothing but mouths and hands and sighs and moans. Running into Keller should have quelled this urge. It really fucking should have, but it didn't.

I'm not sure anything ever will.

Chapter 17

VANESSA

"Wine?"

I shake my head at Auden's offer. "No, but thank you."

She nods, grabs a pitcher of water from the fridge, pours me a glass, and slides it my way. The last thing I expected this morning was a text from her inviting me over for a girls' night, but I suppose I shouldn't be surprised. I'm sure she's getting antsy being home alone with the baby and is likely dying for a night of fun. I know I would be in her position.

"I'll take whatever she doesn't want," Lilah says. She shakes her empty glass at her best friend, then gives me a wink.

I smile back. I wasn't quite sure what to expect tonight, especially given that my last group of friends dropped me so fast after everything came out about

Neal, and I haven't exactly worked on making new ones. So far, it's been nice. Auden's twin sister, Rory, and Hayes's girlfriend, Quinn, are here too. According to them, they get together like this often when the guys go on road trips. They call it their Seattle Serpents Singles Support Group. I'm not quite sure what that means, but it made them all giggle when Auden said it, so I laughed too. It's the first time I have since Gavin walked out the door yesterday.

The Serpents are only gone for four days, but given how much I miss him, it feels like so much longer than that. It's been like that every time he's left since we started sharing a bed. A night away seems like a lifetime, and I always end up sleeping on the couch, unable to stand being there without him. My bed *still* hasn't been delivered, but lately…I'm not mad about it. I like being next to Gavin so much that I don't mind.

I try not to think about that too much.

"Ew. She farted." Rory wrinkles her nose as she stares down at the baby in her arms. "Someone else take my niece, please. She's being gross."

Auden rolls her eyes at her sister as she sets a bowl of chips on the counter next to the stunning charcuterie board. "Stop being dramatic. You fart too."

"I do no such thing," Rory argues, handing baby Alana to me. "Your turn."

I cradle the baby in my arms and grin down at her, tickling the little fat roll on her arm.

"Hi there," I say to her. "Are you being gross for Auntie Rory?" I swear she smiles. "Yeah? You are, huh?"

"Now be gross for Auntie Vanessa too," Rory instructs, taking a swig of her white wine.

Auntie Vanessa.

Logically, I *know* Alana is my niece, but it still feels so strange to hear it. I'm sure it's just because Reed and I don't exactly act like siblings, but it still makes me sad that I don't *feel* like her aunt. I wonder if that's because I still feel so out of place in this new stage of my life. While I'm liking working at Top Shelf more than I thought I might, it's not what I envisioned for myself. And yes, I'm getting back into my art, but it still feels like a whole new venture for me.

The only thing that feels comfortable is Gavin. I hate that I feel this way because of Neal. I loathe that someone who did me so dirty has been able to dictate so much of my life and has made me question everything about myself and my worth. He's not worth the time or energy, but as much as I hate to admit it, he still has a grip on me.

I wish he'd let go. I wish I could snap my fingers and move on easily, put it all behind me, maybe even laugh at the whole situation. But I can't. It changed me, for better or for worse. It's part of me now. He'll be a stain on my heart forever.

I rock Alana back and forth as I refocus on the conversation.

"…like a butthole."

What the hell did I just hear?

Auden barks out a laugh. "You should see your face right now, Vanessa."

"I won't lie, I tuned out there for a minute because I got distracted." I wiggle the baby. "What exactly did I miss?"

"Just Rory being disgusting and comparing the smell of Lawson's gear to a butthole." Auden tosses a chip at her sister.

"He farts a lot!" Rory exclaims. "Did I ever tell you about the time he ripped one while I was waking up?"

The girls laugh.

"To be fair, their gear does smell absolutely atrocious," Quinn agrees. "But I think seeing them out there on the ice all sweaty is worth it." She waggles her brows and shimmies her shoulders, the pair of penguin earrings that dangle from her ears swaying back and forth.

"It truly is," Lilah agrees.

I almost chime in too, complaining about how Gavin's stuff is stinking up the apartment, but I keep my lips zipped.

"Oh my gosh!" Quinn gasps. "I just had the best idea!"

"Share, share," Auden chants, getting as worked up as Quinn looks, and yeah, she *really* needed this night.

"We should set Vanessa here up with one of the guys."

"Yesssss," Lilah says, dragging the word out. "We totally should. But who? The only ones still single are—"

"Locke and Keller," Rory finishes. "And Keller sucks, so that only leaves Locke."

"Keller does not suck," Auden argues. "You're just saying that because he picks on Lawson, which he only does because your boyfriend is such an easy target. He does it to himself half the time."

Rory's lips twitch, and she looks so smitten. "That's fair."

I've only known them for a short time, but it surprises me that Rory and Lawson are together. They're so different from each other. I guess that just seems to work out sometimes. The phrase opposites attract doesn't exist for no reason.

"Locke it is, then," Lilah announces, slapping the counter like this is happening.

"Uh, do I get a say in this?" I chime in.

"No," Rory says, then turns back to the other girls,

who are all now plotting ways to get me and Gavin together.

Oh, if they only knew we've already been *together*. Many, many times. Ugh, just thinking of it makes me miss him all the more.

Just three more days, Vanessa, I tell myself, even though I shouldn't be counting down to anything at all. That's girlfriend behavior, and it's not like Gavin and I are actually dating one another.

"Oh! Puck drop is in five minutes," Lilah announces.

We grab our glasses, Quinn carries the fancy meat-and-cheese smorgasbord, and Rory gets the bowls of chips. Lilah snags an extra bottle of wine, and Auden takes Alana, who is now fast asleep in my arms.

"Looks like someone is a baby whisperer. Kind of wish you hadn't moved out now," she jokes. "I'm just going to put her down in her crib. I'll be right back."

She hurries off toward the bedrooms, and I awkwardly stand at the edge of the room as the girls get comfortable. With the way they snuggle onto the couch, Rory even tucking her feet under her and a blanket around her, it's clear they've done it a time or two. I feel like an imposter. I don't belong here. This is for fiancées and girlfriends. This isn't the place for me.

"We're only teasing, you know?" Auden says, coming up next to me and bumping her shoulder against mine. "We aren't going to set you up. Unless you want us to, of course. You have to admit Locke is pretty good-looking, though."

My cheeks heat because he's good-looking, all right. *More* than good-looking, actually. He's downright hot.

She tips her head to the side, and alarm bells go off in my mind.

"What?" I ask.

Her lips pull upward. "Nothing."

"Nothing what?"

She shakes her head. "It's really nothing. I just thought maybe I saw interest in your eyes."

I force a laugh. "What? No. That's… No."

The words sound weak to my ears, and I hope like hell Auden doesn't notice that too.

It takes her a moment, but eventually she nods. "All right. But if you change your mind…I have his number."

I have his number too.

"Thanks," I say with a laugh.

We each find a spot on the couches and settle in for the next two or so hours.

"Is anyone else horny?" Lilah asks as they flash to Fox on the ice, who is dropped down on his knees, stretching.

"Over your *good boy*, not a chance," Rory tosses back.

She's then smacked by a pillow, and we all laugh. That's how it goes for the first two periods as the Serpents score twice in each one, now up 5–3. We joke around, and they have far too much to say about the game. They go from cheering for their partners to bitching about the refs in two seconds flat. It's cute how passionate they are about it.

Meanwhile, I sit quietly by, too afraid to make any commentary for fear they might read too much into it. Auden looked at me a little too closely earlier. I don't need to give her any more reason to become suspicious.

When the third period starts and it's 5–4 Serpents, the mood in the room changes. We all get quiet, watching as the team tries to hang on to their lead.

"Come on, Fox," Lilah says, her nails between her teeth as she sits on the edge of the couch. A puck just got dangerously close to going over the line, and while they're still reviewing it in the arena, we can see at home that it didn't completely cross.

"He's doing good. It's our defense breaking down. No offense, Auden," Quinn says.

"None taken. They're being outskated. Locke especially."

I snap my eyes to her, physically having to bite my

tongue from saying anything. How dare she single him out? It's a damn team sport!

Or maybe it's just because I know that's such a sore subject for him. He doesn't talk about it often, but I know he's worried he's getting too old and slow for the game. At first, it made me laugh. He isn't even old, but I guess it makes sense when you look at it from the league's perspective. They don't want to give long contracts to people over a certain age because what if they can't live up to them? No sense putting your teammates in a bad spot like that.

Auden probably knows all this, though, which makes me even more annoyed she's called him out. But I can't say anything, so I bite my tongue—literally.

"Sorry," she says out loud, and I don't miss the way her eyes flick to me. "I didn't mean that to sound so rude. I'm sure he's just as frustrated as we all are watching this."

I drag my eyes back to the TV just as the puck is dropped after yet another icing from the Serpents. It happens so quickly—an exhausted-looking Lawson wins the puck, and it's picked up by Gavin, who zings it right over the goalie's glove. The girls jump off the couches, cheering loudly until Auden shushes them, reminding them of the sleeping baby just down the hall.

"Holy smokes!" the commentator shouts. "What a

shot! What a goal! Another top shelf back breaker from the veteran defenseman, Gavin Whitlocke!"

Pride swells in my chest, and I want to look right at Auden and say, *Ha! See? He can play just as well as anyone else out on that ice.* In reality, I just grin to myself, watching as a still-serious-looking Gavin skates down the bench, hitting gloves with his *very* excited teammates.

Fox throws his arms in the air, hugging him, and if you look closely enough, you can see the defenseman say, *We've still got work to do, boys.* There's no excitement from him, just determination, like he's more than ready to prove wrong everyone who thinks he's too slow for the game.

The sudden urge to have him here so I can kiss him slams into me, and along with it comes sadness because I know that won't happen for another few days. I try not to pout about it, focusing back on the game. In the end, the Serpents win 7–4 after putting an empty net goal from Lawson up on the board, leaving Rory grinning proudly as she hugs her sister goodbye.

"Thanks for inviting me," I say to Auden when it's my turn to say good night.

"Thank *you* for coming. I'm really glad you came. I…" She sighs, then pushes her hair over her shoulder. "I think I might have misjudged you when we first met, and I'm sorry about that. I thought you were everything Reed said you were, and that's not fair. I've talked about it with him a lot, about how he calls you 'the evil stepsister' all the time, and it's not cool. He knows that too, but he's a little too…well, *him* to say anything about it. So, I'm saying it to you. Not for him, but for you, because you deserve to hear it. I'm glad you're here, Vanessa. *We're* glad. And I'm so happy I'm getting a chance to get to know you."

Her words shock me. The first time I met Auden was just a week after The Video. I didn't tell anyone about it at the time. I held that card close to my chest. I only told people Neal and I were over, didn't elaborate on anything else, and to be honest, I was a brat that Christmas. I was mean and hateful, and I made it as uncomfortable as possible for Auden and my brother. It was easier that way when seeing them happy and in love. I had just had my heart torn out and didn't want what I was missing out on to be rubbed in my face.

I realize now how misplaced that anger was. It wasn't Auden and Reed I was mad at. It was Neal… and myself. How could I have let that happen? After everything I did to make the perfect life, how could I let it slip through my fingers so easily?

I was wrong about that, too. It wasn't my fault Neal cheated. I know that now. I…I wasn't too much.

You're not too much, Nessa. You're just enough for me.

"Well, since we're apologizing, I'm sorry too. I was terrible that Christmas and deserved all your ire."

"You were kind of scary. And a little badass, if I'm being honest."

I laugh. "I'd say that's not the real me, but I can be mean. Or a brat, so I've been told."

Her brows rise at that, but she doesn't say anything. I still get the sense she might know something is up. Not necessarily *what*, but I have a feeling she knows it has to do with Gavin.

Alana's cries echo through the house, and Auden smiles.

"Duty calls." She squeezes my arm. "Call me. I want to hang out again."

"Sure thing," I promise, and to my surprise, I really mean it.

"Are you still working?"

I smile at the deep voice on the other end of the line. Gavin came home from the short trip, and everything feels right in the world once again. I hate how much his absence affected me, and I try not to read too much into it.

"Sort of?" I say. "I'm off in thirty minutes. Why?"

"Because the guys are going to Top Shelf tonight."

"What?!"

The Seattle Serpents haven't been in again since that first time, and I've been grateful for it. Not because it means I don't have to act like I'm not interested in him whenever Gavin finds himself on the other side of the bar, but because it means I don't have to be with him and my brother in the same room. We haven't all been together since… Shit, I think since Auden was in the hospital.

"Is that okay?" he asks, and I hear a horn honk in the background. He must be in his car, on his way to the bar.

"Uh, yeah. I mean, I can't stop you."

"Right." He clears his throat. "Hutch will be there. The girls, too. Auden's dad has insisted she take a night off, so he has Alana."

I knew that, but I don't tell him. It's been a week since I went to her house for girls' night, and since then, we've been texting regularly. Sometimes it's just funny memes about hockey or whatever ridiculous thing the Serpents' social media team has posted now, and sometimes it's pictures of Alana. Occasionally, it's personal updates, and the text I got earlier asking if I was working tonight was just that. We've been slammed since people like to take the game in here, so

I haven't had a chance to answer her. I suppose it doesn't matter now.

"It's fine," I tell Gavin. "Besides, it's not like I can avoid my brother forever."

Usually, I'd say something snarky, like *even though I wish I could*, but that's not exactly true anymore. After talking with Auden, I kind of *want* to hang out with Reed, get to know him properly. Even when I was a young girl, I wanted a sibling. We may have already been technical siblings for years, but we certainly haven't acted like it. Perhaps it's time to.

"All right. I'll be there in ten, then."

"Ten? Didn't the game just end?"

"I showered fast. No way I'm waiting hours to kiss you."

I smile. "Careful, Gavin. It sounds like you might have a crush on me or something."

He mumbles something I can't quite make out, but it sounds a lot like, *Way more than a fucking crush.* I don't comment on that as we hang up, and I go back to work. Now that the game's over, it's a lot less crowded, though I assume that won't last long when everyone catches wind of the team being here. That won't be my problem for much longer, though.

I'm wiping down the sticky countertops when I feel him. Not see—*feel.* I snap my gaze up to find him striding through the bar, heading right for me.

"Josh?" I call to my manager.

"Yeah?"

"Do you need me to do anything else?"

He looks up to see Gavin standing there, staring at me, eighteen inches of bar top keeping us apart.

"Nah. You're free to go. I'm sure your brother isn't far behind."

I don't bother undoing my apron—I just walk around the bar and grab Gavin's hand, tugging him toward the darkened hallway. Once we've slipped into the shadows, I'm on him. I push up on my tiptoes and smash my mouth against his, loving the muffled growl that leaves him as he pulls me closer, his hands digging into my waist so hard it might bruise.

"Fuck," he says against my lips, biting at me gently. "Missed you."

I chuckle. "You just saw me a few hours ago."

"No." He shakes his head. "Too long ago."

I want to roll my eyes at his ridiculousness, but I can't. I'm too busy being assaulted by his touch, his mouth now on my throat on that spot he knows drives me wild. Besides, he's right. It *does* feel like too long. We make out like high schoolers for I don't even know how long, and it's me who comes up for air first.

"Gavin…" I whine, wanting more but knowing I can't have it. "We should stop."

"We should."

"It sounds like there's a *but* at the end of that sentence."

"Because there is."

He kisses me again, and I melt into him. It's always like that. I'm always sinking into his touch, no matter how small it is. That's a problem. I know it is, but it's one I'll deal with later. Right now, I just want to enjoy it.

We eventually get our wits about us and manage to keep our hands off each other long enough to catch our breath properly.

"We really should head out there," he says. "They're probably wondering where I am. I did leave first, after all."

I nod. "Good point. Want me to go first?"

"Please. I, uh, kind of have a situation going on right now." He gestures toward his crotch, and I let my eyes fall right to his *situation*.

"Yeah, I guess that would be kind of noticeable, huh?" I chuckle, patting his chest. "All right, big boy. I'll go first. See you out there."

I make it two steps before he grabs my wrist, hauling me right back to him and kissing me until I'm weak in the knees and my head is all kinds of fuzzy. I have no doubt my lips are swollen when I finally make it out into the bar. Auden spots me first.

"Vanessa!" she yells, waving me over.

I grin as I approach her and my brother, who has his arm wrapped tightly around her waist.

"Hey," I say to her, then look to Reed. "That was a nice goal tonight."

He looks surprised by my words. "You watched?"

I wave my hand around. "Uh, I work at a *sports bar* that caters to the hockey crowd."

"Right. Duh."

He rolls his eyes with a grin, and it's so strange to see. Not just because Reed tends to be grumpy as hell —though that happens a lot less often now that he's with Auden—but because he's smiling at *me*. We're joking around. We're *getting along*. It's weird, but I like it.

Guilt swirls in my stomach, and it's so much different than the butterflies. It feels icky, and I wish I could reach inside and pull it free. I suppose technically I could. It would just mean coming clean about what's going on with Gavin, and there's no way I'm ready to do that. So I swallow it down and pretend I never felt anything at all.

"Hey, have you seen Locke around? I thought for sure he'd be here first."

I don't know why I do it, but I look right at Auden…and she's staring back.

I quickly divert my gaze back to my brother, then point toward the bathrooms. "Think I saw him go back there."

Reed nods, then shifts from right to left. "So, uh, how's work going?"

Holy shit. He's inquiring about my life!

"It's, uh, it's good," I say. "I make great tips when you guys are playing well."

He snorts cockily. "We always play well."

"Not always," Lawson says, slinging his arm around Reed's shoulder. My brother shrugs him off, glaring at him. The guy doesn't look the least bit deterred, putting his arm right back where it was. "Sometimes we suck. We sucked the other night in Texas."

I grin, thinking of Gavin's goal that shocked the crowd.

"We still won, though," Reed points out, shaking Lawson away yet again.

His arm goes right back where it was until Rory reaches over and yanks her boyfriend away, and I have a feeling she does it often. I also have a feeling Lawson doesn't mind her being mean to him one bit, based on the lovesick grin on his face.

Warmth spreads over my back, and I know instantly it's Gavin. His fingertips graze so softly across my lower back that I wonder if I'm imagining it.

"Hey, guys. Auden, you look as beautiful as ever," he says, and a flicker of jealousy sparks through me, though I know it's pointless. I have no reason to worry about Gavin having feelings for someone else. I mean, not that he has feelings for *me*, but still.

"Locke! There you are!" Lawson yells, shoving his way into our space. "Settle this debate: Who is the best kisser? Me or Keller?"

"Are you… Are you asking me to kiss you both?"

Lawson shrugs. "Sure."

When he steps up to Gavin—lips puckered, eyes closed—he's met with a palm to his face.

"Get the fuck out of here, Lawsy."

"Aww, but you're missing out. I give great smooches!"

"Lawson!" Rory hisses at him, wrenching him away once more. She glares at Hayes. "I told you to stop giving him smelling salts. It makes him an idiot."

"I think you mean an *even bigger* idiot," Keller corrects, and Rory shoots him a dirty look, too.

I want to reach over and high-five her just because of how Keller's been since he's known about the secret Gavin and I share. That day in the elevator was *so* unbelievably awkward. Not enough to kill the sexual tension, which led to some incredible sex on the couch since that's as far as we made it, but still uncomfortable.

"Please tell me you at least got our booth since you got here so early?" Reed says to Gavin, as if what just happened is an everyday occurrence, and I think maybe it is.

Gavin tenses behind me. "I, uh, I—"

"I snagged it as soon as I saw him walk in," I say brightly, rescuing him. It's not entirely the truth, but it isn't exactly a lie either. "Come on."

This time when he touches me, there's no way I could possibly mistake it for imaginary, not when his hand latches on to my ass cheek and he gives me two squeezes. *Thank you*, they say.

I roll my lips together and follow my brother and his teammates over to their favorite spot. I finally take my apron off, folding it up and setting it in my lap as the gang slides into the booth one by one. There's nowhere near enough room for everyone, but we all squeeze in anyway, Lawson and Keller pulling up two chairs at the end of the U-shaped space.

I'm highly aware of Gavin sitting next to me, and not just because I imagine sitting next to him is the equivalent of sitting next to an oven. It's so much more than that. I swear there's an electric current that's bouncing off him and me, over and over. There has to be. There's no other reason for the way my body tingles.

Everyone launches into different conversations, and I chime in here and there, but it's hard when all I can focus on is Gavin.

Gavin and his toned arm that keeps brushing against mine.

Gavin and his laugh that rumbles through me.

Gavin and his sparkling hazel eyes that turn me into mush.

I try my damnedest to pay no attention to them, but it's fruitless. Then I feel it—his fingers on my thigh, and I curse myself for wearing a skirt tonight. His touch is soft and hot, instantly making *me* need to catch my breath. It dances closer to where my thighs kiss. We're sitting at a crowded table. If everyone weren't so caught up in their own conversations, they'd easily see what was happening.

Still, it doesn't stop Gavin from dragging his touch upward, and it's so damn frustrating how he continues to talk with Fox as if he isn't torturing me right now. His fingers graze me *right there*, and I jump.

"Oh my god!"

Everyone's eyes fall on me, and I *pray* they can't see Gavin's hand between my legs, the back of his finger sitting against my throbbing pussy.

"Sorry. I just, um, I realized I forgot to clock out. Excuse me," I say to Gavin, shooting daggers at him.

"Sure." His lips twitch as he scoots out of the bench, and though I want to punch him for that, I refrain, making my way to the bar.

I walk around the back of it because it would be

really weird if I didn't, and Josh tips his head at me when he notices me back there.

"I didn't clock out," I explain.

"Oh, I took care of that for you."

"Oh, well, thanks," I say, but I don't leave. I can't. I'm scared they'll be able to see right through me if I walk back out there.

Instead, I order an amaretto sour, then down half of it in one go. Josh arches a brow at me.

"What?" I glower at him. "I'm thirsty."

He laughs, shaking his head as he walks away.

"Funny you should say that—I'm thirsty too, and, baby, you look like you'd quench my thirst."

I turn to my right to find a guy who looks to be about the same age as me. He has one of those modern mullets that are all the rage, but all they do is remind me of a kid who got hold of their daddy's electric razor. He's also rocking a goatee that's uneven—double ick.

Hideous hair choices aside, I wouldn't be interested in him based on that horrible pickup line alone.

"No."

He snaps his head back. "No? What the hell do you mean *no?*"

"*No*," I repeat, sterner this time. "Which is something you should have said to your barber when he decided to give you that hideous haircut."

He takes a step toward me, and I scoot back, not at all liking where this is going. It's not the first time I've had to deal with someone hitting on me in the bar, but it's the first time I haven't had the counter between us to give me protection.

"Come on, baby. Don't be like that," he says, reaching out for me, and I stumble backward to dodge his touch.

It's pointless because suddenly, the guy isn't anywhere near me. No, he's pressed against the counter, his face turning red as Gavin stands over him, hand around his throat.

"She told you no, dipshit. More than fucking once. What about that is hard to understand?" he snarls, his nose inches from Creepy Guy's.

"I-I-I…" the guy tries to say, but I imagine it's hard to get anything out with how tightly Gavin is holding on to him.

"Yo, Locke, let him go, man." Hayes grabs him by the shoulder and tries to pry him off.

Reed is there too, pulling at him from the other side. "Come on, old man. Let him breathe. He's turning purple."

"Fucking good," Gavin says, still holding on.

And while I'm still pissed at the guy for being a total asshat, I'm now worried about Gavin doing something he can't undo.

"Gavin!" I yell, and he instantly whips his head my way.

"What?" he shouts, eyes wide, like he's in some sort of trance.

"Let him go," I say calmly, like I'm trying to talk someone down from the ledge, and I might as well be. It feels like that's what he's teetering on right now. "*Please.*"

The last word is what breaks through to him, and he does. He drops the man so suddenly that he crashes to the floor, holding his throat as he gasps for air. Gavin just stares at me, his eyes raking over me, like he's looking for damage. I want to reach out to him so damn badly and reassure him I'm okay, but I can't with Reed standing behind me. *Especially* not when he's looking between me and Gavin like he's missing something and we're the answers he's looking for.

"You good, man?" Hayes asks, clapping him on the back.

He nods, never once taking his eyes off me.

"All right." Then he looks at Josh and points to the door. "Get this fuck out of here, yeah?"

Josh stands there wide-eyed for several beats before nodding and scrambling around the counter. He picks the guy up and shoves him toward the door.

"You're banned," Josh tells him.

"Banned?!" Creepy Guy says, as if he's genuinely

shocked by this turn of events. "I didn't do shit! That fucking bitch is just being dramatic! I wasn't even doing anything to her!"

Gavin takes a step, ready to go after him to finish what he started, but I step into his path. He stares down at me, eyes hard, jaw set.

"Are you okay, Van?" Reed asks, stepping up next to him.

His eyes are still darting between us, and it makes me more and more uneasy by the second.

Does he know? Did Gavin's reaction just give us away completely?

"Yeah, I'm fine," I answer, finally pulling my gaze from Gavin's. He still looks like he's seconds away from going after the guy, but I think he's calmed down enough that he won't. "Just some creep hitting on me."

"Sorry, I didn't even see it. I just saw Locke jump out of the booth. Everything else happened so fast. Are you sure you're okay?"

There's genuine concern in his voice, and I think it's the first time I've ever experienced that from him.

I nod. "I'm okay. I promise."

He pats Gavin on the back. "Thanks for having her back, man. You're a damn good friend."

Gavin tenses at the words, though I don't think Reed notices. At least I *hope* he doesn't notice.

"Sure," he says. "Nothing I wouldn't do for anyone else."

I don't doubt his words for a second. That's just the kind of man Gavin is. But he didn't do it for just anyone else. He did it for *me*.

He took care of me—*again*.

He stepped up for me—*again*.

He was simply there for me—*again*.

It's starting to be a pattern with him, and I'm beginning to realize that whenever this thing between us, this *fun* we're having ends, I'm not just going to miss the sex. I'm going to miss this feeling of being cared for by someone who wants nothing else in return. I'm going to miss being somebody's.

I'm going to miss *him*.

And that scares me to no end.

Chapter 18

SERPENTS SINGLES GROUP CHAT

Lawson: I forgot underwear.

Hayes: Again???

Lawson: Yes, again! Stop judging me, dammit!

Fox: Dude, we are on day six of a twelve-day road trip. How are you just now realizing this?

Keller: I swear, if you ask to borrow some again, I'm officially done with this group chat.

Lawson: I wasn't going to. Rory very nicely informed me that it isn't cool to ask your bros to borrow their underwear.

Hayes: WE very nicely told you that, too.

Fox: Actually, you were kind of mean about it.

Keller: Everyone is kind of mean compared to you, good boy.

Fox: Stop calling me that.

Keller: Only when you stop reacting to it like you do.

Lawson: Can someone go to the store with me?

Keller: Are you five? Need someone to hold your hand?

Lawson: Yes! It's a big city. I could get lost! Do you really want to be the reason the team's leading goal-scorer goes missing? I'm cute. Someone could kidnap me!

Keller: Twenty bucks says they'd bring you right back.

Lawson: So is that a no, then?

Keller: It's a HELL no.

Lawson: Anyone else?

Hayes: Yeah, no. Not happening.

Locke: Absolutely not.

Hutch: No.

Fox: I'll go with you, Lawsy.

Lawson: OH, FOXY BABY! I
LOVE YOU!

Lawson: At least someone loves me.

Lawson: Speaking of people who love
me... We're still grabbing dinner with
the guys from the Comets, right?

Hayes: Hell yeah, I miss those guys.

Keller: Yes, but only so I can chat with
Adrian Rhodes about that fight with
that tool from Florida. That Superman
punch he landed was a beauty.

Lawson: Your crush on him is so
weird.

Hutch: Just please do not sit me next
to Grady Miller. He's more obnoxious
than you, Lawsy.

Lawson: Aw, I love Miller!

Hayes: Literally nobody is surprised
by that.

> Locke: I can't make it. Got a FaceTime
> thing.

Lawson: With the family?

> Locke: Who else?

Keller: *thumbs-up emoji*

> Locke: What the hell does that mean?

Keller: Uh, it means *thumbs-up emoji*

Locke: Whatever.

Hayes: Stop being so weird, Kells.

Keller: No.

Keller: Better yet, make me.

Hayes: *eye roll emoji*

Fox: Can't we all just get along? *heart hands emoji*

Lawson: I agree. We all need to stop being so mean. If anyone ever sees these texts, they might think we actually hate each other. Especially you, Keller.

Keller: Good. That's the way I intend it.

Lawson: LIES!

Hayes: You act so damn tough, dude, but if you hated us, you wouldn't be in this group chat.

Hutch: Kid has a point.

Hayes: Fuck's sake. I am NOT a kid.

Locke: He's not. You gotta stop calling him that, Hutchy.

Hayes: What the hell are you piping in for, old man? Don't need Gramps coming to my rescue.

Locke: Hey, watch it!

Hayes: Or what? Going to take me out with your cane next time you see me?

Locke: Dude. Rude.

Hayes: You're right. I'm sorry.

Hayes: OR WHAT? GOING TO TAKE ME OUT WITH YOUR CANE NEXT TIME YOU SEE ME?

Hayes: It's in all caps. I was shouting at you. Because you're old and can't hear. Get it?

Lawson: BURN!

Lawson: Nice one, Hayesy! Remind me to give you a high five later.

Hayes: No, thank you.

Lawson: Okay, I take it back. Locke was right. You are rude. Been hanging out with Keller too long.

Keller: I'm not rude. I'm just saying what everyone else is thinking. If anything, I'm brave because I'm the only one who will step up.

Hutch: You're an asshole, Kells. Just admit it.

Keller: I'm okay with that label.

Fox: I don't think you're an asshole.

Keller: You're only saying that because you're too nice to say anything else.

Fox: Not true. I'd call you an asshole if I really thought you were one. I think you're just projecting because you're sad and lonely.

Lawson: HOLY SHIT! That makes so much sense, Foxy!

Hayes: Damn, it really does.

Hutch: Oh, yeah. I can see that.

Hutch: What? Nothing to say now, Keller?

Keller: Just trying to figure out if I'm willing to let that slide because the good boy said it or if I should punch him next time I see him.

Hayes: Look at you, getting all soft on us.

Hutch: Fuck, I can't wait to watch you fall in love, too, Kells.

Keller: It's not happening.

Lawson: Yes, it will. It's inevitable at this point.

Lawson: Just two to go now.

Keller: Hmm.

Hayes: "Hmm" what?

Keller: Oh, nothing. Nothing at all.

Keller: Locke, you still there?

Keller: Whitlocke?

Keller: Lockey Poo?

Locke: Shut the fuck up, Keller.

Keller: HAHAHAHAHAHA

Hayes: I have no idea what's going on.

Hutch: Same.

Lawson: Me either, but we can discuss this more later.

Lawson: Now, do you guys think I would look good in briefs?

Hayes: For fuck's sake, Lawsy.

Keller: Does anyone have any bleach to erase the image I just got of Lawson in tighty-whities?

Hutch: Please stop talking, Lawson.

Fox: Even I have to sit this one out.

Locke: Yeah, too far.

Lawson: What? You guys see me in my panties ALLLLLL the time! Do I have the ass for them or not?

Lawson: Guys?

Lawson: Foxy Baby? Hutchy? Hayesy? Lockey Poo?

Lawson: Kells?

Lawson: Aww, come on! You all muted the group, didn't you?

Lawson: Hello?

Lawson: HELLO?!

Lawson: Fuck you. I'm getting the briefs anyway.

Chapter 19

LOCKE

"Let's do this, boys!" Lawson shouts down the bench, his mouthguard dangling from his lips as he chews on it. "Pick it the fuck up!"

He's right. We do need to pick it up. We let Jersey tie the game with just five minutes to go, and it's not the first time we've done it this road trip. We're exhausted; that much is obvious. Being away from home for so long always does that, though. Being on the road and not sleeping in your bed starts to get to you after a while, and it's even worse if you have someone waiting for you to get home.

While I don't *technically* have someone waiting for me, I have Nessa, and I miss her as if she were mine. She certainly feels that way, and I'm eager as fuck to get back to her. Our late-night FaceTime calls have been great, but they aren't enough. I need to see her, and not just through a screen. I need to touch her. *Worship* her.

We just need to hang on to these last few minutes and send this game to overtime. We can beat them three-on-three, I know it. Hayes drives to the front of the net in an attempt to stuff the puck past the goalie's pad, and we all rise on the bench, watching and praying the puck will cross the line, but it doesn't. We sit back down as the linesman loses sight of it and blows the whistle.

We get set for another face-off, this time sending Lawson, who is damn good on the draw, out there in hopes we can win it back and get a quick shot on net and surprise the goalie. It doesn't work. He catches it with ease. We try again—still nothing. Our time is up before we know it, the buzzer going off and signaling that we are indeed headed to overtime.

"Fuck!" Hutch slams his stick on the boards next to me. "Fuck!"

I get it. He wants to get home to his baby and his girl. I want to get home to his sister.

"We got this," I tell him, trying to calm him down a bit. "They might have more practice with OT this season than us, but we can outskate any of their guys."

He nods, still scowling out at the ice. "Yeah, yeah. I'm just…"

I pat his back. "I know, man."

The puck is dropped at center ice, and unsurprisingly, Lawson wins it back. He scrambles off the ice for a breather, and Peterson, another young guy, takes his spot. He passes the puck to Frederic, who passes it over to Hayes. They're getting set up, drawing the Jersey players to them and distracting them. It works. Lightning quick, Hayes zooms the puck back to Peterson, who takes off quickly toward the goalie, going one-on-one.

Like he took a play right out of my book, he goes top shelf, and the bench explodes when it hits the net.

"Yes, yes, yes! Fucking yes!" Hutch hollers, jumping with joy.

We all meet Dash, our second goalie, at the end of the bench, tapping his helmet as we head down the tunnel to the visitors' locker room. We dress in record time and hit the bus, all of us eager as hell to hop on the plane and get back to Seattle.

My phone buzzes as I settle into my seat. I pull it free and smile.

"What a game!" my dad says as a greeting. "What a damn game, son!"

I laugh. "Thanks, Pop. Though I do have to wonder what you're doing up still. It's way past your bedtime, old man."

"Hey, watch it. You ain't no spring chicken yourself, you know."

Fuck, don't I know it. Part of the reason the game was tied was because I let Jersey's leading goal-scorer slip past me like I was standing still. It was embarrassing as hell, and I'm not surprised I sat on the bench the rest of the game.

"Bet you're glad to be heading back home after this trip."

"More than you know."

"How's everything going with Nessa?"

My parents are fully aware of just how much I've fucked this situation up even more because I couldn't keep my hands off her. While my mother is worried about me and my father thinks I should focus on hockey, neither of them has lectured me about it.

Truthfully, I think they're a little glad about it. I'm the only one of my siblings who hasn't settled down. While it's not an ideal time, I think they're just glad I'm not alone, and I am too.

I knew I was lonely—it's why I slept with Nessa that night in New York—but I didn't realize just how lonely I was until I had her in my life every day. Now, I can't imagine *not* having someone. I can't imagine not having *her*.

"Good," I answer, looking around the bus for

where Hutch is sitting. It's not like I'm going to say anything incriminating with so many ears around, but it's almost a reflex at this point. "Everything is good. I, uh, I'm looking forward to going home."

I can almost hear my dad smile. "I'm glad, son. You're… You're doing good this season."

So don't let anything screw that up, is what he tacks on to the end without actually saying it.

"I know," I say. "I'm aware."

I'm being careful with her, Pop, is what I really say back.

"All right. Well, I'll let you get. I just wanted to tell you I'm proud. Your mother is with your eldest nephew in the kitchen, feeding him way too much ice cream this late at night, so I'd better go check on them."

"Mom's such a troublemaker."

He laughs heartily. "She is, but that's why I love her. Love you, son."

"Love you too, Pop."

We hang up, and I sigh, dropping my head back against the seat and thinking about Nessa and how serious this thing is starting to get with my parents asking after her every time we talk.

Because it *is* getting serious. It's not what either of us intended, I'm sure, but it doesn't mean it's not happening. We should probably address that, but I feel like we might be too deeply invested in this to change it now. Hell, I'm *still* pushing off her bed delivery just to keep her in mine longer. The company gave me a warning the last time that if I postpone delivery again, they'll cancel the order with no refund.

Don't they know that's exactly what I want? To keep her in my bed? In my penthouse? To…well, to just *keep* her? That thought is scary as hell, but it's an honest one.

I keep hold of it as we finally climb onto the plane and settle into the comfy seats for the long flight to Seattle. That's the worst part about being on the coast, having to play games on the opposite ones and deal with the long-ass trips back home. But if it means I'm getting closer to Nessa, I'll endure anything.

I pull my phone out and grin at the text waiting for me. It's from her, just a simple smiley face, but I know what it means—she's waiting up for me.

"Hey."

I flip my phone over just as Hutch settles into the seat next to me.

"Uh, hey," I say back, looking around. Maybe the other spots are taken? But nope. There are plenty of empty ones. "What's up?"

"Just felt like hanging out with someone mature for a change." He settles back into the seat, stretching out his long legs. "Plus, Lawson is watching Rory sleep, and it's kind of creepy. She's almost my sister-in-law."

"How *are* you feeling about the upcoming wedding? Just under three months now." I'm sure it has to bring up some feelings for him since the last time he tried to get married, the bride never showed.

"Me?" He grins. "Oh, I'm fucking great. I cannot wait to marry Auden." He laughs quietly. "It's so funny. I never thought I'd be in this position again. I thought I swore off relationships forever after everything that went down all those years ago, but I'm so glad I didn't. She's the greatest thing to ever happen to me. And it's the little things, too. Like the way she smiles at me in the morning, or how she always wears those ridiculous sweaters that make no sense because they make her sister happy. You know what I mean?"

Oh, I know what he means all right. It's the same way with Nessa. The small things that shouldn't matter somehow do. Like how she always tucks her hair behind her ear when she's nervous. Or how she feeds Pearl and Rufus and Sir Fishsticks the Fourth with such concentration, her lip between her teeth, always making sure they each get their fair share. Or how she always grabs a pack of cinnamon gum when she grocery shops because she knows it's my favorite. It's all the little things that make me feel things for her I really should not be feeling.

"What's the look for?" Hutch asks, brows pulled tight together as he watches me closely.

"Huh? What look?" I try to play it off, though I have no doubt I definitely *did* just have a look. I've caught *myself* with too many goofy expressions since Nessa came along.

He studies me for what feels like far too fucking long. *Shit. He knows. He fucking knows, and I'm trapped on this plane with him, and he's going to murder me. Fuck, fuck, fuck.* But instead of pulling out a knife and ramming it into my gut, he shakes his head with an easy smile.

"Nah, nothing. I'm just tired, that's all." He scrubs his hand over his face. "Did I mention I can't wait to get home?"

He closes his eyes, and I release the breath I was holding. He falls asleep shortly after, leaving me with my thoughts.

I need to tell him. The longer we let this go on, the worse it's going to be whenever Hutch does find out. And he will. I know he will. Secrets always have a way of coming out. Hell, look what happened with Nessa and her shitty ex. He thought he was hiding that so well, and one slip-up later, it was all over.

I don't want that—to be over. I want... Fuck, I think I want *more*. I want real. I don't just want rolling in my sheets without anyone else knowing how damn happy she makes me. I want to tell the world, and that starts with me telling her brother.

Not now, though. But soon. Very soon.

The rest of the flight passes in a blur, and we're landing back in Washington before I know it. I wave goodbye to the assholes I've spent the last twelve days with, then hop into my AMG and gun it for home.

Lights are on when I push the door open, and I hear her tablet playing in the background. I drop my bag and slip my shoes off, expecting her to come running to me any moment.

But she doesn't. I find her curled up on the couch, fast asleep. I'm not surprised. I've picked up on her habit of sleeping out here when I'm on the road. I hate that she's not getting good rest without me, but I also find it sweet as hell. I'd do the same thing if roles were reversed.

I stand there staring at her for far too long, just watching her. She looks so beautiful in the glow of whatever movie she was watching on her device. The lights dance across her cheeks, highlighting her long lashes that fan out against her skin. Eventually, I drop to my haunches, then brush an errant hair from her face. She stirs and her forest eyes flutter open, a smile tugging at her lips.

"Hey," she says, her voice thick with sleep. "Aw, did I fall asleep? I'm sorry, I tried to stay awake. I just—"

Her words are cut off by a yawn, and I chuckle.

"It's fine. It's late, and I know you worked earlier."

"I did, but it wasn't just that. I spent a few hours at the coffee shop down the street drawing. It got too loud, though, even with my headphones, so I left."

"I'm sorry. I wish you had someplace quiet."

"Me too. Maybe when I get my own place."

She says it so casually that it nearly knocks me over. I don't want her to get her own place. I want this to be her home too, but I don't say so. She's clearly not interested in that.

"Yeah, maybe." I brush my lips across her forehead. "Come on. Let's go to bed."

Despite her protests, I swoop her into my arms and carry her through the living room and to my bedroom. She giggles sleepily when I drop her on the bed, then pulls me down right on top of her.

"Hi," she says with a wide grin.

"Hi yourself." I kiss her gently, not missing how she arches her hips up to me. "Are you trying to get frisky with me, Nessa?"

She nibbles on her bottom lip. "Maybe."

Then she yawns again, and I laugh.

"Maybe next time," I say, kissing her again, then rolling away.

"Wait. Where are you going?" she complains, but her eyes are already closed again.

"Bathroom. Go to sleep, love."

She grins, already half asleep as she says, "I love it when you call me that."

I know she does, which is why I do it so often.

When I come back out, she's dead asleep. There would be no waking her up if I tried, which I don't want to. I have something to take care of. I slip out of the bedroom and tiptoe through the living room and down the hall that leads to the other bedroom. Nessa has given me so much since I've known her, and now I want to give her something too.

I step into my spare bedroom and get to work.

"Okay, I really need you to stop being so perfect."

I turn to find a sleepy-looking Nessa in nothing but my shirt. She must have traded it for her own before coming out here, and I'm not surprised. She loves wearing my clothes almost as much as I love seeing her in them.

I finally crawled into bed about two and a half hours ago, but I was restless. I try to blame it on the jet lag, but with how much I travel, I'm immune to it. It's all because of the blonde cutie padding into the kitchen and slipping her arms around me.

"Mmm," she says, pressing her lips against the middle of my back. "It smells good. What are you making?"

"Just bacon, eggs, and hashbrowns. Nothing fancy."

"Anything is fancy if I don't have to make it."

Since Nessa moved in, we've settled into a routine where I make breakfast whenever I'm home and she makes or orders dinner. I tried to argue with her over it at first because I didn't let her move in so she could take care of me, but she wasn't hearing it. She claimed it was the least she could do for giving her somewhere to live.

She doesn't know I'd give her anything. All she has to do is ask.

"I'll grab the plates," she says, moving to the cabinet I know she can't reach.

I watch in amusement as she struggles to get them out. I could move them lower, sure, but what would be the fun in that? I enjoy the view of her trying to reach them far too much to do that, especially when her shirt —*my* shirt—rides up and gives me a peek of her ass.

When she struggles for just long enough, I turn off the burners and drop the spatula, then go to her. I press against her, just like I have so many other times, and reach over her to grab the plates. I kiss the back of her neck, sweeping the tendrils of hair that have managed to escape her messy bun out of the way.

She sighs, leaning into my touch. "You do this on purpose, don't you?"

"Maybe," I say against her skin. "It is a nice show."

"Show? Is that what you think I'm putting on when I can't reach the plates?"

"No." I slide my hand down her back, cupping those beautiful cheeks she just gave me a glimpse of. "But I'm sure you're genuinely annoyed. Thing is, sometimes I like to annoy you. You turn into a bit of a brat when I do."

She laughs lightly. "I knew it. I knew you like it when I get sassy."

"To be fair, I like everything about you, love."

I feel her shiver in my arms at the nickname, remembering how she said last night that she loves it.

She groans. "You're not being fair."

"How so?" I tease my fingers under her panties, my other hand sliding up the front of her t-shirt and over her tit that fits perfectly in my palm.

"You can't put me in this position with your hard cock brushing against me and call me love. Not with breakfast sitting there getting cold. It's not fair."

"That's okay. I have something else I'd like to eat far more."

I drop to my knees, taking her underwear right

along with me, and she gasps as my lips land against her.

"Gavin." She says my name on a moan, her head dropping back.

"That's right. That's exactly who is about to eat this pussy. Say it again."

"Gavin."

"Again," I instruct as I spread her, forcing her onto her tiptoes.

"Gavin!" she cries out when I slide my tongue along her, from her pussy right back to her hole that I haven't yet played with.

She tenses, then melts against me.

"Oh my god," she whines as I lick her again. "Holy… Don't stop, *please*."

She's begging now, and I'm more than happy to accommodate her. I do it again, slipping my tongue into her cunt for a moment before running it back over her tight ring. She pushes back when I do it, and I grin against her. This time, I focus on her ass, tasting her and thriving off the moans filling the kitchen.

"I think I could come like this," she says through pants. "I just need…"

She puts her hand between her legs, and I know exactly what she's doing, drawing tight circles over her clit. It's fucking hot. My tongue in her ass, her hand on her cunt. *Too* hot, in fact. Before I even realize what's happening, I blow my load right into my pants like some out-of-control fucking teenager instead of an almost forty-year-old man.

It would be embarrassing if Nessa weren't coming right along with me.

"Gavin, Gavin, Gavin," she chants as she shakes harder than I've felt her shake before.

When she finally comes down, I realize it's not enough. Even though I just came, my cock is still rock hard, and I need to be inside her. I rip my cum-soaked pants down, toss her leg up on the counter, and slide inside her.

"Oh god!" she shouts as I slam into her again and again. It's rougher than I've fucked her before, and I can't help myself.

I don't know what's come over me. It feels animalistic or something, like I'm going to go crazy if I don't fill her up right this second. I pound into her, watching as her hands grip the counter tighter and tighter with each thrust. When I'm close, I slip my hand between us and press my finger right against the tight hole I just had my tongue all over.

"Fuck," she groans, pushing into me, the digit sliding into her.

Watching her fuck herself on my finger is exactly what I need to send me over the edge, and I empty myself inside her as she comes right along with me.

When the last of my orgasm leaves me, I drop my head to her shoulder, trying to catch my breath as I pull out, settling her back on the floor.

We stand like that for a long time, and I'm not exactly sure who moves first, but we eventually make our way to the shower. We rinse each other off with gentle hands, unable to look away from one another.

Breakfast never gets eaten, and it's still somehow the best meal I've ever had.

Chapter 20

"Oh, fuck, that's good."

He moans.

"Fucking yes."

I stare up at him.

"Incredible, love. Just incredible."

I blink. "Are you finished?"

He swings a grin my way. "No, but I will be later." He winks, then stabs his teriyaki chicken and takes another massive bite.

I was too tired to cook after my shift at Top Shelf tonight, and while Gavin offered to take me out, the idea of sitting on the couch with him surrounded by takeout containers was much more appealing. That was before he started making those noises.

"Stop being so annoying." I push at him with my feet, hunkering even farther down into the couch, a cardboard container sitting on my chest. I pick out another green bean, then suck it into my mouth.

"I'm not being annoying. You just have a perverted mind."

"Do not," I say, kicking at him again.

He grabs my foot, tickling me right where he knows it affects me the worst. I yelp, trying to wiggle away from him, but it's pointless—he's too damn strong for me.

"Gavin!" I say through loud giggles. "Stop it!"

"Not until you admit you're a naughty, horny little thing."

"I am not!" I argue.

I *so* am. Honestly, if he'd have kept those moans up much longer, I would have had to crawl over and *really* give him something to moan about, but I'm not doing that now with him tickling me to death.

"Stoooop!" I whine, still trying to get away.

My green beans go flying to the floor, but neither of us seems to care about the mess. We're too busy having fun. But Gavin makes a mistake—he pauses *just* long enough for me to get free, and I run. Straight down the hall, toward the other bedrooms.

"Where are you going?" he calls, racing after me. "My bed is the other way."

"Exactly! You think you're getting lucky after that? Not a chance!"

I grab the handle to the bedroom that houses his hockey stuff, knowing he won't dare mess around in there. He's too worried about breaking any of his things.

The door doesn't give way, though. In fact, it's locked. I stop, my senses rapidly switching from fun mode to suspicious. Why the hell is the door locked? Does he not trust me? Does he think I'm going to steal his stuff and sell it online? Is he…hiding something?

No, no. Gavin would never.

I thought Neal would never, too. The thought crashes into me, and all those feelings of betrayal and hurt slam back into me. I don't want them. I don't want to be thinking this way, but try as I might, I can't shake them. Not even when Gavin catches me, boxing me in against the door.

"Ha! I gotcha," he says, his mouth falling to my neck as he peppers me with familiar kisses.

I let him, even though my mind is now a million miles away, thinking up all the reasons he could possibly have locked this door, the one that's been open since the day I moved in here. I would know because I've come in here a few times when he's been on the road, just needing a piece of him.

Is that why it's locked? Does he know I come here? Is he mad that I look through his things? No, he would tell me if he had a problem. He's always been open.

So, what could it be, then? I don't know, but I can't shake the feeling he's hiding something from me.

Not even when he spins me around and drags his kisses from my neck to my lips, or when he lifts me and wraps my legs around his waist. And not even when he carries me to his bedroom and lays me down before peeling my clothes off me, our mess in the living room long, long forgotten. I don't even stop thinking about it as I finally drift off to sleep.

What the hell is Gavin hiding?

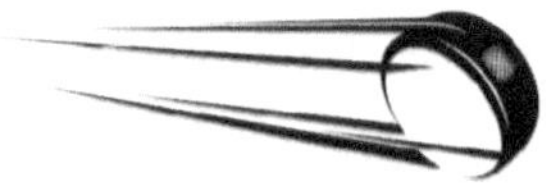

Heavy clouds cover the sky, and cold nips at the air. If I were back in Upstate New York, I'd be inside the warmth of my house, sitting by the fire with hot chocolate and a good book. But this isn't New York, and people are still milling about the city like this cold, rainy weather is nothing new to them.

"Thanks again for meeting me here," Auden says as she settles in across from me at The Coffee Spot, a cute place I found a few weeks ago when I was looking for somewhere new to sketch.

The Serpents are doing a thing at the Children's Hospital for the upcoming holidays, so when she called earlier wanting to get out of the house, I jumped at the chance—anything to keep me from looking at that damn locked door. I've tried it every day for the last four days, but I haven't had any luck. I keep trying not to think about what he could be hiding, but it's slowly driving me mad. I *need* to know why he's shut me out—literally.

"Of course," I tell her, grinning down at Alana, who sits happily in her stroller. I reach over and tickle her chin. "Hi, my beautiful niece. Are you being spoiled? I hope so."

"Oh, she's being spoiled, all right. Hutch brings her something home from every city he visits." Auden rolls her eyes. "And my father is just as bad, always 'dropping by' with something new. Even Rory keeps buying her onesies. It's ridiculous."

You can tell she's not truly bothered by any of it, and I love that Alana is so loved.

"That reminds me…" I grab the small gift bag I brought along and hand it to Auden.

"Stop it. You too?"

I shrug. "She's my niece. I'm legally obligated to spoil her."

Auden laughs, then pulls out the little clown fish stuffed animal I bought her. I saw it in a children's shop last week and knew Alana had to have it.

"Aww, it's so cute! Thank you, Vanessa. That was

really sweet." She hands it to the baby, who lights up at the sight of it.

It's so cute, and it reminds me of Gavin when he talks about Pearl and Rufus, which just makes me sad. Not because of the fish—I love them, and they feel like mine too at this point—but because I'm pretty sure Gavin is hiding something from me.

"Everything okay?"

I snap my gaze back to Auden, who is looking at me with concern.

"Oh, yeah. Just…"

The words die on my tongue as I realize that, as badly as I want to talk to her about this, I can't. She still doesn't know about me and Gavin.

"Nothing," I lie. "It's nothing. Just a little in my head lately."

"Anything I can help with?"

I shake my head. "No, but thank you."

Her eyes narrow, and I hold my breath, waiting for her to call me on my lie.

But all she says is, "Well, just know I'm here if you need to talk about *anything*, even if it's something you feel like you can't. I'm here."

She looks at me so damn closely I *almost* confess to everything right on the spot. Something tells me if I did, Auden wouldn't be all that surprised. She's given me far too many long looks over the last few weeks, and I get the sense she might have picked up on something between me and Gavin a while ago. Even so, I don't say a word, mostly because I don't trust myself.

I shoot her a small smile, and we take our time having coffee, talking about the baby, how much her father fawns over Alana, and a bit about the Serpents, though we don't get into that too deeply. I wonder if Auden can tell it's a sensitive subject for me right now.

When we part, I'm feeling a little better. The closer I get to the penthouse, though, the more aggravated I grow, and when I pull into the garage, I'm just plain pissed. The whole ride up, I fume. The elevator arrives on Gavin's floor, and I punch the code into the door with a bit of extra force. I don't even bother kicking my shoes off by the door. I just drop my purse and go straight for the room to check if it's still locked.

It is.

"Ugh!" I hit it because why not? It's a stupid door hiding something stupid behind it, and *ugh!* I'm just annoyed.

"Nessa?"

I pause my next swing at the inanimate object and turn to find Gavin standing at the end of the hallway.

"What are you doing?" he asks, taking a few steps closer.

"Oh, uh… What are you doing home? I didn't see your car in the garage."

"It's at the shop for maintenance, and I didn't feel like sticking around waiting for it. Keller gave me a ride."

I almost smile at the thought of Keller being forced to hang out with children all day, but then I remember I'm mad.

"Oh."

"Did the door do something to deserve the abuse?"

His lips twitch, and all it does is piss me off more.

"Yes!" I finally explode.

Gavin's eyes widen, but I keep going.

"It's locked when it's never been locked before, and I'd know. I go in there *all the time*, Gavin. When you aren't here, I go in and I look through your pictures and your jerseys and your awards because I miss you and want to connect with you, and now it's locked, and I don't know *why* it's locked, and I…" I gulp in a big breath of air. "I just want to know why? I just want…"

Tears unexpectedly sting my eyes, and I'm not sure why.

No, that's a lie. I know exactly why—Neal.

I exhale heavily. "Open the door, Gavin. Please."

He doesn't say anything for a long time. He just stands there, staring at me, and I can only imagine what's going through his mind. He told me before I wasn't too much, but it certainly feels like I'm too much now. I'm acting like a madwoman over a locked door, and no matter how ridiculous that sounds, I can't stop.

Finally, he moves. He walks down the hall, not stopping until he's right beside me. I watch as he reaches up, up, up to the trim that surrounds the door and pulls down a key.

Oh god. The key was right there the whole time? I'm so embarrassed I can't even look up at him as he pushes the door open and steps aside. I don't move. I'm rooted to the spot.

"Well?" he asks. "Aren't you going to look?"

I lift my head, and my heart stops in my chest. Then it starts right back up again.

Boom boom boomboom boomboomboom.

It's erratic as I take in just what was being hidden behind the locked door. It wasn't anything nefarious. It wasn't some secret life he was hiding. And it wasn't because he didn't want me messing with his things.

I burst into tears. Huge, ugly tears. They roll down my cheeks, and Gavin instantly gathers me into his arms. The cinnamon he always smells like hits my nose, and it makes me cry harder.

"Hey," he says gently, rubbing my back. "Don't cry, Nessa. Please, I hate it when you cry. It... It fucking hurts, okay?"

I *love* that it hurts. How sick is that?

"I'm sorry, I'm just…" I sniffle against him. "You made me an art room?"

He laughs softly. "Well, yeah. You mentioned the coffee shop was too loud, and it's too cold and wet to be up on the roof, so I figured, why not? I'm not using this room for anything important, and you've already claimed the other room as your own personal closet, so it just made sense."

I rub my eyes against his shirt, and it makes his chest rumble again.

I look at his blurry face. "You're perfect, you know that?"

His mouth hitches up on one side. "I thought I was annoying."

"That too. But also perfect." I rise up, my lips ghosting over his. "Perfectly annoying."

He kisses me first, his big hand cradling the back of my head as he holds me close, his mouth moving expertly over mine like he knows my body better than I do. I think he just might.

When we finally part, he grins. "Well? Want to take a closer look?"

I nod frantically. "Yes, please."

He releases me, then ushers me into the gorgeous sage-painted room. There are white shelves lining one wall, each cubby filled with different kinds of art supplies. Pens, pencils, markers, paintbrushes galore… everything. There are at least four different-sized sketchbooks, an easel that captures the little sunlight that's poking through the clouds, and an oversized chair that could easily fit three of me tucked in the opposite corner. A giant—and extremely expensive— drawing table sits in the middle of the room, a stool slid beneath it. It's topped off with a few faux plants to give it a lively look.

It's breathtaking, and everything I could have ever wanted from a space like this.

"Gavin…" I choke back the sob that's trying to work its way free. "I can't believe you did this for me."

"You deserve it."

He says it so simply that I nearly believe him. I pull my gaze from the beautiful room and look at the man responsible for it. He's leaning against the door, his hands in his pockets as he grins at me.

"When did you do all this?"

"I snuck stuff in while you were at work and stayed up late after games."

He sacrificed his sleep for me? His game?

It makes me feel so damn lucky and absolutely horrible for thinking the worst of him.

"I'm sorry," I say quietly.

"Why?"

"Because I…" I wring my hands. "I thought… I

don't know what I thought, okay? I just felt like you were hiding something from me, and I didn't like it."

He shakes his head. "Don't apologize, Nessa. I *was* hiding something from you."

"Yeah, but it was something sweet. That's different."

"No, it's not. Not when you have the kind of past you do. I mean, that is where your mind went, right?"

I nod, hating the emotion that clogs in my throat. "Yeah."

"I get it, and it's fair. I should have told you I was working on something and asked you to keep out instead of just locking the door."

"But—"

"No," he says, pushing off the door and crossing the room to me. "No, no *buts*. That was my bad. Nessa?" He ducks his head to look me right in the eyes. "I'm not Neal. I'm not going to hurt you like he did. I…" He pauses, running his tongue over his lips. "I'm just not going to hurt you, okay?"

Something tells me that's not what he was going to say, but I don't question him. I'm too damn mortified by my behavior and too damn happy about my new art room.

"I know," I tell him, meaning it. "I know."

"Good." He rises to his full height. "Now, how about we christen your new chair?"

He bounces his brows, squeezing my ass, and I laugh. Then I'm not laughing at all because he kisses me, and it turns serious very quickly. He strips me out of my clothes, and I do the same to him, then push him back until he falls onto the chair. I climb over him, and we both groan as I sink onto his cock.

"Fuck," he hisses. "God, I missed you."

I laugh as I lift my hips, riding him slowly. "You just saw me this morning."

"It wasn't enough, imagine that."

But I don't have to imagine it. I know exactly what he's talking about. I missed him too, and I fear that may always be the case. We started this as fun, but it's become so much more than that. I didn't want it to. I didn't want this to mean anything at all. I just wanted to feel like I did in New York, but now… Now, I feel taken care of. I feel cared for. I feel cherished.

I feel…*loved*.

Fuck, I feel so damn loved, and it's scary as hell. I can't feel loved because that would mean… That would mean I love him too, and that's not possible. I cannot love Gavin Whitlocke. I can't love anyone ever again. I'm too broken. I'm too much.

You're not too much, Nessa. You're just enough for me.

His words from before slip into my mind, and I squeeze my eyes shut against them.

"Look at me," Gavin says, like he knows what I'm trying to do.

I peel them back open, meeting his heated stare.

"There she is," he murmurs, and I swear he's not just looking at me as I ride him.

He's looking *into* me. Every part, even the dark and ruined ones. He's looking at everything I've been through, from losing my mom at a young age and the heartbreak that came with that, to what happened with Neal and all the damage after. He's looking at me like he loves me, and just like that, I'm hanging on the edge with just my fingertips, and if I don't come soon, I might lose it. I know Gavin feels the same way.

"Love…" he warns when I swivel my hips again. "I need to come. Need to fill you up."

"Then do it, Gavin. Give it to me. Fill me with your cum. I want to feel it dripping out of me."

He growls, then places his feet on the oversized chair and grabs my wrists, putting my hands behind my back as he takes over from the bottom. He drives up into me fast, my tits bouncing so hard it almost hurts, but I don't care. I want this too damn much, which is why when he leans forward and captures my nipple between his teeth, I explode.

"Yes, love, that's it," he says through gritted teeth as he continues to fuck me through it. "Squeeze my cock with your beautiful cunt. It belongs to me, remember?"

My whole body is racked with shudders as wave after wave hits me. Just when I think I'm done, another one crashes into me, and it's enough to set him off, too. He spills into me with one last hard thrust, and I'm done. Completely fucking spent. I crumple against him, and he holds me tightly, running his hand over my hair as we struggle for air. We sit like that for a long time, taking in what just happened.

"Thank you."

"For the orgasm? You're welcome."

I roll my eyes, which are growing heavier by the second. "No, Mr. Annoying. I meant *thank you* for the room. You have no idea how much this means to me, Gavin. It's… Nobody has ever done anything like this for me. So, thank you. Thank you…"

For loving me.

I leave the words unspoken, letting them hang between us.

He swallows hard, and I swear he hears every one of them as he says, "You're welcome, love."

It's the last thing I hear before I drift off to sleep, feeling happier than I have in a long, long time, and it's all because of him.

Chapter 21

LOCKE

"Yo, Locke, Coach wants to talk to you in his office before you go."

I nod at Frederic to let him know I heard him, then set my phone in my cubby and head toward Coach's office. We just won another home game, and while I'm feeling damn good about that, they always mess me up a bit when they're in the afternoon. Throws my schedule off just enough to make me question what time it is when we get done.

I bump fists with a few of our staff as I pass by, everyone riding a high after beating Vegas—our number one rival team—then knock on the door.

"Hey, Whitlocke," Coach Smith says as he looks up from his desk. "Come on in."

Not too long ago, Owen Smith was in the same position I'm in now. He was the "old guy" playing for the Carolina Comets, and he wasn't looking to get traded and move yet again. He wanted stability. So, he went out and got it himself—he retired.

I don't plan on doing that just yet, but I still admire the guy for knowing when to hang it up. Rumor is he did it for his wife because she worked for the team, but I don't know that for sure. It could have just been Lawson running his mouth again, though he does have a direct link to the Comets, his brother being their goalie and all.

"Please, have a seat." He gestures to the chair across from his desk, and I do just that. "Afternoon games blow."

I chuckle. "Take it you don't miss them?"

"Not a chance. I mean, I miss playing, don't get me wrong, but I also don't miss beating my body up every day."

He's not lying about that. This game is physically taxing in ways most people can't even fathom. The teams release injury reports at the end of the season, but that's just the tip of the iceberg most times.

"But that's not why I called you in here."

"Why did you?" I ask.

"I don't know." He shrugs, leaning back in his chair and folding his hands over his stomach. "Just wanted to check in—old guy to old guy, you know?"

Translation: How are you holding up out there?

"So," he says, "how do you feel the season is going?"

"Not too bad."

His lips twitch at my answer, both of us fully aware of the record season I'm having. "Think it's something you can keep doing?"

"That's the plan, Coach. Going to give it hell."

"Good." He nods. "I'm glad to hear that. And you're feeling all right? Everything okay after taking that puck up high?"

I'd nearly forgotten about that. So much has happened since, and I wasn't as bruised and beaten up as I thought I'd be afterward. I still have some leftover scabbing from the gash on my cheek, but other than that, I'm all healed up.

"Feeling good. Having to work hard, but it's nothing I'm not willing to do."

He grins at that. "I figured you'd say something like that, and that's exactly why we like having you as a Serpent, Locke."

Hope fills my chest. We aren't anywhere near new contract talks, not with it still being so early in the season, but it gives me a bit of faith that they're going to work to keep me around. That's good, because I want to stay, especially with...

No. I can't base the rest of my career on a girl. I won't. I—

Oh, who the hell am I kidding? I would, and that's a terrifying thought.

"So," he says, sitting forward, "between you and me…anything special you're doing? I mean, you're playing next-level hockey here, Locke. What's the secret?"

Nessa.

She's the secret. As soon as I met her, I felt a shift, and it's only intensified since she came back into my life. I'm playing good hockey because I'm feeling better than I've ever felt in my life, and I have her to thank for that.

"Ah," Coach Smith says, leaning back again, his eyes gleaming with understanding.

"What?"

He lifts a single brow. "It's a woman."

"Nah." I try to play it off, but we both know I'm full of shit.

He even laughs. "Right. Sure." He grabs a pen from his desk, clicking it open. "I remember when I tried to deny it, too. Didn't last too long." His smile grows, and I wonder if he's thinking about his wife. "Anyway," he says, shaking himself out of his stupor. "I don't want to keep you. I just wanted to check in and figured since we had an early game and we don't need to rush home after this, I'd talk your ear off a bit." He flicks his chin toward the door. "Keep playing like you're playing out there, and you'll get everything you want, Locke."

"Appreciate it, Coach."

I rise from the chair, and I'm just about out the door when he calls my name.

"Yeah?" I ask, turning to face him.

"Whoever she is, keep her."

Oh, I plan to.

"Thanks, Coach," I say before leaving him sitting there with a knowing grin.

I sport a smile of my own as I make my way back to the locker room to grab my things so I can go home and get back to the girl I'm planning on keeping. I almost told her the other day. It was when I showed her the art studio I built for her, and she broke down in tears over it. I'd suspected before then that what I was feeling was serious, but that sealed it for me. Some very important words nearly tumbled out, but I stopped myself at the last moment. Not because they wouldn't be true, but because it wouldn't mean the same as it would if we weren't hiding this.

All I have to do is muster the courage to tell Hutch, and I am going to. I have it all planned out. I'm going to ask him to dinner, sit him down, and explain everything that happened. In fact, I planned on asking him after the game, before Coach wanted to see me. Hopefully, he's still here.

I pick up my pace and am relieved to see him when I walk back into the locker room.

"Hey, man. I was just coming to talk to you. I—is that my phone?"

He looks up from where he's sitting in my stall.

Wait, why is he in my stall? And why the fuck is he holding my phone?

I drag my eyes from my property in his hands, and I'm met with a glare I haven't been on the receiving end of in a long time. Actually, the last time was when he felt I betrayed him. I—

Oh fuck. Fuck, fuck, fuck.

He rises to his full height, which is just an inch shorter than my own. Standing here now? With his features pulled tight and his eyes dark? Well, I certainly don't feel like the bigger man at all. I feel weak and sick, and like I know exactly what's coming next.

"What the fuck is Vanessa doing calling you?" he asks through clenched teeth.

There are a few guys left behind, including Lawson, Hayes, Fox, and Keller. I glance at them quickly, and all their eyes are trained on us. To my surprise, Keller doesn't have a smirk on his face. He looks genuinely concerned as his eyes bounce between me and the captain.

"Who?"

It's the wrong thing to say. I know it the second I

say it. I don't even know why I bothered trying. We know exactly who he's talking about.

"Don't fuck with me right now, *Whitlocke*." He says my name like it's a dirty word. He holds my phone up. "Why the fuck is she calling you?"

I could lie. I could come up with a simple reason, like maybe we exchanged numbers because I was helping her with something, but I can't bring myself to do it. I can't bring myself to lie anymore.

"Is there something going on between you?" he asks.

I nod, and someone gasps. I assume it's Lawson.

I ignore him, staring right at Hutch. "She lives with me."

His eyes widen. "What the—"

I hold my hand up to stop him. "There's more."

"More?" he sneers. "What fucking *more* could there possibly be?"

His voice is cold now, lifeless, and it nearly sends a shiver down my spine.

"She lives with me," I repeat. "She's *been* living with me. She moved out of your place and into mine."

"What the actual fuck?" He gnashes his teeth. "Why the hell didn't you say anything? You've even fucking asked about her!"

I sigh. "I know. I know I have. I just… Fuck, man. I didn't exactly know how to tell you."

"What? That you're roommates?"

"That I'm in love with her."

Another gasp, but I don't dare look away from Hutch. How could I when I know he's two seconds away from swinging on me? I'd deserve it too. Every damn hit.

But he doesn't. In fact, he doesn't move at all, and I think maybe…maybe it'll all be okay.

Then he moves so fucking quick I barely have time to react before an arm is against my throat and I'm slammed against a wall several feet behind me. My head snaps back against it, and it fucking smarts like hell, but I don't dare try to push him away. He's absolutely entitled to this reaction right now. I've been lying to him for months. I would be pissed too if I were in his position.

"What the fuck did you just say to me?" His nose is inches away from mine, his eyes darker than I've ever seen.

"I said I love her, Reed."

His eyes widen at the use of his first name. He's always been Hutchinson, Hutch, and occasionally Hutchy. Never Reed, not with me. But this is serious, and I need him to know that.

"How could you possibly love her? You're *just* roommates, right? Fucking *right*?"

I swallow as best I can with his arm still pressed against my windpipe.

I shake my head. "No. We aren't."

Yet another gasp.

"Shut the fuck up, Lawson!" Hutch snaps, and the forward has the brains to zip his lips and sit down.

I dare another glance at my teammates—the ones who haven't cleared the room by now—and they all appear to be varying degrees of concerned. Lawson is worried *he's* next in line. Hayes is trying to figure out how he's going to pull Hutch off me. Fox is wishing we'd just hug. And Keller? Keller might look the worst of them all, and it's probably because he knows he's just as guilty as I am.

Okay, maybe not *as* guilty, but he's been aware of this for months. He's been lying too.

"Explain yourself," Hutch barks at me.

"Can you let go of me?"

"No."

I nod. "Fair enough." I cough, trying to get some air. "I, uh, I met her in New York."

"What? When? But the last time we were in New York, you already knew her."

"It was last season."

"Last season? How? I… Oh, *fuck*." His eyes widen, and for the first time, he relents on his hold. His wheels are turning, and he's not staring at me. No, he looks through me, going back to that night. "Vanessa was supposed to go to dinner with Auden, me, my mom, and her dad, but she decided not to. It was the day she got divorced. We figured she just needed her space, but…"

"She didn't stay in her room," I tell him. "She went to a bar, and it just happened to be the same bar I was at. I didn't know, all right? I fucking swear to you, I didn't know who she was. She was just a pretty girl in the bar, and I was feeling lonely as hell. All of you guys were partnering off, and I was just… I don't know. I wanted to experience *something*, even if just for a night."

He shakes his head like he can't believe the coincidence, and I want to tell him to join the club. It's the exact same way I felt when I learned who Nessa was.

"Then she came to Seattle, and I was stunned," I continue. "I couldn't believe she was the same girl you told us about."

"Because she's not. I don't know what happened, but she's changed."

He doesn't know what happened? She got her heart stomped on, that's what fucking happened, but I don't get into that now. He needs to know the rest.

"We didn't want to lie to you, Hutch. I swear. We

just didn't think it mattered. It was one night months prior, and that was it. It wasn't supposed to be anything else. But she…"

I can't help but grin thinking about Nessa, and apparently, it's the wrong thing, because Hutch tightens his hold once more.

"She needed a place to stay," I tell him. "She knew how you felt about her and that you wanted her out."

"So, what? You just offer up your spare bedroom in hopes of getting lucky again?"

For the first time, I return fire and shove on Hutch, and he staggers back a bit. He can say what he wants about me, but he needs to keep Nessa out of this. She's off the table.

"It wasn't fucking like that." I shove him again, and this time he lets me go. "I was trying to *help* her."

Unlike you goes unsaid, but Hutch hears it loud and clear. I suck in breaths of air, trying to get my bearings straight again, but Hutch just keeps going.

"So why not tell me? Why not just explain what happened if it was nothing?"

"Because it wasn't *nothing*," I say, pushing off the wall. "It was never nothing. Not back in New York and not fucking now."

He stares at me, seething, literally flexing his hands at his sides as if he's holding himself back from hitting me. I wish he would. I wish he'd take a swing at me.

Anything to make me stop feeling like absolute shit right now, to stop seeing that untrusting look in his eyes. The last thing I wanted this season was for us to be split up, so I worked my ass off to keep my position on this team.

Who would have thought it would be actions off the ice that would tear us apart anyway?

"Why her, Locke? She's my sister."

I laugh humorlessly. "Oh, so *now* she's your sister? Before, she was your *step*sister or the *evil step*sister. It's pretty fucking convenient that when she does something you don't like, she suddenly becomes your sister and you care about her."

"Don't fucking tell me what I do and don't care about. I have always cared about her."

"Yeah, well, you have a piss-poor way of showing it. She thinks you hate her."

"What?" He rears his head back like I've just hit him. "She thinks that? I don't...I don't hate her. I just don't... Fuck, I guess I just don't really know her."

"You never gave her a chance. You wrote her off the second she stepped into your life. Why?"

"I..."

He's at a complete loss, having no answer for that, and I watch as it dawns on him that he truly doesn't know his own sister.

"Fuck," he mutters, stumbling back and dropping

into a stall. "I really did that, didn't I? I didn't even put up a fight when she said she was moving. I just told her bye. Didn't even question it. Didn't even *think* about checking the place out for myself. I'm…" He scrubs a hand over his face. "I've held her at arm's length this entire time, and even when she came to me to mend things, I couldn't be bothered." He shakes his head like he's disgusted with himself. "I'm a fucking dick."

"You really are," I agree.

I look over at the guys, who are watching all this unfold. I nod toward the door, telling them to get lost. They do, minus Keller. He pauses in the doorway, then turns to face Hutch.

"I knew," he confesses, and dammit, I respect the guy just a little more for that. He's doing the one thing I couldn't do—being honest with him.

Hutch's jaw drops. "Did *everyone* know?"

"I did," Fox says, popping his head back into the room.

"What?" Hutch and I say at the same time.

The goalie shrugs. "I got the feeling something had happened between you two when she first arrived. You got really pale, and it was obvious you were into her."

"For the record, I knew nothing," Hayes says, his head appearing right beside Fox's.

"Me either," Lawson adds, jumping over them to indicate who's talking, as if we didn't know. "But now I know"—another jump—"and this gossip is *so* good." Jump. "Can I tell Rory?"

"No!" we all shout at the same time.

"Boo!" he says, still bouncing up and down.

"Go away. All of you. I'll deal with you later, Keller."

He doesn't even make a smartass comment, just nods and shoves the other guys out of the way. Then it's me and Hutch. He turns to me, his eyes still heated but not nearly as incensed as they were.

"So you love her, huh?"

I sigh and drop into the stall next to him, nodding. "Yeah, man. I really fucking do. I don't know when it happened, but it did, and I don't regret it. I wish I did, because it would mean you're not mad at me, and it would mean I'm not breaking that unspoken rule about siblings being off-limits, but fuck. I can't, Reed. I can't regret it. I love her too much to."

"Good. Don't. I'd be pissed if you did."

The guilt that's been weighing me down since Nessa came to town slithers away, and while I'm still worried Hutch might clock me at any moment, I feel okay. Also, I *really* feel like I want to see Nessa. I want to tell *her* how I feel. She deserves to know, even if she doesn't feel the same way. I hope like hell she does, but if she doesn't, I'll wait.

I don't think I have any other choice.

"All right," Hutch says after several quiet minutes. "Tell me everything."

So, we sit in stalls that aren't ours, and I start from the very beginning.

Chapter 22

VANESSA

I've kept one eye on the door for the past hour, waiting for Gavin to walk into Top Shelf after that win, but I'm starting to think he's not going to show.

I'd understand if he didn't. I'm sure he's tired and likely ready for a hot meal and a nap. But he's never not called or texted me back, and worry is starting to sit heavily in my stomach. I check my phone again and frown when I find nothing. I pour another beer for Sid, one of our regulars, and that itch that's been nagging at me since I started drawing again comes back. I wish I had a pen or pencil so I could sketch this moment, do anything to take my mind off why Gavin isn't here.

But I don't, so I go back to staring and willing the door to open and him to step through and give me one of those smiles I love so much. Twenty minutes later, the door opens, and in steps a tall hockey player.

Only it's not Gavin. It's Reed, and he's alone.

"Hey, Josh?"

He looks up from making a tequila sunrise, takes one look at Hutch, and nods. "Go on. I got things covered."

"Thanks," I tell him, already taking my apron off. I owe him big-time for covering for me yet again.

I round the bar, meeting Reed on the other side. He looks uncertain, maybe even a little scared.

"What's wrong? Is everything okay with Auden and Alana?"

"Huh? Oh, yeah." He nods. "Everything is fine with them. Why?"

"Uh, because you're here?"

His brows slant together, like me saying that perturbs him, but it's true. It's weird that he's here alone. It's weird that *we're* alone. I don't think we've ever been in the same room without a buffer before.

"Okay, so, then, what's up?" I ask.

"Can we talk?"

My hackles rise instantly. He wants to…talk to me?

"Um, sure." I point toward the booth where the Serpents always gather. "We can sit over there. Want something to drink?"

"I probably should. Whiskey, tw—"

"Two cubes. I remember. I'll be right over."

I go back behind the bar and grab him a double

shot of top-shelf whiskey, add two ice cubes, and pour myself a shot of vodka. I'm still on the clock and shouldn't technically be drinking, but something tells me I might want to for this conversation, whatever it's about. I mean, I have a feeling I know, but I could be wrong.

I'm not sure I want to be, though. I want this thing with Gavin to be out in the open. I'm ready for Reed to know, even if that does mean I have to be honest about my feelings toward his teammate.

I slip into the booth opposite my brother, sliding his drink his way, and settle in. We don't talk for a few moments, and I try my best not to stare at him because all it does is make me nervous. That's sad in its own regard. I shouldn't be uneasy talking with my own brother, but I am. The longer I sit there, the more my nerves build, and the urge to say something just bubbles out of me.

"So, I—"

"How—"

We start at the same time, both of us chuckling uncomfortably at that. *Good gravy, look at us. Neither of us knows how to act around the other.*

I motion for Reed to go ahead.

He takes a sip of his whiskey first, then says, "How are you?"

This is the second time he's asked about me, and I

find it just as disarming as before. Something about this time feels different, and I don't think it's just because he's here alone.

"I'm good." *Really* damn good, thanks to Gavin, though I don't tell him that. "How are you?"

"I'm not here to talk about me."

Suddenly, the reason why this feels different hits me—he knows. He knows about Gavin, and he's here to tell me off. My heart hammers in my chest, and my hands begin to shake. I hide them under the table, pinching myself to try to get it under control. I'm used to Reed being disappointed in me, so why is this messing with me so much?

I take a deep breath, trying to calm myself, and ask, "Then what do you want to talk about?"

"Us."

For the second time, his words shock me. He wants to talk about *us*? As in me and him? What is there we could possibly talk about? Is there even an us to discuss?

He finishes off the rest of his whiskey and wipes the back of his hand across his lips. "I'm sorry."

I don't say anything. I don't even move. I'm not quite sure I could if I tried because it's not at all what I expected him to say. Reed is...*sorry*? What the hell is that even supposed to mean?

I ask him as much, and he laughs dryly. "It means

I've been a really fucking shitty brother." He sighs loudly, leaning back against the booth like a weight has been lifted, and I have no doubt it's because those words were just very hard for him to say. "And don't try to argue with me about it. I—"

"I wasn't going to. You have been a shitty brother —but I've been a shitty sister too."

We've both been mean to one another in so many different ways over the years that it's hard to keep track of. Like when I ruined his Christmas break, and when I didn't show for his game that night in New York. Even before that, too. I was snotty to him whenever he'd come home during the summers, and I know it's because he was disrupting the life Dad, Angie, and I had built. It's so silly to feel like Reed being there ruined it all, especially since he's Angie's son, but that's exactly how I felt. I'd already lost one mother, and I didn't want to lose another.

I know now that wouldn't have been the case, but back then, I had no idea. I was just trying desperately to hold on to something that felt good after feeling crappy for so long.

He nods. "Maybe, but you were young. I wasn't. I was old enough to know better and do better. And I should have, but I didn't. I was fine with being a jerk to you, so it's no surprise that your brattiness toward me has kept up."

All I can think of is Gavin calling me a brat. He loves it now when I get sassy with him, but what if I get to be too much for him, too?

"You're thinking about him, aren't you?"

I snap my gaze back to Reed. "What?"

"Whitlocke. You're thinking about him, aren't you?"

I have no doubt I look like one of the fish in Gavin's tank at this point, my mouth floating open, then closed.

"You know?" I finally manage to ask.

"He told me earlier." His eyes narrow. "Well, not so much told me, but I pieced it together. I saw your name light up his phone."

Shit. I knew I shouldn't have called him so soon after the game. I couldn't stop myself, though. He was worried going into this game because it was against Vegas, and they're always tough competition for the Serpents. They have a history together. So when Seattle kicked their ass and Gavin earned two points on top of that, I wanted to talk to him.

"I hate that you felt like you couldn't tell me about this," Reed says. "I mean, I don't *love* that you're… doing whatever it is you're doing with my teammate and close friend, but I would have understood eventually. I've grown a lot in the last few years too, you know."

He doesn't have to say it has to do with Auden. We both already know it does.

"I don't want to be the kind of brother you hide stuff from. I don't like that you feel you can't tell me things. And I really, really don't want you to think I hate you."

Emotion clogs my throat, my nose grows heavy, and my eyes begin to water. I know exactly what it means—I'm about to cry.

"I don't, Van. I don't hate you, okay?" Reed says, his voice shaky and pleading. "I…I love you."

I break. Tears fall down my cheeks, and my shoulders shake as sobs rack through me. I don't know when Reed scoots over to me, but suddenly his arms are wrapped around me and he's hugging me for the first time in… God, I don't even know how long. Maybe ever? I don't know. I just know that it feels *good*.

I throw my arms around him, holding him just as tightly, and I let the cries come. They're not just because of Reed and his words; it's more than that. It's everything we've missed together over the years we've been at each other's throats. It's the support we could have been showing, the cheering for the same team, the sibling camaraderie, like making fun of how much our parents love each other together. It's all those things we never got to do because we were too busy thinking the other was enemy number one.

"Fuck," he mutters, releasing me first, and not that I'd ever bring it up to him, but I see it when he swipes under his eyes. "I didn't mean to make you cry."

I shake my head, grab a napkin from the dispenser, and wipe my wet cheeks. "It's okay. I just didn't realize how much I needed that."

"Me either," he agrees, and I believe him.

Reed scoots back to his side of the bench, and we sit there for a few quiet moments, trying to collect ourselves. This is a lot more than what I bargained for today, but I can't deny how much lighter it makes me feel. My relationship with Reed has always bothered me, and I wonder if deep down, that's why I came to Seattle when I needed to get out of New York. Maybe it was just another part of my life I felt I needed to heal.

"You know," Reed eventually says, "I think I didn't like you because you represented everything I had lost."

I understand that completely. "And I think I didn't like you because you *had* everything I had lost."

He nods. "We missed out on so much because of that. I don't want that for you anymore. I don't want things to pass you by. I don't want you not to know what love is like. I want you to be happy, Van. I want you to get everything you ever wanted."

"I want that too."

"So why not get it? With him."

"With Gavin?"

"Yeah. Why not?"

I sling back my vodka, grimacing from the burn, and set the shot glass on the table. "I... It's complicated."

I want to smack myself for using that excuse, given my history with it, but it's the only way to describe the situation we're in. We said we were just having fun, and even though my feelings have definitely changed since we first agreed to that, I'm still unbelievably scared of them. I mean, there's no way I found someone so perfect so soon after my divorce...right? That only happens in the movies, not to me. I couldn't possibly be that lucky. Not after everything.

"There's always a reason to not be with someone—and trust me, I thought I had a very good one at one point—but I promise you, Van, there are a million other reasons *to* be with them, and they always outweigh that one."

I know he's right, but fear still sits heavily on my chest.

"He loves you, you know."

I don't even try to act surprised by his words. Why should I? I think Gavin and I have been telling each other we love one another for weeks, not with our words but with our actions and our bodies. That's certainly what I tried to tell him in my art room the other day, and I think it's what he was trying to say, too.

"I'm scared, Reed," I confess out loud for the first time. "I can't get my heart broken again. The divorce…the cheating…it broke me. I can't be broken again. And with the way I feel about Gavin, I'm not sure I'd recover."

"I've known him a long time, and I know he'd never do anything to hurt you."

"That's what everyone says."

"Yeah, but sometimes they mean it." He leans across the table. "Besides, do you want to go through your life alone because you're too afraid to love again? If I had done that, I wouldn't have met Auden, and I wouldn't have Alana. And that would suck, because my baby is cute as hell."

I chuckle. "She really is."

"She is, and she wants her auntie Vanessa to be happy."

"Using the kid against me isn't cool, Reed." I glare at him.

He shrugs unapologetically. "If it gets you to admit you're in love with him, then I'm fine with it."

I scoff. "As if that was ever a question. Of course I'm in love with him. I love him more than I could possibly explain. I—"

"Is that true?"

I pause. I can usually tell when he's near, but I was so wrapped up in talking to Reed that I missed it.

He's here.

Gavin is here.

Slowly, I turn, and a grin breaks out over my face like I haven't seen him in years rather than hours.

"Hi," I whisper.

"Is that true, Nessa? Do you love me?"

I push from the booth, rising to my feet, and I wish I hadn't. My knees are shaking so hard they're nearly knocking together, and my whole body is buzzing in a way it never has before. I tuck a piece of hair behind my ear, then convince myself to look up at him.

Greens and golds and browns meet my stare, taking my breath away. Will it always be like this when I look at him? Will I always get these butterflies? Will he always make my heart feel like it's doing cartwheels? I already know the answer to those questions, which is why he needs to know too.

"Gavin, I…" I take a deep breath. "I've been hurt. *Badly*. I gave away my heart and my trust, and it was given back to me in shards. Because of that, I was mean. I was cold. I was just a shell of the person I set out to be. And then you happened." I smile softly, thinking of the night we met. "You came into my life on the worst possible day and somehow made it the best. You didn't judge me. You didn't care that I was broken. You listened. You understood. You were simply *there*, and that meant more than you could know. And when I moved out here to run away from my problems, there you were again. By accident, of course, but it didn't feel like an accident. It felt like fate. It felt like this was where I was meant to be, and I think that's because of you. No, I *know* that's because of you. That day when I walked into Reed's and saw you, I couldn't believe it. It took everything in me not to react and fling myself at you. You were real. That night wasn't a dream. Then reality set in, and I was scared. I was so damn scared because I didn't *want* to feel that way. I didn't want to feel the butterflies or feel like my heart was ready to beat out of my chest for someone else. But I did. I *do*. I always will because it's you, Gavin. It has always been you. And I..." I gulp in another breath. "I love you."

Three long seconds. That's how long he stares at me without saying anything or moving.

Then he's doing both at once.

"Thank fuck," he murmurs, and it's the last thing I hear before he's kissing me.

His hands cup my face, tilting my head as I push up to my tiptoes to meet him. I sigh when his tongue slides against mine, and he swallows the sound. I am nothing but air, and he's the anchor keeping me from floating away.

Yeah, that's what he is—my anchor, but he's not there to hold me down. He's keeping me steady. Keeping me on my feet. Our kiss turns from hard and rushed to soft and sensual. When we eventually part, Gavin rests his head against mine.

"I'm not sure if I was clear or not, but I love you too."

I giggle. "I kind of figured that, but it sure is nice to hear."

"Good. I plan on telling you a lot." He presses another soft kiss to my lips. "I'm sorry, Nessa."

"What?" I pull my head back. "What do you have to be sorry for?"

"I shouldn't have hidden you, and I shouldn't have made you lie to Hutch."

I dare a peek to my right, but Reed is nowhere to be found. He must have slipped away when Gavin showed up, and I'm okay with that. We'll talk more later. I feel confident in that now.

"I shouldn't have insisted this was just something fun and meaningless when it was never that," Gavin continues. "It always meant something more to me, even that first night."

I smile, because it meant something to me then, too. "You did tell me I belonged to you."

"I did, and I don't think I realized how much I truly meant it until I woke up and you were gone."

I wince. "I'm sorry about that."

"Don't be. A part of me wishes you hadn't left, of course, but the other part… I'm glad. I think we needed to find each other again, needed to prove our night together wasn't just some fluke and was as meant to be as it felt."

"It felt so real even then."

He nods. "It did, and that's why it was scary. But you don't have to be scared now. I've got you, and I have no plans of letting you go. We'll take this slow. We'll go at your pace. I know you're still dealing with the repercussions of what your ex did, and that's okay. If you need to wait…if you need more time…I'll be here. I'm not going anywhere, love. How could I? Not when I love your laugh and your smile so much. Or how you try really hard to wait up for me after my games. How you sleep on the couch because our bed feels too empty without me. How you order takeout in the perfect combinations."

I chuckle, and he grabs my chin, tipping it up toward him.

"But more than that, I love *you*. I love your passion, your fire, and your drive. How your lips always taste like cherries, and how much you care about others, even though you try to hide it. I just… I love you, Nessa. You could never make me go anywhere. You're never too much and you're never not enough either. You're perfect just as you are, and it's what makes me love you so fucking much."

I close my eyes against his words. Not because I don't believe him, but because I do. Every single word. He would never hurt me. He's proven that time and time again, and it's time for me to trust that. It's time for me to let myself be loved, this time for real.

"I'm not going anywhere either," I promise him.

He grins. "Good."

Then he's kissing me again. It's hard and it's hot and it's *so* inappropriate, especially since we're standing in the middle of my workplace right now, yet I can't seem to care. I'm still scared, maybe even more than I was before, but with the way Gavin is kissing me… I don't know. I think everything is going to be all right.

"Fuck," he says against my lips. "I need to touch you right now."

"You are touching me." I pull him closer as if to prove it.

"Not enough," he grunts, his hands falling to my ass. "Need more."

"Home?" I ask.

He pulls away, his eyes sparkling with something,

and it's not just lust. It's something more. Something grander. Something…a lot like love.

"Home."

Chapter 23

We race back to the penthouse, my tires squealing against the pavement as I pull my car into the garage.

Home. This isn't just my place anymore, it's ours. It's felt that way for a long damn time, but it's official now. She loves me. *Nessa* loves me.

Hearing her say those words… It filled in a pit I didn't even know I had within me. I've been lonely, sure, but I didn't realize just how badly I wanted what the other Serpents Singles were finding until she sassed at me in a bar in New York City. I didn't realize just how damn badly I needed that in my life, just how badly I needed her. But I did, and I do, and now that I have her? There's no chance she's going anywhere.

We're both antsy as we wait for the elevator, and when it finally arrives, the doors are barely open before we're rushing in. In a silent conversation, we agree to keep our hands to ourselves, both of us knowing that if we start, we aren't going to stop. We manage to keep it up when the car reaches our floor, and we practically sprint down the hall to our door.

The second I have it open, all bets are off. I have no idea who reaches for the other first, and it doesn't matter. All that matters is that Nessa is in my arms and her mouth is on mine. I sweep her off her feet, loving the way her legs fit around my waist and her arms wind around my neck as I carry her through the penthouse.

I take her straight to the shower, knowing she likes to take one after her shift. We strip out of our clothes, then take our time washing each other, teasing and touching and building this up, up, up until I slip into her and fuck her soft and slow against the shower wall until the water runs cold.

When we're finished, I clean us both again, then towel us off and drop her onto the bed. The second I set her down, she's reaching for me like we haven't touched in days, and I laugh at her impatience until I'm not laughing anymore. I can't with my breath gone as she sucks me to the back of her throat without warning. Then it whooshes out of me all at once, and I gasp for air.

"Holy shit," I mutter as I stare down at her. She looks like a fucking dream as she sucks on me, and I have to bite the inside of my cheek to keep from coming down her throat right there.

She uses her hand to work me over as she releases all of me except the tip, teasing me before swallowing me down again. Over and over, and I can't fucking take it. Without warning, I pull away, and I enjoy the stunned look on her face far too much.

"Gonna come," I say, struggling to catch my breath.

She pouts. "That's kind of the point."

"Yeah, but I want to come inside you." I slip my hand into her still-wet hair, tipping her head back with a tight grip. She leans into the touch, loving the bite of pain. "Don't you want that? Don't you want me to fill that pretty pussy of yours, love? Don't you want to feel me dripping from your sweet cunt?"

Her eyes glaze over at my words like she could come from them alone, and she nods.

"Yes. *Please*," she begs, voice raspy and filled with want.

"Then get on your hands and knees," I tell her, and her eyes widen just slightly before she flips over for me.

And fuck, what a vision she is. Ass in the air, peeking at me over her shoulder with innocent eyes, though she's anything but. I could slide into her and fuck her senseless. That's what she wants, after all. But I don't. I need to taste her first.

I drop to my knees, pulling her to the edge of the bed so I can get better access, and I eat her. Oh, I fucking eat. I lick and suck and taste every damn inch of her. I bury my face in her pussy, then her ass, and start all over again until she's making a mess all over me.

And yet, it's still not enough. I want more. I want *all* of her.

"Have you ever been fucked here?" I ask her, slipping my thumb over her hole and pressing on the tight ring.

"Yes," she says on a moan. "I mean, no. Never. But yes to you. I want that. I want to give that to you. Only you."

"Only mine is fucking right," I murmur, nipping at her cheek.

I rise behind her, reach into my bedside table, and pull free a small bottle of lube I put in there after that morning in the kitchen, just in case. I pop open the top and drop a generous amount between her spread cheeks, adding a bit more to my fingers just to be safe.

Slowly, I press a single digit into her tight hole. At first, she resists the foreign feeling, but it doesn't last long as the pleasure sets in. I back out, then push in farther, and each time she wiggles, searching for more. I work her over, every pass getting easier until I can slip another finger in.

"Gavin…" She practically sighs my name, and I grin.

She's so fucking lost in the bliss that she either doesn't notice when I add a third finger, or she just loves it that much and doesn't care. When she's loosened up enough and her body is relaxed, I slowly pull my fingers free one at a time before pressing the tip of my cock to her ass. She tenses at the new, bigger pressure.

"Breathe, love," I instruct her. "Just breathe and try to relax."

She nods, her hands flexing against the bedsheets as I push in more.

"Relax," I say again, and I feel her do it. "That's it, Nessa. You're doing such a good job. Fuck, you should see you right now. You should see how good you look with my cock in your ass. Stretching you so beautifully."

My words melt away the rest of her anxiety until she's languid on the bed and I've completely bottomed out. I officially have all of her. Every inch of her…it's mine. *She's* mine.

"Oh god." She moans. "You're so… It feels so big. Fuck, Gavin, you feel *so* good."

I stay still for a moment, letting her adjust to me, then slowly—so very fucking slowly—I move, and she cries with pure joy.

"Yes, yes. *More.*"

And I give it to her. I pick up my pace, thrusting harder and faster each time but still being gentle and conscious of her body squeezing me and the sounds she's making. She's loving this. Who knew? I'm loving it too, and I *need* to come. But Nessa first.

"Touch yourself, love. Let me see you finger your cunt."

"God, yes," she says, slipping her hand between her legs.

I can't see her, but I know when she slides in. I can *feel* it. Her entire body is taut as she fucks herself on her fingers while my cock fills her ass, and it's too much. All of this is too much.

I come with a roar, the most intense orgasm slamming into me as I fulfill my promise and empty myself inside her. It must be enough to set Nessa off, too, and she squeezes me tightly as she crests the edge right along with me. I wait until the twitches subside before carefully pulling out of her.

"Stay," I tell her, giving her a light swat on the ass.

She giggles softly as I grab a washcloth from the bathroom to clean her up with. She shivers as I run the wet cloth between her legs, then her cheeks, soaking up the mess I've left behind. I clean myself next and wash my hands before returning to bed. Nessa is already curled up in the middle, the sheets pulled up around her chin, her eyes heavy as she grins up at me. I slip in beside her, tugging her close until her head is resting on my chest.

"Hi," she says.

"Hi," I say back, and she laughs again.

It's such a sweet sound, and I swear I could listen to it for the rest of my life. That's a good thing because that's what this is—it's not some fling, it's not just fun. It's more. It's *real*.

We lie there like that in silence for so long that my eyes grow tired and I'm starting to drift off.

"Gavin?" she asks when I think she's asleep.

"Yeah?"

"I don't think I'm going to need that bed now."

I chuckle. "Good thing I canceled it weeks ago."

"Weeks?!"

"Yep. They actually tried delivering it about a week after I ordered it, but I kept putting it off because I didn't want to give you up." I shrug. "They finally threatened to keep it without a refund, so I canceled it."

"That's incredibly sneaky of you," she accuses, yet I don't feel the least bit sorry. "Sweet too, if I'm being honest."

"Yeah? Well, get used to it, love."

She sighs happily, drawing short circles on my

chest. "You know, we should move Sir Fishsticks the Fourth somewhere else."

"We should?"

"Yeah. He's seen *a lot* of dirty things since I moved in. Poor fella is likely traumatized."

"That's okay. I'll just replace him with Sir Fishsticks the Fifth."

"Gavin!" She swats at me, and I laugh. "You're terrible."

"Maybe, but you love me."

She snuggles closer, and I hold her tightly. "I do. I really, really do."

"I love you too."

She sighs. "I like it when you say that."

"I plan on saying it for a long, long time, you know? We're talking old-and-gray kind of long time."

"But you already are old and gray."

I growl. "Woman."

She cackles loudly, and I laugh too. This is what I was waiting for right here—her. Her kind heart, her smarts, her sense of humor, her talent, her bratty moments. Just…her.

And I have her. Forever and more.

Chapter 24

"No."

"But—"

"They don't play well together."

"I—"

"That lionfish will destroy them. Do you want to be responsible for the death of my sweet little clown fish? You already thought you killed them once and could barely live with yourself." He raises his brows pointedly.

I huff, frustrated I can't have the beautiful creature, but also…I get it. I love Pearl and Rufus, and I can't imagine anything happening to them.

"All right," I relent. "I'll keep looking."

"That's my girl," Gavin says, patting my ass as we meander through the fish store.

Not a day has gone by since we finally gave in to this

thing that he has not taken care of me. Take last night, for example: I was holed up in my studio, so completely lost in the painting I'm making for Gavin's parents—who I met via FaceTime last week—for Christmas, that I forgot to eat lunch *and* dinner. But Gavin knew that somehow, and he came home after his game with a bag of cheap burgers and a chocolate shake.

That caring quality of his is exactly why we're at a fish store just five minutes before they close as I try to pick out a fish for myself. I mentioned it earlier in passing, and he insisted we get me one for Christmas. I told him he was ridiculous, then somehow found myself being put in the car and driven here. We argued in the parking lot for ten minutes, then made out for five, which is why we're cutting it so close.

I grin over at the associate behind the counter, who is shooting daggers our way.

"Okay, we need to hurry this up or that guy is going to charge us double," I whisper to Gavin.

"Pretty sure he's not allowed to do that."

"He could! You don't know that."

Gavin gives me a look, then shakes his head at me, his lips twitching.

"What about that one?" He points to another fish.

"Ew. No."

"Ew? What? Puffers are so cool!"

"Nope."

"Fine." He gestures toward another tank. "This one?"

"Hmm, no. He looks mean. And kind of ugly."

"Ugly? Foxfaces are awesome. Are you really just picking fish based on their cuteness?"

"Um, yes? That's the whole point, right?"

"No!" He sighs, exasperated, and I grin.

He notices.

"Wait, you're doing this on purpose, aren't you? Being bratty?"

I shrug. "Maybe."

"Nessa…" he warns.

I giggle, skipping away to look at more fish. He groans from behind me, and I know it's not because he's annoyed. No, he's turned on, and I am too. To be fair, I don't think I've stopped being turned on since we finally accepted this. I can't believe how freeing it is to just be together now. We don't have to hide. We don't have to lie. We just get to be *us*.

I like us. I like us so much that I grab Gavin by the shirt and drag him down to me, kissing him hard and fast. He returns it with the same fervor, his hands roaming all over me, tugging me closer.

A throat clears, and we break away. The guy behind the counter flips the sign from *Open* to *Closed*, then narrows his eyes once again. We laugh and keep browsing.

Then I see him. Or her. I have no idea.

"This one!" I press my face to the glass like a kid looking into a toy store. "This is the one."

"That's a goldfish."

"I know. It looks just like Sir Fishsticks the Fourth."

Gavin frowns. "Goldfish are freshwater. We're looking for saltwater."

"But…" I look at the little thing in the water, already half in love with it. "But…"

He sighs. "Are you sure this is the one you want?"

"Yes, I love him."

"It's a girl."

"What? How can you even tell, fish nerd?"

He ignores the jab and points at my new friend. "Look at her shape, for one. And her vent is protruding instead of being an innie."

"I have no idea what that is, but I'll believe you, and I'll take her. She's perfect."

"Then we'll get another tank."

"Really?" I throw my arms around his neck, hugging him tightly, inhaling the cinnamon I love so much. "I love you, I love you, I love you, fish nerd!"

"I love you too. *Clearly.*" He laughs as he squeezes me back. "Now, come on before this kid blows a fuse or something."

The associate checks us out, not looking up a single time, and by the time we make it out of the store, fish in hand, we're laughing like fools.

"Oh my god, he *hated* us," I say.

"He hated *me*, he loved you."

"He did not! Did you see the way he grimaced when I told him that joke?"

"Because the punchline was arti*fish*al coloring."

"That was hilarious! And clever!" I argue as he opens the door to his SUV and helps me inside.

"So," he asks, "what are you going to name her?"

"Madam Fishsticks."

Gavin stares at me blankly.

Blink. Blink. Blink.

Then he bursts into laughter, and I grin as I settle into the passenger seat, my brand-new goldfish sitting cozy on my lap for the trip home. I could get used to this. I could get used to him.

And I fully plan on letting myself.

Epilogue

LOCKE

"Here's to another year and another Serpents Single down!"

Lawson raises his glass in a toast, and Nessa giggles beside me as we stand around in a group at a very packed Top Shelf on New Year's Eve. I tighten my hold on her waist, grinning down at her. She surprised me at the game tonight by showing up in a Serpents jersey. She's still wearing it, and it's taking everything I have not to haul her off somewhere private and have my way with her.

Sure, I'd seen her in my team t-shirts before, but not a jersey. One look at her in the dark green and gold, and I was enraptured. Couldn't have taken my eyes off her if I tried. Then she turned around, and I swear I became a caveman for a moment. All that was running through my mind was *Mine, mine, mine, mine,* and it had everything to do with seeing my name and number on her back.

Whitlocke

46

It was perfect. *She* was perfect, standing in the crowd, cheering for me. I played the best fucking game of my career. There wasn't a person in that arena who wasn't chanting my name by the end of the game. Still, her voice was the only one that mattered.

And I think it will always be that way. When my agent called to tell me that, while nothing was certain yet, my future with the Seattle Serpents was all but determined and I'd be sticking around for at least the next few years, she was the first person I wanted to tell. It wasn't my teammates, who have been with me since the beginning. It was Nessa. Always Nessa.

We clink our glasses together, the best eleven people can, and cheer. I didn't believe this day would come, but here we are. Nearly all of us are now paired off. All except for Keller, who stares sullenly down into his beer.

"So, I heard you're considering opening your own art studio. Rotating displays, space for classes, and those sip and paints that are all the rage," Auden says to Nessa, pulling my attention off my teammate.

"Reed!" Nessa admonishes.

"What? I'm just passing on the good news." He winks at her, and it's still so damn strange to see.

They've spent the last few weeks working on building a relationship, which has included several long phone calls—some of which ended in yelling—and a lot of texting. I know the importance of a good sibling relationship, so I couldn't be happier for them as they mend their connection.

"So it's true?" Auden asks.

Nessa shrugs, trying to play it cool, but she's been talking about it nearly nonstop for the last two weeks. "Maybe. I mean, I have a business degree, and I love art, so why not combine them? I'm looking at a place next week, but there's no guarantee. Besides, if I do decide to, it's going to take a lot of work and time and money and—"

"Breathe," Auden says with a laugh. "You know we'll help you out."

"You will?"

"Of course we will," Lilah answers. "Do you have any idea how good I am at planning shit?"

"It's true. She's incredible," Fox says, staring at his girlfriend like a dope.

"And I would totally come if you offered a parent-and-kiddo night. Flora would love that," Quinn adds.

Hayes nods. "She would. She's really into making pictures for people right now. She won't stop drawing her cat, Pickles, as a kaiju wrecking cities. In retrospect, it probably wasn't the best idea to introduce her to Godzilla so young."

"It's never too early for Godzilla," Hutch argues.

"Or—and hear me out—a dog night. Because they're better than people."

"For the record, I'm with her," Lawson says, pointing to Rory.

"Settle down, golden retriever. Pretty sure she meant actual dogs, not humans who act like them," Keller gripes.

I frown. He seems more down than usual tonight, and I can't help but wonder if it's because he's the only one not with someone. Could Keller…actually have a heart under all the grumpiness?

Nah. Not a chance.

"You guys are amazing," my girl says, her voice getting thick with emotion. "Truly. Thank you."

"Of course. We take care of our own." Auden bumps her shoulder against Nessa's.

She buries her face into my side, and I know it's because she's trying to keep from crying. I squeeze her tight, kissing the top of her head. We all fall into easy conversation, waiting for the countdown to midnight, which is just five minutes away.

"Guys, I have an announcement," Lawson says, and we all turn to look at him. "I love you all."

We groan in unison.

"Knock it off, Lawsy," Hutch grumbles.

"What he said." Hayes points at the captain.

"Yep," I say.

"Aww, I love you too, buddy." Fox grins, patting the forward on the back.

"Finally!" Lawson throws his hands in the air. "Someone cares about me! What? No comment, Keller?"

But when we all turn to him, ready for whatever smartass thing he's going to say next, he's not looking at us. He's staring across the room, his knuckles white as he grips the glass in his hand.

"Keller. You okay, man?"

"Fine," he bites out, though it's clear he's anything but.

Something is up, and based on where he's looking and how he can't take his eyes off her, it has everything to do with the redhead who just walked into the bar. She's arm in arm with some guy, and she throws her head back with a laugh. Keller gnashes his teeth, and I can't tell if he's two seconds away from marching over there or two away from walking out altogether.

"Do you know her or something?" Lawson asks.

"You could say that," Keller says, not shifting his gaze in the slightest. "She's my wife."

. . .

**

THANK YOU FOR READING!

I hope you loved Locke & Vanessa! If you enjoyed this book, I encourage you to leave a review on your favorite platform.

Want more?
Keep reading for a bonus scene!

Bonus Scene

VANESSA

"This place is incredible, Van."

I grin over at Auden, whose eyes are shining with pride. "Thank you. I couldn't have done it without your help."

"Or mine," Lilah chimes in."

"Or yours," I agree with a laugh.

It's true. If they hadn't been here for me—Quinn and Rory too—then I wouldn't be able to say I'm a business owner.

I wouldn't be opening my very own art studio.

The bell over the door chimes, and I wish I could say that's what draws my attention, but it's not.

I felt him before that.

Gavin walks through the door, and I swear time stops. Everything else—even this studio that I've spent the last nine months working on—ceases to exist. It's just him.

He runs a hand over his jaw, eyes scanning the room until they snag on me.

He smiles, and everything in me lights up.

The world snaps back into place, and that's when I hear the girls giggling from beside me.

"What?" I ask, my cheeks heating from their stares.

"Nothing. You just look so happy every time you see him," Auden says.

"That's because I am."

She grins, reaching over and squeezing my hand. "I'm glad, Van. You deserve it." She turns to Gavin just as he strides up to us. "Hey."

"Auden," he says, not taking his eyes off me.

All it does is elicit another round of giggles.

"I'll take that," Lilah says, grabbing the bag of ice from his hand.

He doesn't even bother acknowledging her. It's not because he's being rude—I don't think he ever is. He's just that engrossed in me.

Truthfully, I love it. It's been that way since the beginning, and I still haven't gotten tired of it. I doubt I ever will.

"Now that they're gone…" Gavin says once Auden and Lilah have hurried away. Then he grabs me by the waist, tugging me to him so quickly I gasp. "I can do this."

Then he kisses me like he hasn't seen me in years,

when he ran to the store just fifteen minutes ago to grab more ice for our party.

I didn't want to make a big to-do about the opening, but Auden and Lilah insisted. When Gavin backed them up, I gave in.

Now that we're here, I'm glad I did it, and not just for this moment as Gavin's lips move over mine.

It's being able to share this with so many people I love.

"Can you please stop mauling my sister?"

We break apart, and I smile over at Reed, who is scowling at his teammate.

"Reed, be nice," I tell him.

"I *am* being nice, trust me."

I believe him. While he's supportive of me and Gavin and everything we've built these last few years, he still doesn't care for our public displays of affection.

I would be annoyed by it if I didn't find it so sweet. We've grown close since my relationship with Gavin became public, and if this is what that means, then I'll take it.

Gavin just laughs. "Don't you have a kid to catch?"

"What? I don't—"

Almost as if Alana heard him, she starts to run through the shop, and then Reed's off, chasing after her.

"She's grown so much," I say, watching my niece as she darts away.

"She has. You should have seen her the other day when he brought her to the rink. She was adorable on those skates."

He smiles fondly, and it's not just because he loves Alana like I do. It's because at the beginning of the season, Gavin announced he's retiring. I know he's excited for whatever the next chapter of his life looks like, but he's going to miss the game, too. He's been doing this for so long, it's almost like he doesn't know anything else. It scares him, but it gives him purpose, too.

As much as I'll miss seeing him on the ice, I'm kind of glad he's hanging up his skates. It means more time with him, and that's always my favorite.

"Speaking of adorable..." He presses a kiss to my cheek. "Have I told you how beautiful you look today?"

I laugh. "Yes, many times, but I still love hearing it, so go ahead and say it again."

"You look beautiful. I always loved this dress." He leans into me, his nose brushing against my cheek as he says. "And as good as it looks on you, it looks better on my floor."

That same blush from before steals up my cheeks at

his words. This is the dress I was wearing the night we met, and the floor is exactly where it ended up.

I'm hoping that's where it'll land tonight, too.

"I'm proud of you, you know," he says. "You're doing something amazing here, and I can't wait to see this place packed to the gills with little artists learning from you. You deserve it all and more."

Suddenly, tears sting my eyes, and I blink them away quickly. It's my studio opening, and my makeup looked incredible this morning. I can't cry, even if I really want to.

"Thank you," I say softly, though it feels so silly when what he just said was so moving. "I love you."

He smiles like it's the first time I've ever said it, something he always does, and it makes my heart pound.

"I love you too, Nessa. Always."

I don't doubt him. Not one bit.

This thing? We're for real. We're always.

And I wouldn't have it any other way.

Other Titles
by Teagan Hunter

SEATTLE SERPENTS SERIES

Body Check

Face Off

Delayed Penalty

Empty Net

Top Shelf

Match Penalty

CAROLINA COMETS SERIES

Puck Shy

Blind Pass

One-Timer

Sin Bin

Scoring Chance

Glove Save

Neutral Zone

ROOMMATE ROMPS SERIES

Loathe Thy Neighbor

Love Thy Neighbor

Crave Thy Neighbor

Tempt Thy Neighbor

SLICE SERIES

A Pizza My Heart

I Knead You Tonight

Doughn't Let Me Go

A Slice of Love

Cheesy on the Eyes

TEXTING SERIES

Let's Get Textual

I Wanna Text You Up

Can't Text This

Text Me Baby One More Time

INTERCONNECTED STANDALONES

We Are the Stars

If You Say So

STANDALONES

The DM Diaries

Best Friends for Never

Stay on top of my new releases, cover reveals, sales, and more by visiting:

www.teaganhunterwrites.com

Thank You

My husband, Henry. Thank you for being there to support me through this one. It was a long journey, and you never stopped showing up for me. I love you.

Laurie and Kristann. Always my biggest cheerleaders! Thank you both for your endless support.

My editing team. Caitlin, Julia, Judy… You ladies are incredible. Not just for catching all my mistakes but for being so damn patient with me. Thank you.

Kim, Nina, and the VPR team. Have I mentioned lately how much I appreciate you? You made this journey easier, and I'm forever grateful to be part of the VPR family.

. . .

Tidbits. Thank you for sticking by me, even when I suck and don't show up. Your continued support means the world.

You. Thank you for joining me on this rollercoaster ride of a career.

With love and unwavering gratitude,
    Teagan

TEAGAN HUNTER writes steamy romantic comedies with lots of sarcasm and a side of heart. She loves pizza, hockey, and romance novels, though not in that order. When not writing, you can find her watching entirely too many hours of *Supernatural, One Tree Hill,* or *New Girl.* She's mildly obsessed with Halloween and prefers cooler weather. She married her high school sweetheart, and they currently live in the PNW.

www.teaganhunterwrites.com